Dare the Devil

Roger L. Conlee

Pale Horse Books

This work of fiction is based in part on events that actually occurred to real people in places that existed in the middle of the 20th century. It is mostly, though, a product of the author's imagination.

Library of Congress Control Number: 2014907458
ISBN: 978-1-939917-11-9

Cover Design: Mark A. Clements
Author Photo: David Friend Productions (www.DavidFriend.com)
Vintage car courtesy of Robert Withem

Also by Roger L. Conlee

Every Shape Every Shadow: A Novel of Guadalcanal
Counterclockwise
The Hindenburg Letter
Souls on the Wind
Fog and Darkness

www.PaleHorseBooks.com
www.RogerConlee.com

ONE

I didn't shoot Bugsy Siegel," I told my Uncle Dieter.

"Of course not, Jacob," he replied. "You would never kill anyone unless it was in defense of your family or yourself."

Uncle Dieter was about the only one in the world who called me Jacob. To most everyone I was Jake. Jake Weaver, military writer and investigative reporter for William Randolph Hearst's *Los Angeles Herald-Express*.

I hadn't seen Dieter Weber, pronounced "Vayber," in more than four years. It was swell that he'd been able to come from the old country for a visit, just bad luck that the visit happened to coincide with this gangland slaying that had the whole town buzzing.

In my opinion, Dieter was the finest German who ever lived. He was a retired Berlin cop now, but during the Nazi period he'd been a colonel in the SS. He had worked from the inside to save Jews and other "undesirables," figuring that was the best way to help save Germany's honor during that horrible time. He'd slipped them into Switzerland or, when that wasn't possible, obtained better treatment for some of them in the concentration camps. Working secretly and in great danger all that time for the Resistance. A brave man. A man I loved as much or more than my own father.

Somehow, miraculously, Dieter had managed to keep his clandestine doings undiscovered. In the last weeks of the war he'd surrendered to the British. When he got home after release from a POW camp, he'd found Berlin a shambles of rubble and ruined buildings. People were busy trying to clean things up. Fortunately he lived in the American Zone, not the Russian, where things were worse.

I had also been involved in World War II, but in a very different way. I'd been our war correspondent and I'd also done some unofficial work for MI-6, British intelligence.

It was now June of 1947. Dieter and I sat drinking beer and catching up in the living room of our home in West Los Angeles. I lived in that Craftsman-style house with my wife Valerie and my German-born daughter Ilse. Valerie worked at North American Aviation and was one of the very few female tool designers in the country. Ilse was a sophomore in high school. Dieter had known her in Germany before I even knew she existed, but that's another story. I'll get to that in a bit.

Dieter took a sip of his beer and asked about the bloody shooting of Bugsy Siegel in the Beverly Hills house he leased. He'd seen the big headlines and the gory photos. Who hadn't?

"Jacob, why ever do some folks think that you, of all people, killed this gangster?"

"I had some bad experiences with him in the past few months," I said. "It's a long story, Dieter. Let me start at the beginning. Back in November . . ."

TWO

I blinked. I felt my facial muscles tighten.

"You start talking and talk fast unless you want a belly full of lead," the guy holding the .38 Special snarled. A black fedora and cheap suit. Lips twisted into an ugly sneer.

"We know you know where the loot is stashed, so you better give." Such words and that gun should have had the hairs on the back of my neck standing at attention. But they didn't.

Another menacing step forward by the punk with the pistol. "This is your last chance. Spill, 'less you want some new ventilation on that puny chest of yours." Right index finger slipping inside the trigger guard.

I said nothing. What could I say? I didn't know where any loot was stashed.

"Okay, have it your way, wise guy. You asked for it." *Bam! Bam!*

"Cut!" the director called out. "And print."

Shaking my head and getting up from the canvas chair from where I'd been watching this dumb scene, I said, "That's about the worst dialogue I ever heard, Mick." Mickey Cohen had asked me here to this sound stage at Warner's because he thought I might enjoy the making of this film, in which he was a minor backer.

"I know, Jake," he said, pulling his thick-as-an-oak body up from his chair. "Hey, it's just a cheap little B movie, but it'll turn a profit." He winked at the girl who worked the clapperboard, then patted her fanny. The cute little thing smiled but her eyes told me it wasn't a genuine smile, just one she felt was required.

I liked Mickey Cohen, God help me. He'd been a boxer in the Thirties, won a few more bouts than he lost, then somehow fell in with Lucky Luciano and Meyer Lansky, the hoods who ran the crime syndicate in New York. Big-time crime got more organized across the country following the days of Dutch Schultz and Al Capone. The Luciano guys got it through their heads that they could make more by working together instead of killing each other. Now the syndicate had branches in Chicago, Los Angeles and elsewhere.

Under a thug named Jack Dragna, though, some of the L.A. boys still tried to practice a bit of independence. So Luciano sent Ben Siegel out here to make them toe the line. But before long they told Cohen to keep an eye on Siegel, honor among thieves being what it was. Luciano suspected that Siegel, who hated being called "Bugsy," was skimming on them. There was a good chance he was.

How do I, Jake Weaver of the *Herald-Express*, fit into this? William Randolph Hearst, our aging but still involved owner, decided to launch an anti-crime crusade, a campaign designed to sell papers and possibly even help to clean up L.A. a bit, get a few crooked politicians voted out of office. The gangsters had cops, councilmen and judges in their pockets—seemed like half the town was on the take—and the old man wanted us to go after them. He'd put me in charge.

Since the war ended more than a year ago, our circulation, once L.A.'s largest, had slipped some. Readers had begun turning to the morning papers.

Hearst had taken a liking to me since I'd written some good stuff as an overseas correspondent during the war and then coauthored a book on it with a Marine Corps officer friend. "Write hard stuff, sell papers," he always said.

Mickey Cohen, knowing my reputation, made a point of cozying up. He took me to the fights at the Shrine Auditorium and to a couple of Coast League ball games at Gilmore Field. We got along okay but it was obvious he was keeping an eye on me as well as on Siegel. I didn't mind. The guy was likeable, and maybe the contact would lead to some good info.

My wife minded, though. Valerie hated the idea of me keeping company with a notorious hood. "They can't go around shooting reporters," I tried to assure her. "It'd be obvious to a blind monkey who was behind that, and even the crooked cops would have to come down on them. Besides, Cohen hasn't threatened me or warned me to cool it."

Valerie was a strong woman and clever as a cat. Six years younger and taller than me when she wore heels, her hair was silky black, her eyes a stunning blue. Valerie had been widowed in 1941 when her husband was killed in an auto accident. I met her eighteen months later and, lucky me, she liked me right away. We got married in 1943 after I got back from Europe with my German-born daughter Ilse.

It was my Uncle Dieter who'd brought Ilse and me together in Berlin in 1942. She was twelve then, the product of a brief hot fling I'd had on a trip to Berlin twelve years earlier. Her existence came as a shocking surprise to me, but a very happy one as it turned out.

But back to my gangsters. The survival plan I'd come up with was to go after Jack Dragna and the punks who'd been running L.A. crime ever since Prohibition, more so than their watchdogs Cohen and Siegel.

During the Thirties, I had briefly moonlighted doing some publicity for MGM. I'd enjoyed being on a movie lot in those days and I still do. So now, standing outside Sound Stage Six, Mickey was saying, "I know that was a pretty bad scene, Jake, but Georgie"—meaning Raft—"and I don't have a huge stake in this.

It'll always get packaged with somethin' big budget, like *Meet Me in St. Louis*, and so we'll come out ahead . . . Got time for a drink?"

"Not now, Mick, thanks. I gotta be getting back."

"Okay, Scribbler. See you in church, kid." His favorite parting line.

Climbing into my Chevy Ridemaster coupe, I glanced up at the sound stage's high white exterior wall. Above it, Burbank's November sky hung in stark contrast, a ceiling of deep blue. I closed the door and was about to step on the starter pedal when I looked back through the window. Mickey Cohen still stood there, staring. He offered up a little grin. I didn't discern much warmth in it.

Did I really believe the assurances I'd given Valerie?

My team consisted of two investigative reporters, Richie Millsap and Marko Janicek, a second-generation Serbian. Janicek had been part of a special U.S. Army Rangers team during the war.

Agness Underwood, our new city editor, was an ex-officio member of our little group. She was the only female city editor in L.A. and I figured maybe one of the few in the whole U.S. of A. Aggie previously had been our police reporter. She knew where the bodies were buried and which cops—and there were plenty—were on Jack Dragna's pad. She called our team the Unholy Trinity.

Our building was a three-story stone affair on South Trenton Street just below downtown, with a small penthouse on the roof for the Associated Press. This old neighborhood, just off Pico Boulevard, was filled with rowdy juke joints and pool halls and was bordered by a Bekins Van & Storage building and the Electric Railway's trolley-car barns. One of my boxer friends said the area "had no class," but what did he know? I loved it.

I parked in front of my favorite tavern, the Continental, crossed Trenton and went inside the paper to have a little meeting with my team. We were working on a story about a cop who was in Dragna's pocket. Millsap said he had some proof. Aggie Underwood ambled over and pulled up a chair to join us. "And how's the Unholy Trinity today?" she said.

We sat around a desk in a far corner of the city room beneath fat, load-bearing pillars and between the Coke machine and the sports department. "Boy!" Aggie called out. When a copyboy trotted over, his white sleeves rolled up, she said, "Bring four coffees over here."

"Make it three, Bobby," Richie Millsap said. "I got a bottle of Coke going here."

When we got down to business, Millsap said he'd seen his cop accepting a fat envelope, surely filled with bills, from one of Dragna's boys in the back of a bar up on Olympic. "If I'd had a little camera with me, maybe I coulda snuck a picture."

"Well, take one of our new 35-millimeters from now on," I said. "If you see something like that again, get a shot if you can."

"But be damn careful about it," Aggie put in with a serious look. "Don't get caught."

Marko Janicek said he'd tailed a cop we thought was crooked but hadn't come up with anything. "Unless you wanta count him spending an hour in a whore's apartment near Echo Park."

"Irene Slattery?" I asked.

"Or Sluttery, as we call her," Marko said. "She spreads her thighs to half the force, that one."

"Don't be too hard on old Irene," Aggie said. "I happen to know she's done some snitching for the cops."

"So she helps 'em out in more ways than one," I said unkindly.

Before the Unholy Trinity parted, I made some assignments. Millsap was to keep after the cop who'd taken that envelope, and

Janicek was to see what Irene Slattery might know. "But keep your fly zipped up," I said.

I was going to keep an eye on Jack Dragna himself. He lived out in Brentwood, and I knew some of the bars and restaurants he frequented, always with bodyguards close by. Musso & Frank, Chasen's, the Brown Derby.

I went back outside, was going to have a beer at the Continental. Damn, my car had a parking ticket on the windshield. That hadn't happened before. Not here. I knew all the cops who worked this neighborhood. They knew my car and had always given me a free pass. I guess our crusade was hitting some nerves. I snatched up the ticket and was about to slip it in a pocket when I noticed something scribbled on the back: "Be careful, asshole."

THREE

Disgusted, I went inside and plopped myself down on a stool at the counter. "Don't Fence Me In" was playing on the jukebox. Bing Crosby and the Andrews Sisters. "Hi ya, Red, want a Falstaff?" asked Shaker, the bartender. Because of my reddish-brown hair I'd often been called Red.

"Mind reader," I said.

"Gal over there was asking about you. Nice looking dame." He placed a bottle of beer and a glass in front of me.

I turned and saw a slim, attractive woman get up from a booth and head in my direction. I thought I recognized her. Dark blond hair tied back in a bun, oval face, pearl gray suit with padded shoulders. She slid onto the stool next to me with an elegant move of her hips. A coy smile on her lips, mischief in her deep green eyes.

It was the nose that sealed the deal. The bridge was a little crooked. It had been broken. Holy cats! This was Gretchen Siedler, the German war widow turned British agent. She'd helped me in Berlin four years ago. We'd had a one-night stand back then, an impulsive, explosive wartime roll in the German hay. I'd been sure I would never see her again. What the hell was she doing in L.A.? Shaker stared at her approvingly.

"Excuse me," Gretchen said, "I am looking for the *Volkspark*. Can you direct me?" We had used this coded phrase back in 1942. Hearing it again after all this time made me chuckle. The years had been good to her. As beautiful as ever, just a few more lines of experience in that lovely face, a face not at all diminished by that bumpy nose. I'd always felt it added a touch of character.

"Well, well, Tapestry," I said, using her old code name. "What the heck brings you here?" She laid a hand on top of mine. I felt a little flutter inside my chest.

"It is very good to see you, Jake," Gretchen said with that glacier-melting look she had, and a German accent I remembered so well. "You have been a busy boy. Colonel Freeborn"—her boss at MI-6 in London, often called the Pope by his agents—"told me how you collected von Braun and most of his rocket team for you Americans. And I have heard about your book. I am looking forward to reading it." The book I'd coauthored on World War II had been out for several months now.

"Thanks. I'm darn glad to see you survived the war, Gretchen. I guess the Gestapo never caught on to you."

"It was not easy. I had some difficulties." She took a sip from her glass and made a face. "This wine, it is not very satisfactory."

Shaker, who'd been wiping a glass with a towel, said, "I'm sorry, ma'am. It's jug wine from the valley. We don't get much call for vino. Most folks in here want beer or hard stuff."

Gretchen gave him a "that's all right" smile and turned back to me. "Why am I here, you asked? Well . . ." she said in a low voice, looking around furtively. I didn't want my bartender friend to hear what she was going to say next. "Shaker, I think those folks at the other end of the bar need some service." Good guy that he was, Shaker could take a hint. When he was gone, Gretchen continued.

"The Pope says that one of the worst of the Nazis is here somewhere. This man managed to avoid capture, create for himself a new identity, and slip out of Germany. He was one of those doctors who conducted horrible experiments on prisoners. He was notorious for his methods of torture. Colonel Freeborn wants me to find him and he thinks that perhaps you too can help, knowing the city as you do, and the people."

"And here I thought I'd heard the last of our Mr. Freeborn. Well, that's a tall order, Gretchen, but I'll see what I can do."

She raised her glass and clinked it against mine. "Good," she said. "I was hoping you would say that. You see, in addition to the MI-6 I also work as a volunteer for Konrad Adenauer's Social Democrats, who hope to establish a provisional government in the western occupation zones."

"I see. What's this guy's name and what's he look like?"

"His name was Otto Woolf, and his medical degree is from the University of Greifswald. We don't know what he is calling himself now. He is one-point-seven meters tall, husky, and fifty-four years old. His ghastly experiments were conducted at Buchenwald on women Russian prisoners, Jews, and even some Gypsies."

"That's beyond depravity, Gretchen. What else do you know about him?"

"He has relatives in New York, second cousins or some such."

"In that case, seems like he'd be hiding there. Why do you think he's in L.A.?"

"Because Colonel Freeborn says so. MI-6 has its ways, you know."

"Yeah, they sure do. Say, how'd you know where to find me?"

"Give me a little credit, *Shatzi*. I merely asked someone at your newspaper where I could find you and he said here in this establishment most any afternoon after four." Gretchen, clever as ever.

She touched my hand again. Before I could stop myself I leaned close and kissed her cheek. And immediately regretted it. Damn. Shaker, thirty feet away, had noticed.

Gretchen's eyes closed dreamily. She smiled. I pictured my sweet wife Valerie and hated myself.

I picked up my sixteen-year-old daughter Ilse after school.

"Hello, *Vati*," she said as she hopped into the car. We often used words in her native language and I was pleased she still called me by the German word for daddy. Valerie wouldn't be home from North American Aviation for more than an hour, so I said, "Would you like to get a Coke or maybe a malted?"

"Sure, *Vati*." I headed for Stan's Drive-In over at Sunset and Highland.

As I drove, Ilse watched my every move, the way I handled the steering wheel, how I changed gears. I knew she would be taking driver education in school and that I'd soon be giving her some lessons too. Could this maturing young woman possibly be the same little girl who led me through the Berlin Zoo four years ago? "How was your day?" she asked.

"I got a doggone parking ticket, *Liebchen*, first one in years. I guess the cops are sore at us for some of these stories we've been writing." Without thinking, I added, "And I ran into Gretchen Siedler, a big surprise."

"Your friend Gretchen who drove us to that airfield so we could leave Germany? You kissed her before we got on that plane." I nearly choked. I had hoped she'd forgotten all that.

"That's right, Ilse. She gave us some great help when we needed it. If not for her, you and I probably couldn't have gotten out of Germany."

"You knew where she lived—in Schöneberg. We were there, remember? Whatever is she doing here?"

"Some kind of work for the British government again."

Back at the Continental, Gretchen had told me she was staying in an apartment building the British Consulate leased near Wilshire and Union. She'd given me the address and phone number. I told her she could contact me at the paper but never at home.

When we parted, she put her hands on my face and kissed my lips. I wished she hadn't. Shaker saw that—of course. "*Auf wiedersehen* for now, Jake," Gretchen had said.

I pulled in at Stan's, a circular building with parking spaces all around it, and a huge neon sign. A pretty girl with blond pigtails zipped up on roller skates to take our order. Ilse asked for a chocolate shake, me a Coke.

When the kid skated away, Ilse asked, "Will your friendship with Gretchen cause difficulties with *Mutter*?" This kid was sure savvy.

"Of course not," I said, though I was trying to persuade myself of that. Some disturbing thoughts had churned in my head since meeting Gretchen at the Continental. "I keep nothing from my dear Valerie. I'll tell her all about it." And I would too. Well, not *all* about it.

"Would you like to be a carhop?" I asked Ilse after our drinks arrived on a tray which attached to the driver-side door.

"No, *Vati*, I would rather start as a copygirl on a newspaper."

On the way home fifteen minutes later, I tried to get my arms around the immensity of this Gretchen business. After Ilse and I arrived here from Germany in the winter of '42 I told Valerie—she was then my fiancée—about the British agent who'd helped us escape. But of course not about what happened in her bedroom one night. Valerie was surprised and a bit unsettled learning that the agent who saved us was a German woman. She asked several questions about that.

But the far bigger surprise to Valerie was the existence of my daughter, the result of that brief affair I'd had in Germany in 1930, and she shot many more questions at me about *that*. Being a good woman with a kind heart, Val decided to let the past be the past. After all, before we hooked up, she'd had a little fling of her own with a kid from the factory, Corky or Pinky, some cutesy-pie name. Nothing wrong with that—she was then a young widow. We married the month after my return and she willingly accepted the role of stepmother. The subject of Gretchen never again came up.

Back at our house on Saturn Street, Ilse went to her room to tackle her homework, and I sank onto the sofa, where I began to ponder where a Nazi on the lam might be in this big, sprawling town. There were a couple of German restaurants in Santa Monica and Culver City, and there'd been a chapter of the German-American Bund here before the war. After Pearl Harbor it either disbanded or went underground.

Before long, I heard Valerie's Plymouth pull into the driveway and stop.

I cooked up a batch of spaghetti for our evening meal. Since we both worked, Valerie and I took turns making dinner. Ilse usually helped. She hadn't done much cooking in Germany but under Valerie's tutelage she was learning fast. I steamed some broccoli to go along with the spaghetti. French bread, too, and a bottle of pinot noir.

I didn't tell Valerie about Gretchen, not yet. I was still working on how to bring up that subject.

Over dinner we talked about Ilse's day at school and also about the troubling developments in Europe. Stalin had seized control of Poland, eastern Germany, Hungary, and Bulgaria. Winston Churchill had made a speech at a little college in Missouri, with President Truman at his side. Valerie, as much of a news junkie as me, quoted word for word one of the expressive Churchill's most disturbing phrases: "From Stettin in the Baltic to Trieste in the Adriatic, an iron curtain has descended across the Continent."

"Does this mean that Stalin rules Berlin?" Ilse asked.

"Most of it," I said. "The Western Allies control part of it, though."

"Oh, my poor hometown, divided like that, and most of it in ruins. I have seen the awful pictures. I wonder if my old classroom is still standing." Ilse and I exchanged a meaningful look. Don't mention Gretchen, I was trying to convey.

Valerie noticed. "What?" she said. "What's going on with you two?"

"I think father and I were feeling sorry for those poor people. Is that not so, *Vati*?" I nodded agreement at my clever daughter.

"Here, dear, just one sip," Valerie said, handing her wine glass to Ilse. It was common for European teenagers to drink wine, and we sometimes allowed Ilse to have some, though just a little.

After dinner, Valerie and I washed the dishes, while Ilse went to the living room to listen to the radio. It was time for *Fibber McGee and Molly*, a comedy program she'd grown fond of.

I decided not to put this off any longer. I motioned Valerie to one of the kitchen chairs and I took the other one. "Val," I said, "you remember Gretchen Siedler, the British agent who helped me in Berlin?" She gave a lukewarm nod.

"She's here in L.A."

"She is?" Looking surprised and a little concerned. "Whatever for?"

"She showed up at the Continental this afternoon. I was surprised as hell. She's been ordered to find an escaped Nazi criminal who's supposed to be holed up in L.A. They call him the Buchenwald Butcher. She said MI-6 thinks maybe I can help."

"And I suppose you're going to?"

"I probably should, don't you think?"

"No I don't. You've got these other things on your plate, the crime lords and all."

"I know, and that's my top priority, but maybe I could ask around a bit."

"You don't owe the MI-6 a thing, Jake. You've already done more than enough for them."

"I know, but—"

"You'll be seeing more of this Gretchen then, I suppose. I

know she helped you and Ilse escape. Maybe I should meet her." A determined look on Valerie's face. "Yes, I would like to meet this woman."

I didn't sleep worth a damn that night.

FOUR

I switched cars with Valerie the next day. Jack Dragna's goons most likely knew my Chevy Ridemaster and I didn't want to get spotted cruising his place. But Valerie's Plymouth probably wouldn't mean anything to them. I hadn't said anything more to Valerie about her meeting Gretchen, an idea I still didn't like one bit. I knew it would happen, though, one of these days. Val would make sure of that.

I wore dark glasses and a San Francisco Seals ball cap when I took a look at Dragna's big house near the Brentwood Country Club. My usual brown fedora sat on the seat beside me as I approached. Sure enough, two of his bodyguards were there, one sitting in a black Packard parked in the street, the other smoking a cigarette and chatting with a Chinese gardener on the front lawn. Dragna always had some muscle close at hand. No sign of Fat Jack himself. The guy in the Packard glanced at Valerie's car as I passed, but I was pretty sure he didn't make me.

That accomplished a whole lot of nothing, I thought as I drove on. I had a stop to make before going on to the *Herald-Express*.

Twenty minutes later I pulled up in front of Sachsen Haus on 17th Street. Sachsen was an ancient tribal word for the north German lands. I'd looked it up. Before the war this had been sort of a "meet the nice Germans" place where tourist information and flyers had been handed out. Back then, they'd made a big effort to entice Americans to attend the 1936 Olympic Games in Berlin. The Aryan Bookstore had been located there, featuring all kinds of white-supremacy bullcrap.

A German-American Bund rally held there in 1939 had brought out a large group of protestors, shouting and waving anti-Nazi placards. A riot broke out and scores of cops came to break it up. In the melée several demonstrators were injured by pro-German toughs. Some were hospitalized.

After the Nazis invaded Poland, Sachsen Haus went low-profile. A boys' choir practiced there, but performed only privately. After the war, though, the house reopened to the public, claiming to be a friendly place where people could learn about the "cheerful new Germany" that was beginning to emerge under Konrad Adenauer and the Social Democrats.

I donned my regular hat, put on a casual air, and entered. I found a stern-looking, bespectacled woman of about fifty at a reception desk surrounded by brochures about skiing at Garmisch-Partenkirchen, and posters of pretty blond girls dancing on a grassy Alpine plateau in bright native costumes.

"Velcome. How may I help you?" she asked.

After I asked some trivial questions about sightseeing, she told me that Germany was recovering, that Americans again would find it a fine place to visit. Transatlantic ships would soon resume sailing to Bremerhaven, and the airport at Frankfurt had reopened. I knew that most German cities were sad piles of bombed-out rubble and that the recovery she boasted of would be a long time coming.

I picked up a brochure on Rhine River cruises, then asked where she was from—Cologne, she answered—and how long she'd been here. "It is seven months now."

"How do you find Los Angeles?"

"It is *wunderbar*. Such lovely, sunny weather."

A somber-looking man emerged from an office and with quick, efficient steps went to a water cooler to fill a cup. Double-breasted gray suit, rimless eyeglasses. He gave me a quick looking-over, nodded rather coldly, and went back to wherever he'd come from.

"May I book something for you, sir?" the woman asked.

"Not right now, thanks, but I'm interested. My wife and I might think about one of your tours. I'll be back."

I left, having learned nothing except that I'd found Sachsen Haus a curious place. The woman who'd "velcomed" me hadn't smiled at me once. As I drove to the paper I wondered what else was going on in there.

While I navigated the traffic on Figueroa, the car radio played Ernest Tubb singing "Walking the Floor Over You." I'd liked country music ever since I was a kid and dad took me to hear Uncle Dave Macon at the Shreveport Auditorium.

Reaching South Trenton, I parked in a public lot close to the paper—didn't want Valerie's car to get a darn parking ticket. Once inside, I called Gretchen Siedler's apartment—it was a Normandy number—to suggest she have a look at Sachsen Haus, but she wasn't in. The phone just rang and rang.

After I hung up, Richie Millsap came over and showed me a story he'd written on a cop taking a big vacation at Yosemite, paid for by Jack Dragna. It was well documented. Richie had managed to see the receipts at a travel agency and copied down the dates and amounts. I approved it and told him to take it to the city desk. This would ruffle some feathers big time and Hearst would love it. Good.

One of our reporters, Dick Lafferty, was working on a story about why the actor John Wayne hadn't been in the service during the war. He thought Wayne was a draft dodger, and I tended to agree.

Lafferty plopped himself down at my desk and showed me his notes and a few draft paragraphs. I'd been the paper's military writer and war correspondent, so guys often came to me with things like this.

Under his original name, Marion Morrison, Wayne had played football at USC in the late Twenties. He'd gone on to appear in a string of B Westerns, nothing special, until John Ford's big hit in 1939, *Stagecoach*, made him a sudden star. These days Wayne was sometimes seen with Bugsy Siegel. I knew Siegel liked palling around with celebrities.

When war with Japan broke out, Wayne got a draft-deferred 3-A status, supposedly because he was a little old at 34 and had dependent kids.

"Looks to me like Republic Pictures pulled some strings to get that deferment," Lafferty said after I'd looked over his material. "Whatta you think, Jake?"

"They probably did," I said, "and since other actors his age enlisted—including Henry Fonda and Clark Gable—a lot of people, me included, turned a jaundiced eye on Mr. Wayne. He claimed he tried to volunteer for John Ford's military camera unit that filmed combat at Midway and Italy, but I wasn't buying that."

"Me neither," Lafferty said. "Wayne kept insisting he'd join up after finishing one more film, but it became just one more and then yet *another* one more. He fell in love with the idea of winning the war on celluloid and was making good money at it. So, do you think I've got a story here, Jake? Was he a draft dodger?"

"Looks pretty clear to me," I said, "that he conspired with Republic to keep his deferment. Go ahead, write it."

If this story ran, Wayne would get apoplectic, and Siegel wouldn't like it, either. Perverse old me, I didn't mind ruffling Bugsy's feathers. "Let's see what Aggie Underwood and W.R."—meaning Hearst—"say about it," I told Lafferty.

The things I get into being one of the senior guys around here.

A few minutes after Lafferty left, Mickey Cohen called and invited me to go to a basketball game with him and Bugsy Siegel the next night at the Pan-Pacific Auditorium. UCLA would play Pepperdine in a mid-November season opener.

"Sure," I said. An evening with Cohen and Siegel was always

an experience, and I liked UCLA's young assistant coach, John Wooden. He was ticketed to succeed the head man, Wilbur Johns, in a year or so. Besides plying me with hot dogs and beer, these guys would probably slip in a warning or two to lighten up on them in the paper. Fine, let 'em.

FIVE

I got home that evening about twenty minutes before Valerie did. When she pulled into the driveway in my car she tooted the horn, which she never did, so I trotted on outside. Right away I spotted the gash on my left front fender and a little splotch of maroon paint there. Valerie hopped out—gosh she was pretty, even when upset—and her face wore a whole lot of upset.

"Before you get mad," she said, "this wasn't my fault."

I put my arms around her. "I'm not getting mad, Sweets. Are you all right? What the heck happened?"

"Some goon tried to run me off the road, tried to kill me! On La Cienega, down near Stocker where there's all those oil wells and that big dropoff." She was talking fast, her eyes dilated.

I gently brushed her cheek with my fingers. Pretending to be calm, I said, "Relax, Sweets. Take a deep breath—atta girl—and tell me about it. Take your time."

"I'm in the right lane and this big maroon Buick roars up on my left and starts crowding me. Tries to push me down that ravine. I give a little ground but not much. I'm not going to plunge down that hill, even if your car gets all banged up. As he hits me, he looks right at me and you know what? He's startled, real surprised, like he expects me to be someone else. He floors it and roars away. I'm a little out of control, the right tires throwing up gravel from the shoulder, but I give it a touch of gas, don't overcorrect, and get it straightened out again."

"You're a darn good driver, Val, I've always said that. What did this guy look like?"

"A wide forehead, deep-set eyes. Couldn't see his hair—he had a hat on."

"Anything else?" I asked.

"No, I only saw him for a second or so. Maybe big shoulders, I'm not sure."

"Val, I think some guy thought that was me. When he saw *you*, he figured he had the wrong car. The important thing is that you're okay." My arms still around her, I held her even closer. "Great job!" I was trying hard not to let her see how really angry I was.

Valerie pursed her lips, pulled away, and scuffed at the grass with the toe of her shoe. She's a damn strong woman, I knew.

"Was it one of Siegel's boys?" she asked. "Or Cohen's?"

"Not too likely. Those guys aren't real happy with me right now, but they don't wanta kill me. More likely it was Dragna." That's when I saw Ilse standing there on the front porch. She probably heard it all. Well, it didn't matter. She was strong, too, and was well aware of what was going on with me and the Mob.

"Don't you be worryin' about the car," I told Valerie. "Billy V can bang out and repaint that fender." Billy Vukovich, a friend of mine and a champion race-car driver, had an auto-body shop in Culver City.

I realized my fists were clenched. I could almost taste my rage. In the process of trying to kill me, somebody *almost killed my wife!*

Should I call this in to the cops? Nah, even though some of them were fairly straight and not beholden to the Mob, that'd probably be useless. Here was a better idea: Billy Vukovich must know most of the town's other body-shop guys. Maybe he could find out if a Buick had just come in for some fresh repair work.

I wasn't certain, but I thought Jack Dragna had a maroon Buick Super in that stable of seven or eight cars of his.

* * *

In the morning I dropped my car off at Billy V's and one of his guys drove me to work. I'd hardly got there before I got a call from Gretchen Siedler, my British agent friend.

With some reluctance, I met Gretchen at the Continental that afternoon. She ordered a vodka martini, saying, "One glass of that jug wine was enough for me, thank you." I had my usual bottle of Falstaff beer. I asked how she was getting along and if she'd made any progress.

"I have checked several of your hospitals and medical clinics to see if they have any recent new employees who were Swiss or perhaps Austrian. This man surely would say he was not German. I said I was in search of a relative with whom I had lost contact during the war. So far I have come up empty—isn't that your American saying?"

"Yes, but those were good places to start." I suggested she could also look into the German restaurants in Santa Monica and Culver City, and named some of them. She wrote those down on a notepad. Then I told her about Sachsen Haus, and suggested she might snoop around there a bit. She took a sip of her martini, put the glass down and grasped my hand. "Thank you, dear Jake, I am so glad you are helping me with this."

I pulled my hand away. "Gretchen, no offense, but I don't think any public displays of affection are a good idea." Her eyes twinkled with mischief, but she said, "Yes, I am sure you are right." Was she thinking *private* displays were okay?

The jukebox was playing "To Each His Own." Eddy Howard.

"Just why do you and Colonel Freeborn believe this Dr. Woolf is in L.A.?" I said.

"One of our agents found that he flew here to this city from New York on your TWA airline." I knew TWA had begun making transcontinental flights on DC-4s, flights which required fueling stops in places like Chicago and Denver.

"Say, are you familiar with Tijuana, the border town just across from San Diego?"

"Yes, I have heard of it."

"TJ has a hospital and a few medical clinics," I said. "This guy might think he'd be safer in Mexico. Those might be worth checking out, too." Gretchen nodded and wrote Tijuana on her notepad.

I'll never know why I did this, but then I said that my wife would like to meet her, adding, "I'm not sure that's a good idea, but—"

"Yes, I would like that. I am sure she is a fine woman."

"She sure is, but let's not rush into that. Let's see if she brings it up again." Which I knew damn well Valerie would do.

Out on the sidewalk as we were about to part, Gretchen inched up to me, real close. Oh hell, I thought, she's going to kiss me. She hesitated, finally pulled back, and said with a sly grin, "*Auf weidersehen* for now, dear Jake."

We'd written a piece on Bugsy Siegel helping to bankroll his girlfriend Virginia Hill and her prostitution ring. This had been corroborated by her ex-accountant, who'd had enough of faking stuff on her tax returns and dropped her as a client. We assured the guy we wouldn't name him in our story—and we didn't—so he'd nervously agreed to our using his information. Siegel was seriously upset when the story broke. He didn't tell me so, but Mickey Cohen did. That was no surprise. Of course Siegel would be pissed.

This not only embarrassed him, it must have hurt his marriage too. Siegel had a wife and kids somewhere. New York? Here? None of us really knew.

So I was a little nervous about going to a basketball game at the Pan-Pacific with him and Cohen.

* * *

That night, Bugsy didn't seem too engrossed in the game, but Mickey did. He was a real fan and he knew a lot about basketball. "That's traveling, that's traveling," he called out at one point when a Pepperdine guard carried the ball for a full step between dribbles. "Shoulda been whistled for that."

The two of them sat on each side of me in front-row seats close to the UCLA bench, Siegel resplendent in a double-breasted gray suit, two-tone wingtip shoes, his fedora cocked at a jaunty angle. Cohen wore a suit too, but it was a little baggy. Alongside Siegel, Mickey—who was much shorter at about five-six—looked sort of scruffy. Just as I'd expected, The Mick had bought me a beer and a hot dog. Beer wasn't sold on campus, but it was available at college games away from school, like here at Beverly and Curson.

Siegel had a habit of telling jokes, some of them pretty funny, but right in the middle of the action. Darn distracting. I wanted to follow the game.

With UCLA leading by six at halftime, we climbed the stairs to the concession stand, where Mickey bought me another beer.

He asked if I'd like to go back to Warner's and see another scene being filmed in that flick he was backing. "Some of those actors are pretty bad shots. One of 'em might fire at you by mistake." Was that supposed to be funny?

But Cohen added, "Don't worry, Scribbler, they're using blanks."

"Even so, no thanks," I said. "I heard enough of that bad dialogue the other day."

Cohen then asked about our anti-crime crusade—I knew one of them would bring that up. "Don't be too hard on us, Jakester. Hell, we're just businessmen tryin' to make an honest buck or two. Well, mostly honest," he added with a chuckle.

"Yeah, well, I've got my orders, fellas," I said.

"It doesn't bother me much, Jake," Siegel put in. "I know it's Hearst's doing, not yours. It'll run its course and not change things a bit." The chilly look in his eyes belied those words. "But Jesus, man, ease up on me, will ya?" he added. That was more like what I'd been expecting from the man.

"It may not bother you, Ben, but it's bothering the hell out of Fat Jack," Cohen said, referring to Dragna, the guy the Mob didn't trust. And whom Cohen hated.

I probably shouldn't have—these guys didn't need to know my business—but I mentioned the Buick that tried to force Valerie down that steep hill along La Cienega. "Musta thought it was me driving. Damn it, they almost killed my wife. Dragna's got a maroon Buick sedan, doesn't he?"

Siegel shrugged. For just a second I caught a guarded look on his face, almost as if he hadn't liked the question. Cohen, though, said, "Yeah, I think so. That bastard. We don't want your wife hurt."

"Or me either?" I asked.

Siegel put a hand on my shoulder. That made me nervous. "Don't worry, Jake, us guys only kill each other."

"In that case," I said, "Dragna stepped way over the line. My wife sure isn't one of you guys."

"Yeah, he did." Siegel turned to Cohen. "Maybe it's time for Fat Jack to have a little accident. Whatta you think, Mickey?"

I shuddered at that.

"Maybe so," Cohen said. "I think I'll check that out with Genovese."

That conversation depressed the hell out of me during the second half of the game. I sure didn't want a gangland murder taking place on my account.

I knew Lucky Luciano was in Italy. He'd been deported by the feds last year, but he still ruled his U.S. crime family with an iron hand. Vito Genovese and Meyer Lansky ran things for him in the States, taking their orders by transatlantic cable.

During a time out in the second half, I asked Cohen, "What's the story on Jack Dragna anyway? What makes him tick?"

"Dragna started out bootlegging during Prohibition," Mickey said. "Then in the Thirties he got into runnin' drugs and whores, sellin' protection, plus he set up a race wire. He drove out the competition, ran the whole town. Now that we've got all organized, he ain't got as much control, supposed to play ball with all of us, but he don't like it. That's why Ben's here, to keep an eye . . . hey, whatsa matter with me, Scribbler? Why the hell am I telling you all this?"

I grinned and said, "Because I'm such a sweet guy, of course. It's just background, Mick, I'm not gonna write this." The buzzer sounded; the time out was over.

With four minutes to go, Pepperdine had cut UCLA's lead to four points and the Bruins called a time out. I noticed that it wasn't Coach Johns, but his assistant, John Wooden, who talked as the players huddled around. We were close enough to hear Wooden, holding a rolled-up program, say, "You know what to do, fellows, four-corner stall. Keep the ball away from them."

And that's what they did, executing a textbook stall, keeping the ball away from Pepperdine the rest of the game with some sharp passing. When Pepperdine turned to some desperate fouling, UCLA sank most of its free throws, winning in the end by eight points.

As we parted outside, I said, "Thanks a lot, fellas, I had a great time."

"Sure thing," Cohen answered.

As they walked off, probably thinking they were out of earshot, I made out Siegel saying, "I'm calling Genovese in the morning, see what those guys say about Fat Jack's life expectancy."

I didn't like the sound of that at all.

That night while Valerie was listening to *Your Hit Parade* on the radio, I went to the crawl space above my closet and pulled down the box containing my Luger. I worked the pistol's toggle-lock action, then proceeded to oil and clean the thing. I also checked the little box of 9-millimeter ammunition before putting it all back again.

SIX

The fender on my Chevy Ridemaster had been banged out, straightened and repainted. When I picked it up at Billy Vukovich's, I told him we'd go to the midget-auto races that night at Gilmore Stadium. "Great, it'll be good to have a couple more fans there," Billy said.

The bill came to thirty-seven dollars. I was pretty sure he'd given me a big break on the price. I then drove to the paper to put in a day's work. There'd be another meeting with my anti-crime team, Richie Millsap and Marko Janicek.

When the Unholy Trinity got together I asked if either of them had been threatened in any way, had been tailed, or even just had a sense of being endangered.

"Why do you ask?" said Millsap.

I told them what had happened to Valerie when she was in my car. "The bastards!" Janicek uttered. "Who do you think it was?"

"Probably one of Dragna's boys. That's just a hunch, but I'm sure as hell going to find out."

"Now that you mention it," Millsap said, "it seems to me Dragna does have a big maroon Buick."

"Yeah, I think so too. I've got a body-shop guy asking around to see if it turns up somewhere with some collision damage. Okay then, we have stories to go over and leads to follow."

Valerie, Ilse and I showed up that night at the Gilmore speedway. This was a quarter-mile dirt track with black-and-white striped wooden crash walls along the outside. Pits and their crews occupied the edge of the infield.

I bought a program, fifteen cents, and we took seats far enough from the turns so we wouldn't get sprayed with flying dirt. There would be qualifying heats, a trophy dash, a semi-main event, and then the main event, called the Grand Prix.

I told Ilse that these cars were smaller versions of those that raced at the Indianapolis 500. I also had to explain what the Indy 500 was. "These cars are powered by Ford V-8 engines," I said, "and some by Offenhausers. Those are German engines, Ilse, very powerful. We call them Offies."

"I see," she said with interest. "Then I hope an Offie wins." As the races took place, some of them did. "See how they whirl and skid in the turns," Ilse exclaimed, "and pick up speed in the straight places." She was enjoying all this.

Finally came the Grand Prix. In a red and white car, Number 15, Vukovich battled and battled most of the way with fellows named Troy Ruttman and Rodger Ward.

"Is Mr. V driving an Offenhauser?" Ilse asked.

"Yes he is, *Liebchen*."

In the final stretch, Billy gunned past Ruttman and got the checkered flag by less than two car lengths. We all clapped and cheered.

"A German engine won the race," Ilse cried out. "*Wunderbar!*"

We went down to the pits to congratulate Billy. Dirt from the track covered his face except for two big round patches around the eyes where his goggles protected them. As he took off his crash helmet, Ilse said, "You look like a raccoon, sir."

"I wouldn't if I'd stayed in front all the way, little lady, but I couldn't manage that tonight. And who might you be?"

I introduced Ilse as my swell daughter—Billy V had already met Valerie. He took off his gloves and shook Ilse's hand, saying,

"I'm real pleased to meet you." Turning, he said, "And how are you, Valerie?"

"Just fine, Billy. Congratulations. You drove a great race." A track official came up to present Billy his trophy. He cleaned off his face with a towel, and we stepped back to keep out of the pictures that were about to be taken.

When that was over, Billy said, "Jake, I've asked around and so far no maroon Buick has been brought in to any shops for repair." I had told him why my fender needed fixing up—Valerie's nasty experience on La Cienega—so he said, "I'm sure sorry about what happened the other day, Valerie. I hear you handled Jake's buggy real well. You wanta try some midget-auto racing?"

"Maybe I should," Valerie said with that coy little grin of hers.

"*Muti!*" Ilse exclaimed, unaware that her spunky stepmother was kidding. Wasn't she?

That's when I reached one of my dumb decisions. I would go to Jack Dragna's myself and nose around in that big garage of his, stupidly dangerous as that would be. But I had to *know*, to really find out who'd done this to Valerie.

I may be stupid but I'm not a fool, so on Monday morning I arranged a little insurance policy. I left word with our city editor, Aggie Underwood, that I was heading out to Dragna's. If I didn't come back, she would inform the police commissioner, Clem Horrall, one L.A. cop we knew to be clean, and Fat Jack would be in the soup. I hadn't told Valerie what I was about to do. She'd probably brain me with a potted plant.

So I drove to Dragna's place and parked right in front. Sometimes brazen is better than stealth. As I got out, one of his goons came up, scowled at me, and looked over the car, giving special attention to the front left fender. He had a broad forehead and deep-set eyes, probably the same guy who'd tried to waste Valerie.

"What the hell you want?" he snarled.

"Just to have a look around."

"The hell you will. That's trespassing."

"No it's not. Your boss knows me. He'll be glad to see me."

"Mr. Dragna's not home, so scram out of here, pal."

I noticed the bulge under his jacket. Shoulder holster, some big artillery under there. "I appreciate fine cars," I said. "Jack told me to stop by anytime and have a look. I was in the neighborhood, so I'll take him up on it, check out some of those buggies of his."

I started toward the wide garage but this guy grabbed my arm. I shook off his grip and broke into a trot. He followed, walking fast and yelling, "Hey!"

One of the three big garage doors was open and another of Dragna's punks stood there blocking my way. "Good morning," I said. "Would you stand aside, please?"

He threw a punch at my face. I'd done some boxing in the Navy a few years back. I ducked the blow, then drove a right hand into his solar plexus, putting all I had behind it. He grunted and doubled over while I scurried inside.

I passed an elegant Duesenberg roadster and a shiny red Caddy, then came to a maroon Buick Super. Beside it, a guy had some mallets, a sander, and a spray gun. "Have a little accident there?" I asked, seeing a banged-up right fender and a splash of black Chevrolet paint. *My* Chevrolet paint.

The punk I'd just clocked staggered up, his face a contortion of pain and anger. Before he could grab hold of me, I quick-stepped away. "Got some fine cars here," I said. "Well, since Jack's not here, I'll be on my way."

Big Forehead arrived at that moment with a large black .45 pointed at me. "Yeah, you'll be on your way," he growled. "For a little ride. With us!"

Jesus! It felt like my body temperature just dropped ten degrees.

"To a tugboat down at the harbor," I asked, "or maybe a hole in the ground out in the Mojave? No thanks. Now put that pop gun away. The chief cop knows I'm here, the commissioner himself. If I go for a ride with you, Fat Jack will be taking a ride himself. To San Quentin."

"You're bluffing," Big Shoulders snarled.

"I never bluff," I said, trying to put a brave face on it. "I've got a good hand here. Believe me, the commish knows all about it."

The two goons gaped, words eluding them.

"So long, fellas," I said. "Have a nice day." To the guy I'd punched, I added, "Take a Bromo Seltzer and lie down awhile. You'll feel better."

They followed when I strode back to the car, but didn't try to stop me. They shouted a few choice obscenities, though.

I got in and started the engine, but there was Big Shoulders standing in front of the car, gun in hand, hateful scowl on his face. When I started inching forward, he stepped aside and gave me the finger.

As I drove off, my hands started to shake. Maybe I wasn't as brave as I thought. "Okay," I told myself, "now I know who tried to kill me—and almost snuffed Valerie instead. Damn it, if anybody's going to knock off Jack Dragna, it should be me, not one of Luciano's boys." Was I really thinking *that?*

Twenty minutes later, Aggie Underwood said, "I'm sure relieved to see you here in one piece, Jakey boy."

I wasn't sure what she was talking about. For a moment I couldn't tell you where I'd just been or what I'd done. I'd had kind of a blackout for a few hours after I'd shot that Nazi infiltrator during the Battle of the Bulge. Had I just had another? The mind does funny things in times of stress.

"Me too," I said uncertainly.

* * *

Gretchen called that afternoon and asked if I'd go to Tijuana with her. Something inside me wanted to say, "Sure." I couldn't deny I had feelings for this woman. There'd been a strong attraction that first day in Berlin four years ago, an attraction that cut both ways. If Gretchen tried to lure me into a bedroom in a Mexican hotel, I knew it would be hard to resist. But I had a darn good marriage to a remarkable woman, a woman I loved very much. I damn sure wasn't going to jeopardize that.

"Sorry, Gretchen," I said. "I can't get a day off." Though I knew I could. "I've got a lot of assignments piling up here. You'll be fine down there by yourself. You know some Spanish, don't you? Most of you Europeans have three or four languages."

"Yes, I speak some Spanish. Well, *mein Leibling*, I am very disappointed."

"So am I," I half lied.

After she rang off I leaned back, put my feet up on the desk, laced my fingers behind my head, and began to think about this evil doctor she was trying to track down. The Buchenwald Butcher.

We'd both assumed this guy would try to connect with a hospital or medical clinic. But since he'd conducted gruesome surgical experiments, he surely knew about knives, scalpels, bone chisels and such. Maybe he'd hooked up with a surgical supply outfit. Or maybe a pharmaceutical company. Those were possibilities I could pass along to Gretchen.

Agness Underwood came by at that moment, winked, and said, "Why aren't you working, Jakey boy?"

I pulled my feet off the desk fast, straightened up, and said, "I *am* working, Aggie. I'm thinking. Thinking always leads to good stories, you know that."

She laughed and said, "Well, think hard then, we've got a big news hole to fill today."

I soon had something to think hard *about*. A couple of minutes later I got a call from one of my tipsters, Lenny Navarro, who told me Billy Wilkerson and Ben Jaffe had overextended themselves on the Flamingo Hotel they were trying to build on the Las Vegas Strip. I already knew that. And that Bugsy Siegel had stepped in with some Cosa Nostra bucks to help them out. Help them out, hell—Bugsy had seized control. I was aware of that, too.

"Tell me something I don't know, Lenny."

"Bet you don't know this, Jake. Bugsy's having trouble too. Big cost overruns. He don't know shit about construction and his contractors are gouging hell out of him, buying material they don't need, padding their bills with phony change orders, crap like that. Meyer Lansky and Luciano are pretty damn upset, wasting Mob money like that."

"Now *that* I hadn't known, Lenny. Thanks, I owe you one. Hell, make that two."

Lucky Luciano sore at Siegel? That got my antenna going up. That was something I would definitely look into.

A few minutes later, a process server showed up and shoved a subpoena in my face, ordering me to appear in Superior Court. Jack Dragna, damn his black soul, was pressing a misdemeanor trespass charge against me. This was Monday and the hearing was set for Thursday at ten. I called the paper's lawyer, Ed Franklin, and told him what I'd done out at Fat Jack's. He asked a lot of questions, like why did I even go, and who saw me there? He agreed to appear with me and we talked a little strategy.

We met in front of the courthouse on South Hill Street on Thursday, beneath that big statue of the blindfolded Lady Justice balancing her scales. As we entered and walked to courtroom six, Franklin told me to keep my mouth shut, that he'd do the talking.

Inside, Big Shoulders was already there, sitting beside a guy in glasses and a blue suit, obviously Dragna's attorney. We took seats at the defendant's table opposite them.

A bailiff called out, "Superior Court, County of Los Angeles, is now in session. All rise." As I got to my feet, the judge entered. I swallowed hard. *Oh-oh*. His name was Pasqual Bonadio and it was well known that he'd sided with Dragna and Bugsy Siegel on several prominent cases. His palm had probably been greased but good. I whispered that to my lawyer, who nodded gravely.

After the charge was read, Franklin said, "Your honor, we respectfully request that you step down. We have reason to doubt your impartiality in this matter."

Bonadio scowled, rapped his gavel on the sound block, and said, "Request denied. Attorney for the plaintiff, proceed."

Dragna's lawyer said his piece. When my man's turn came, he said, "What proof has the prosecution shown, your honor? Were any pictures taken? Were my client's fingerprints found at Mr. Dragna's? I request that this be dropped."

"We have the word of two reputable witnesses," Dragna's attorney said.

"Reputable?" Franklin fired back. "Those men are known hoodlums. Again, where is any real evidence of trespassing? On the other hand we have the word of a respected journalist. It's his word against that of two men known to be involved in criminal activity. I move again that this matter be dropped."

"Motion denied." Again, the rapping of the gavel. "I find the defendant guilty of trespassing and fine him one hundred dollars. Court adjourned."

I shouted, "Aw, what a damn fix this was."

"Two hundred dollars!" Bonadio snarled. "Want to try for three? Or would you rather be locked up for contempt?" My mouth opened but I forced the choice words I had there to stay put. Big Shoulders flashed me an evil grin of triumph.

Franklin took me by the arm and hustled me out of there. In the hallway, he said, "I'm sorry about this outcome, Jake, but we were dead ducks in there, and an appeal would probably be pointless. But I will see that the *Herald-Express* pays your fine."

Thank goodness for small favors, I thought. Now I had a rap sheet.

SEVEN

Hearst hadn't been showing up at the paper as often as he used to. I'd heard that he wasn't doing well—no surprise, the old buzzard was eighty-four years old.

He and Marion Davies had closed up their huge waterfront home in Santa Monica and now were living in a smaller place in Beverly Hills. Not much smaller, though—it was a three-story mansion. They seldom went up the coast anymore to his castle at San Simeon. But even though he'd slowed down a lot, Hearst's interest in his papers remained as strong as ever. He kept sending in notes, often delivered by Miss Davies, saying, "Do this, do that, play this real big, use this angle," and so on.

It was no big surprise then when Aggie Underwood called me at home that night and said we'd been summoned to Beverly Hills the following day for a personal meeting. It would be Aggie, managing editor John Campbell, and me. If the king couldn't get out to see his knights, they must come to him.

Before going there, I cornered our man who covered the courts and asked him not to write anything about my little conviction. I prayed it would escape the notice of our competition, the *Times* and the *Mirror*. I hadn't even told Valerie about that or about my visit to Dragna's, which had led to it. I would tell her soon, though. I kept only a few things from her, like my one-nighter with Gretchen in 1942, and the fact that I'd shot some Germans during my second incursion into Nazi Germany in '44.

Johnny Campbell drove Aggie and me out to Hearst's in his four-door Dodge, me riding shotgun and Aggie in back.

"Let's not tell him anything about your wife's close call," Aggie said as we rolled along Olympic Boulevard. "He'd probably get excited and order a big play on that. I can see the head he'd dictate: 'Gangsters Try to Kill *Herald-Express* Reporter's Wife.' "

"Absolutely," Campbell agreed. "We don't need that getting out."

"Thanks and amen to that," I put in.

Aggie said Hearst had scrubbed Dick Lafferty's John Wayne draft-dodging story. "W.R. says Wayne's so popular now that a lot of our readers would take offense. He's worried about circulation."

"Aren't we all?" I said. "Afternoon papers are starting to slip. I guess people would rather read the news with their morning coffee."

At the front door of the Hearst manor, a butler took our hats and led us to a large walnut-paneled library. There we found W.R. seated in a gray velvet wingback chair. He looked pale and drawn and many pounds lighter than the last time I'd seen him. It made me sad seeing this vigorous man looking old and frail.

Marion Davies sat in an identical chair drawn up next to him. She, on the other hand, looked a little puffy, no longer the gamine of her acting days.

As always, Hearst greeted us warmly and formally, preceding our last names with Miss and Mister. "Thank you for coming all the way out here. As you can see, I'm not quite myself these days." His voice rusty and weaker than I'd ever heard it. That too saddened me.

A servant brought in a tray of coffee, cream and sugar, cups, saucers, and assorted pastries. "Thank you, Charles," W.R. said.

Turning to me, he said, "And how is my favorite bloodhound?" He'd begun calling me that during my days as a war correspondent.

"Your anti-crime team is doing a splendid job, Mr. Weaver. That story of Mr. Millsap's on Dragna paying for a crooked cop's vacation in Yosemite was excellent."

I thanked him and went on to explain what else we were working on.

"Good," he said. "I do hope this will help our circulation. I've been growing concerned about the numbers."

Marion Davies spoke up. "Willie is thinking of merging the *Herald-Express* with the *Examiner*." That was a rumor I'd heard and dreaded, didn't like the idea of combining with the *Morning Examiner*, our sister paper.

"Oh please, no," Aggie uttered.

"I hope it won't come to that, Miss Underwood," Hearst said, "but it may become necessary at some point. We've been losing too much money. Rest assured, no matter what, there will always be a job for you three.

"And speaking of circulation, my Detroit paper, the *Times*, is lagging behind the *News* and *Free Press*. I wouldn't like to have to close it down. An anti-crime campaign might help them. Would you be willing to go there for a few days, Mr. Weaver, and give them some advice on setting up a team like yours? They could go after the Purple Gang, and my favorite bloodhound could show them how to go about it."

I knew that the Purple Gang had operated in Detroit ever since Prohibition and was one of the few syndicates that had managed to elude Lucky Luciano's grasp. I also knew this was more order than request. "Sure, Chief, if that's what you want."

"Splendid, Mr. Weaver, thank you."

As I poured a cup of coffee for Aggie and one for myself, the old man asked questions of Johnny and her, like how we'd play the mayoral election. Aggie, direct as always, voiced her misgivings about the incumbent, Fletcher Bowron, who'd been in office more than ten years. She called him "as crooked as Canyon Drive."

"If you have something good on him, by all means go after him," Hearst said. He then told Johnny he wanted a strong editorial supporting Douglas MacArthur for the Republican presidential nomination in 1948. "That brilliant general"—two words I wouldn't link together—"is doing marvelous work as military commander of Japan." Johnny nodded.

A big supporter of MacArthur, W.R. wasn't happy that the book I'd coauthored, *Two Men at War: A Retrospective*, had criticized some of the general's actions in the Pacific. And yet the old man, ever faithful to his minions, made sure all his papers and radio stations gave it favorable reviews, for which I was immensely grateful.

"I'm pleased that young Richard Nixon, whom we backed so strongly," Hearst said, "knocked Voorhiss right off his Congressional seat last week. Be sure to play Nixon up after the first of the year, what committees he gets on, so forth." It had been a rough and tumble campaign, during which the young man from Whittier had thrown a lot of dirt. I knew Johnny had hated being told to pimp for Nixon during the race. "Sure, Chief," he managed.

W.R. then asked about our plans for Thanksgiving, which was coming up. Aggie said she was having some friends over, while Johnny and I said we just planned quiet dinners at home.

"With your good wife and daughter," W.R. said to me. "I hope that fine girl of yours is adjusting well to life in America." I had told him about Ilse on my return from Germany in 1942.

"Yes sir, thank you, she's doing well. She's on the school paper, and wants to become a reporter someday like her old dad."

"Excellent. She can always have a job with one of my papers."

"That's kind of you, sir, but only if she proves good enough."

Miss Davies said they usually threw a big party at Thanksgiving but regretfully wouldn't be doing so this year. W.R.'s condition made the reason for that obvious.

Johnny nibbled on a cupcake as Hearst asked more questions.

Finally the audience was over. W.R. again thanked us for coming, and we knights took leave of the king.

I'd been cogitating a bit more about Sachsen Haus, so back at the paper I called a friend of mine in the Federal Building—a Thornwall number—a guy who worked for the State Department, and asked about that place's ties to the German government.

"*What* German government?" he said. "The Allied occupation forces still run that country. Some municipal elections have been permitted in the western zones—strictly local—and the Social Democrats have won most of them. A national German government is still a few years away."

"So Bernie, there's no German authority that would have control of, say, the Sachsen Haus here in L.A.?"

"None at all. That place, as well as the House of Germany in that big park down in San Diego, are on their own, run by volunteers."

Ach so, I thought, using the German equivalent of "Oh, really?" I would have to tell Gretchen to move that curious Sachsen Haus up higher on her list.

That night I bit the bullet and finally told Valerie about going to Fat Jack's, where a gun was pulled on me, and also about what happened in court.

"Oh, Jake," she uttered, frowning in despair.

"I know, hon, it was risky, but I got what I came for: proof that Dragna was the one who almost got you killed."

"But . . . oh you reckless fool of a husband you. And now you have a conviction?"

"Just a misdemeanor, Sweets, just a misdemeanor. Still, I'm gonna take down that crooked judge somehow. Get a picture of him being wined and dined by Bugsy at Ciro's . . . showing up at Dragna's place . . . accepting a case of whisky from one of the goons, something like that. Maybe I'll even figure a way to sneak a peek at his bank account. Say, it looks like I've got a trip coming up. W.R. wants me to go and help the *Detroit Times* set up an anti-crime team like our Unholy Trinity."

"Oh, shoot," Valerie said, "and here I thought you were through going off to the wars."

"A different kind of war, Val, but a war just the same. I won't be gone long and this time I'll try not to get shot at."

When we made love later that night, she was better than ever, really throwing herself into it. She took me places I'd rarely been. I knew her concern for my safety had a lot to do with that.

On Saturday Valerie and I took some canvas camp chairs and soft drinks and watched Ilse's soccer game at the West Los Angeles Playground.

Only boys played in athletic competition against other high schools, but Ilse had joined a girls' soccer team in a Department of Recreation and Parks youth league. Games were played on Saturdays. A German man, Klaus Schäfer, and a Hungarian woman, Miss Kardos, coached her team. They were immigrants who'd fled the war in Europe. The team, called the Tigers, was a mix of girls of European, American and Mexican backgrounds.

The game was a dandy. "These girls are in great shape," Valerie said at one point during the contest. "They run and run, always moving. Look at Ilse's ponytail flying up and down."

On a corner kick, Ilse gathered in the ball with her left foot and deftly goaled it with her right, the ball skittering past the keeper by inches.

Valerie and I and the other parents jumped to our feet. "Atta girl!" I shouted.

At halftime the girls sat around their coaches, drank water, and listened to words of instruction and encouragement. The German coach, a big man with straw-colored hair and thick glasses, obviously had played the game. He knew what he was talking about—talking in a thick accent.

The Tigers went on to win 3 to 1, Ilse setting up one of the additional goals with a nice pass to one of her teammates. The three of us celebrated afterward with sandwiches and ice cream at a nearby deli.

The next day, Sunday, I played golf at the Lakeside course in Burbank with Marko Janicek and two of our sportswriters. I'd recently bought a new set of clubs with steel shafts and was eager to try those babies out. They replaced the old hickory ones I'd had from before the war.

One of the sports guys wanted to play four bits a hole but I said no way. I didn't golf often enough to be very good and I'd probably owe him nine bucks at the end of the day. My aim was to have some fun and fresh air, see what the new clubs could do, and forget about criminals for awhile.

That didn't prove entirely possible. The Unholy Trinity had captured the imagination of the whole darn city room, and the sportswriters kept bringing up Jack Dragna, the crooked judge, cops on the take, and so on. "I hear Bugsy Siegel's a golfer," one of them said. "I wouldn't know," I answered. "Now shut up and let me putt."

In the end I took 102 strokes, not a good round. I'd been in four or five sand traps. I blamed it on the new clubs I wasn't used to. On the other hand, Marko hit a lot of fine shots and finished with an 86. Good thing I hadn't been betting with the athletic former Army Ranger.

*   *   *

When the Unholy Trinity met in the city room the next day, I congratulated Marko on his fine round, then asked him to tail Judge Bonadio for a day. "See what he does when he's not in court, where he goes, where he takes his meals, where he lives. If he goes into a bank be sure to get the name and location. But Marko, be real careful that he doesn't catch on."

Marko liked the idea and accepted the chore, saying, "No sweat."

On my desk was a note from Hearst saying he wanted me to go to Detroit right after Thanksgiving. Man, the Motor City would be cold at the end of November, snow probably sweeping in off Lake St. Claire. Good thing I still had the overcoat Valerie gave me before I went to Germany in '42. I'd make damn good use of it.

After reading the note, I called Gretchen at her apartment to ask how it went for her down in Tijuana.

"It is a peculiar, rather shabby town," she said, "but interesting. Unfortunately I learned nothing at their hospital and medical clinics. Only one place had a doctor who was not Mexican. This was an overweight man from San Diego, clearly not Otto Woolf. But I made two discoveries: mariachi music and the taco. The trumpets, violins and guitars, *sehr schön*, so unlike any music I had ever heard. And the taco, it makes a tasty little meal."

What wasn't to like about mariachi music and tacos?

I told her she might want to look into surgical supply places in L.A., and repeated my earlier suggestion about Sachsen Haus. "I've learned that place has no connection with any authorities in today's Germany. It's completely independent."

She thanked me for those tips and asked when we could meet again.

"How about noon tomorrow at Moran's?" I said. "We shouldn't always be seen at the same place. Moran's is a joint on the same side of the street as the Continental, two doors down."

"Good, my dear. I will look forward to seeing you."

EIGHT

My daughter's Americanization was rocking right along. Ilse liked the movies, especially mysteries. The Alfred Hitchcock film *Spellbound* was a favorite of hers. In the whodunits she often figured out who the culprit was before the end. She'd also enjoyed the midget-auto races. So when Mickey Cohen invited me to the Friday night fights I decided to take Ilse along. Why not? There was no school the next day and she was a savvy girl who took genuine interest in my work. I couldn't see any harm in her meeting The Mick.

But Valerie could. When I floated the idea she put her foot down but good. I tried to persuade her it would be okay and that Mickey and I would refrain from cussing, or so I hoped. "It'll be educational for her, Val, and she'll have a swell time."

"Sometimes I wonder about you, Jake. Exposing Ilse to an evening with a hoodlum in a loud, smoky place like that would be—what's the word I'm looking for?—oh yes, *stupid*."

She was right. I gave Valerie that round. Besides, I'd recently won my share of these little debates with her.

Artie Aragon, a flashy welterweight of Mexican background, would headline the main event. Aragon had a lot of personality and the local press loved him, though in my opinion they overrated him. He'd won a lot of bouts—lost a few, too—but didn't have the skills to challenge on the national level against top-notchers like Ike Williams and Sugar Ray Robinson.

Cohen left a ringside seat for me, so on Friday night I met him there at the Shrine Auditorium. The place was hot, noisy and filled with smoke, cigarette and cigar both. As the preliminary bouts were fought, droplets of sweat and blood splashed us. Ah, front-row seats. Yeah, Valerie, I thought, good thing Ilse's not here after all.

Between bouts I mentioned my upcoming Detroit assignment, and asked, "What do you know about the Purple Gang, Mick?"

"A wop named Tripolani runs that outfit. He's a strange one, that guy. His number two is a fella called Columbini. They don't take any guff from Luciano. Don't know why Lucky don't move in on those punks. Maybe it's too small time or maybe Lansky's holding him back." I knew Luciano took advice from his pal Meyer Lansky, who was known as "the Mob's accountant."

"Lansky might figure it'd be too ugly a mess," Mickey went on, "though a little blood ain't never bothered Lucky before."

"Do you think Luciano will be back in the States someday?" I asked.

"For sure. He's got connections like you wouldn't believe. He'll get in here before you know it, probably through Cuba. Old Lucky's got all the Havana casinos under his thumb, ya know."

Before the ten-round main event, Artie Aragon entered the ring in a gaudy robe in the Mexican colors, green, white and red, and raised his arms to some loud cheering. His opponent, Joey Gonsalvez, a pretty fair fighter himself, slipped through the ropes and began hopping up and down in his corner, antsy to get on with it.

The first three rounds were pretty close. I didn't see how the judges could give either man much of an edge. Before the bell sounded for round four, Mickey, who'd done some boxing in his younger days, said, "I hear you used to box too, Scribbler."

"Yeah, I had a few bouts in the Navy. Won most of 'em till the day I ran up against a Mexican kid with fists like thunder."

"Then whatta you say we strap on the gloves one of these days and spar a round or two?"

"Maybe so," I answered. Valerie would love *that*. There was no way, though, that I would ever step into the ring with Mickey Cohen.

In the later rounds, Aragon opened a cut above Gonsalvez's left eye and his corner men were busy plastering that up during the breaks. Gonsalvez went down for an eight-count in round nine, and at the end of the tenth the ring announcer took his mike, raised Aragon's hand, and bellowed, "The winnah, seven rounds to three, Artie Aragon!" bringing on a thunderous ovation.

"Wanta go down to the locker room and congratulate the greaser?" Mickey asked.

"Nah, I've met Artie before. I'll leave him to the sportswriters."

We made our way to the exit among a mob of others leaving the arena. Outside, Mickey said, "I know you got yourself a good wife, Jake, but anytime you get the urge to slide your dipstick into somethin' real sweet—"

"Thanks just the same, Mick, but I'm gonna play it straight in that department. Hey, it was fun tonight. Thanks for the ticket."

"Sure." His eyes narrowed just a little. "I been pretty good to you, so . . ." He stopped right there but the point was made: return the favor, he was saying. "Well, be careful in Detroit, Scribbler. It's a tough place. See you in church, kid."

I'd already decided that Dragna, not Cohen, was the main target of our campaign, but I knew that beneath his good-guy façade, Mickey Cohen, runner of whores, numbers, heroin, loan sharks—you name it—was one ruthless son of a bitch.

Driving home, I thought back on my meeting with Gretchen at Moran's. Over ham sandwiches and some drinks, we'd talked about the leads she'd been following and thankfully she didn't get overly flirtatious. She was surprised to learn I'd be going to Detroit.

"The place where they make all the cars," she'd said. "I will miss you. How long will you be gone?"

"Not long, a week or less. Say, since you've discovered the taco, there's a little joint called Juanito's at Pico and Olive that has great tacos. You'll have to try it."

She said she would, then asked about my Uncle Dieter, whom she'd met in Berlin back in '42.

"I've had some letters from him. He's fine, working as a detective now in the American Zone of Berlin. Dieter's a little old for that, sixty-eight, but the occupation forces are hard up for experienced men who weren't hard-liner Nazis. He'll retire in a year or two. He plans to come visit us one of these days."

When I got home from the fights, Valerie was still up. She held a small glass of cognac and poured one for me. We sat in the living room and I told her about Aragon's victory. "We were sitting ringside and the violence of boxing is pretty damn graphic when you're up that close. You were right about keeping Ilse at home."

"Of course I was," Valerie said. She went on to mention some things she'd done that day at work, blueprint modifications and such. Also chores she'd lined up for me to do that weekend, like fix the latch on the garden gate and fertilize the lawn.

Then she said, "Say, your friend Gretchen apparently is all alone in this town. It can't be easy for her. Let's have her over for Thanksgiving dinner."

"For Thanksgiving?"

"Sure, we have a big turkey and it would do her good. Ilse would be glad to see her again too. It's been—what?—four years now?"

I didn't like that at all. The woman I'd slept with in Germany and my wife together? But I knew this would be another round I would lose to this determined wife of mine.

* * *

Gretchen happily accepted the invitation and so about noon on Thanksgiving Day, Ilse and I drove out to her apartment at Wilshire and Union to pick her up.

"My, Ilse, I would not have recognized you," Gretchen said. "You are a young lady now and a very lovely one." My daughter blushed, gave a little head bob, and took Gretchen's hand. "It is most good to see you again, *Frau* Siedler."

"None of that now. You must call me Gretchen." She pulled Ilse into a hug.

"Please sit in front with my *Vater*," Ilse said before climbing into the back seat. As I drove west on Wilshire, fretting a lot, Gretchen asked Ilse about school and how she was getting along in America. They talked—I worried.

Before long came the moment I'd been dreading. To my surprise, though, Valerie and Gretchen quickly took to one another. Soon they were calling each other by first name as if they'd been friends forever.

"It smells wonderful in here," said Gretchen. Valerie told her that was the turkey roasting in the oven. "Dinner will be in a couple of hours, so come out in back with us and we'll have some champagne."

We'd placed a table and chairs on a shady spot on the back lawn—it was a nice day for November—and Valerie had glasses there, some cheese, crackers, and champagne in a bucket of ice. While the women conversed, getting comfortable with one another, Ilse was having a glass of lemonade, though I also gave her a sip of my champagne. I just sat quietly and listened to the gals chat for several minutes. So did Ilse.

"Jake tells me your code name is Tapestry," Valerie said at one point, "and that his was Colonial Four, and maybe it still is, since he's helping you again."

"Yes, MI-6 amuses itself with such code names. During the

war, Colonel Freeborn ran an agent in Berchtesgaden known as Meatloaf." Valerie laughed at that, glanced at me and said, "You're not saying much, dear."

I'd been having the odd sense of being on display, that both of them were thinking about me and what they knew of me, and were trying too hard to disguise it by talking about anything *but* me. "You two are getting along fine without any input from this old reporter here."

"You are not old," Gretchen said with a little smile. That remark, plus the smile, brought a curious look to Valerie's face and a blaze of panic to my mind. But my clever wife masked it, saying with a quick, sly grin, "Well, he's *kind* of old."

Ilse asked Gretchen if her place in Schöneberg had survived the air raids.

"*Ja*, thank you for asking. To our neighborhood some damage was done but luckily none on our block."

"I am so glad," Ilse said. "I remember your nice kitchen there."

As the champagne mellowed us and the women's rapport grew, Valerie asked Gretchen about her late husband. Gretchen explained that he'd been a *Luftwaffe* pilot who was killed attacking England. "I loved Friedrich very much and this was a difficult time for me, but his death only reinforced my already strong dislike of the Nazis."

"I'm sure it did," Valerie said. "Now this assignment that's brought you all the way here, why is it that you think this man you're hunting could be in Los Angeles?"

"We had learned from a reliable source that he came here from New York. It is possible that he may not be here at all, that this was merely another jumping-off point. If I learn nothing more in a month or so, MI-6 will recall me to Europe. But enough about me, Valerie. I understand that you are an aircraft engineer."

"Not exactly. What I really am is a tool designer."

"And one of the few woman tool designers in the whole country," I cut in proudly.

"That is most impressive," Gretchen said, and raised her champagne glass in salute.

To my surprise, Valerie then inquired about Gretchen's somewhat twisted nose: "If I'm not out of line and you don't mind my asking."

"Not at all," Gretchen said, and told how she'd been banged about in a brawl with some tough factory women during the Blitz in London, where she'd briefly been stationed. "My accent they did not like. They called me a dirty German."

Ilse jumped in and said the same thing happened to her on her first day of school.

"I am so sorry," Gretchen said.

"I hit one of them pretty good. After that I had no more trouble. Now I like my school very much."

"I used to do some boxing," I put in, "so maybe some of that's in Ilse's genes."

"Oh, let's hope not," Valerie said.

Later, we trooped back in to have our meal. All in all, dinner proceeded well. Besides the turkey, Valerie had prepared a green salad, sweet potatoes, stuffing, and cranberry sauce. We had chilled chardonnay too.

"So this is a typical American Thanksgiving meal," Gretchen said. "In *Deutschland* we have no such holiday. It is all so delicious. Thank you so much for including me."

To my relief, Valerie asked nothing about Gretchen's dealings with me in Berlin and the women continued to get along thick as thieves.

That evening Valerie went with me when I drove Gretchen home. When we said goodbye in front of her building, the two women hugged and lightly kissed cheeks. Gretchen thanked us again. "Today was *wunderbar.*"

"Please come again anytime," Valerie said.

Back in the car as I drove toward home, she said, "I like Gretchen, she's a remarkable woman. I hope she succeeds in her mission out here. She's lovely, too. Oddly enough, I don't find the bridge of her nose unattractive. It adds a certain allure to her face. I'm happy to know her."

When I said nothing to that, Valerie added, "She thinks the world of you—that's obvious. Who wouldn't? I certainly do, you charming old galoot."

I still didn't know what to say.

"I'll never ask what went on between you two in Berlin, but I know you couldn't have got out of Nazi Germany without her help. If you were, well, indiscreet with her back then—and please don't ever tell me—I wouldn't mind."

I was stunned. Was this wife of mine on a fishing expedition? Or was she just being uncannily intuitive as women are wont to be? Either way, it was no wonder I was a little in awe of her—and loved her like I did.

"We weren't married at the time," Valerie went on, "so there would be nothing to forgive."

But we were *engaged*, I thought, with the tacit obligations that entailed. I still kept my silence but when I stopped for a red light on Olympic I reached over, grasped her hand, and gazed deeply into those warm blue eyes that never failed to excite me.

"I know how much you love me," she whispered, and planted a kiss on my cheek.

Was I a lucky son of a bitch or what? "Am I really kinda old?" I asked her.

NINE

Valerie's words played over in my mind as I drove to the paper on Friday morning. "We weren't married at the time so there would be nothing to forgive." If Val felt that way, could she herself have been "well, indiscreet"—her words again—when I was in Germany in 1942? I'd never even considered that before and was mad at myself—real mad—that it surfaced now. Had a tad of doubt about that been buried somewhere deep in my mind all along? Damn me, I trusted my wife, obviously more than I trusted myself.

I had to put those troubling thoughts aside, because the Unholy Trinity met again that morning. "Have you tailed Judge Bonadio yet?" I asked Marko Janicek when we'd got together around my desk in the city room.

"Nope. Court wasn't in session on Thanksgiving."

"Oh, right, I forgot."

"I figured he'd be at home, wherever that is. I'll do it Monday."

"Fine, Marko, and do be real careful about it." We then went over the leads we were following.

Richie Millsap said one of Cohen's prostitutes had been beaten up in a cheap hotel where she turned her tricks. "Maybe a john who thought he was overcharged, or maybe one of Mickey's boys 'cause she was skimming on him."

"Maybe she was," I said. "She hurt bad?"

"The cops say a bloody nose and black eye is all."

"Okay, Richie. I don't see that being a story, though. Let the poor gal nurse her bruises in private."

Before the meeting broke up, I gave them assignments for when I'd be gone, for the first thing I did after that was call TWA and book a flight to Detroit for Monday. I wasn't eager to leave town for a week or so, but orders from Hearst were orders from Hearst.

The flight would stop in Chicago for the night before going on to Detroit the next morning. I thought about calling Kenny Nielsen, my coauthor on our book about the war to see if he could meet me there, but decided against it. He lived a hundred and fifty miles from Chicago and we'd only be able to have a short visit. Too much to ask of Kenny.

I strolled to the wire room to see what was coming in on the teletype machines, something I often did. The United Press teleprinter was clattering out a story on an anti-French uprising in Algeria. The AP machine had a story on a trapped coal miner in West Virginia. At the Palace of Nations in Geneva, the League of Nations had been officially dissolved. That gave me a laugh. It had been "unofficially" dissolved for years after being too gutless to do anything about German and Italian aggression in Europe and Africa before the war. I hoped its successor, the new United Nations, would have more spine.

We also had a teletype connection to our inland bureau in San Bernardino. It filed a sad story about a young female patient in the Loma Linda Hospital near Redlands who'd died in a tragic mishap. A fatal saline solution had somehow been inserted in her intravenous feed. She had died in screaming agony.

Gretchen's Otto Woolf popped into my mind. Maybe she and I should go out to Loma Linda one of these days and do some poking around.

* * *

That night Valerie, Ilse and I had turkey sandwiches for dinner. Ah, Thanksgiving leftovers! Later, after Ilse went to bed, Valerie and I nestled down on the living room sofa. We had some Duke Ellington platters going on the record player. His man on the alto sax, Johnny Hodges, was real smooth. We were feeling pretty mellow and before long we started to mess around, necking like a couple of horny teenagers. I got rid of any concerns I might have had. My beautiful, devoted wife surely hadn't played around back when I was in Germany.

Loma Linda Hospital would have to wait. Detroit came first.

It's funny what thoughts can crowd a child's imagination, and as I gazed down on the Rocky Mountains from my window seat in a TWA Constellation, I thought back to a silly little concern I'd had as a kid. When I was growing up in Louisiana I never saw a mountain and I wondered what they were like. Were they gray and blue as in the pictures? Were they solid rock or did they have some dirt? Were the roads safe? Could you pass through them okay?

Later, of course, moving to California I'd learned that mountains were cool. They came in all shapes and sizes. Things grew on them. They were pretty. They were safe. I enjoyed taking trips up into the San Bernardinos and the San Gabriels.

It took more than twelve hours, spread over a day and a half, but at last I reached Willow Run Airport. It was close to noon on Tuesday when we touched down there, twenty-five miles west of Detroit. Along the way, we'd stopped in Denver and then Chicago, where we overnighted, to exchange passengers and take on fuel.

This airfield butted up against the world's largest factory building, one I'd been anxious to see. Henry Ford had built it early in the war to turn out B-24 bombers for the air forces and, under contract to Consolidated Aircraft, he'd turned them out by the thousands. Someday I might write about Ford's German subsidiary, *Ford-Werke*, continuing to operate and reap profits throughout the war.

A wind as frosty as any I'd ever experienced in Germany lashed at me as I climbed down the portable stairway. The sky was as gray as putty. My overcoat helped but darn it, I'd forgotten to bring a scarf. I hurried to the terminal building as fast as I could, my teeth chattering like castanets, to find out about ground transport. I found that a station wagon, a woody, could take me and a few others into town for two dollars each. It was a Ford of course.

Although the airport was closer to Ann Arbor than Detroit, the trip along the Willow Run Expressway didn't take long. I found this smooth highway even nicer than that new shortcut to the valley, the Hollywood Freeway, though a few Michigan winters might change all that.

I knew Detroit was bustling. Its factories were turning out cars again instead of tanks, half-tracks and artillery haulers. I saw more skyscrapers here than in low-slung L.A., and bundled-up, prosperous-looking people on the sidewalks. Before we pulled up at the Book-Cadillac Hotel, I glimpsed an impressive suspension bridge leading across the Detroit River to Canada.

After settling into my room and unpacking, I walked over to J.L. Hudson's, less than two blocks away along cold and blustery Woodward Avenue, to buy the much-needed scarf. I'd heard that this was one of the largest department stores in the world and that it had movable stairways called escalators. I suppose going up a floor or two without having to climb stairs must have been quite a wonder when these engineering marvels were introduced.

Hudson's was big all right. It took me several minutes to find menswear, but I didn't mind—there was plenty to see.

Later, I picked up a copy of the *Times* to read while I had a burger for my supper at a sports bar called Lindell's. The sports pages were still crowing about Michigan's 58-6 trouncing of Ohio State in the season's last college football game.

It had been a long, tiring two days of travel, so after that I went back to the hotel to hit the hay.

In the morning, I walked over to the *Detroit Times* building on Bagley Street. It was a three-story concrete affair, Classical Revival style, I guessed, with huge arched windows at the street level.

The newsroom on the second floor was similar to most of the others I'd seen—with desks, typewriters, telephones, and a lot of noise. I spotted the ubiquitous horseshoe-shaped table around which the copy editors perched.

I had met the managing editor, Logan Webb, at some Hearst conference or other. He was short, wiry, and wore black-rimmed glasses. Webb was expecting me. We shook hands and he ushered me into his office, where I peeled off my overcoat and draped it over one of two chairs facing his desk.

"It's good to see you, Jake," he said, "have a seat. I gotta say I'm not exactly sure why you're here. Our circulation has actually gone up lately. The series we ran on those race riots at the Belle Isle Bridge sold a lot of papers. We're up to about 88,000 now, gaining ground on the *Freep*." Which meant the *Free Press*.

"Jesus!" I said, surprised. Hearst thought this paper was hurting.

"Detroit was mostly white before the war," Webb went on, "but when a lot of niggers, sorry, *Negroes*, started coming in from the South for the factory jobs, there was trouble."

Southern California didn't have much racial prejudice but I guessed northern industrial cities were another matter. And I didn't much care for Webb's tone.

"Yeah," I said, "but how could Hearst have been so off base on your circulation?"

"Well, he's pretty old now. Maybe he read the figures with

some dyslexia. How about some coffee, Jake?"

I nodded okay and Webb shouted, "Copy!" whereupon a copyboy soon stuck his young, pimply face in the door and was told to fetch some coffee.

"Well, we still need to go through the motions, Logan," I said, "and set up an anti-crime team. W.R. would have our asses if we didn't."

"I know. I've got two investigative reporters picked out for that. I'll have you meet 'em pretty soon."

The coffee arrived in two big mugs and we each had some.

"What do you know about the Purple Gang," I asked, "and this guy Tripolani?"

"There's actually not much left of the Purple Gang, Jake."

I almost dropped my coffee mug. "Not much left?"

"The cops came down hard on those boys after the Collingwood Manor Massacre."

"The Collingwood Manor Massacre?" I asked.

"Yeah, we had our own little version of the St. Valentine's Day Massacre. The Purples burst into that place and gunned down most of a rival gang. This was back in the Thirties. Ray Bernstein, the kike who ran the Purples at the time, was fingered along with two others, convicted, and hauled off to Marquette."

I took another sip of coffee. I knew Marquette was where Michigan had its maximum-security prison, and also that what sat before me was a bigot.

"The Purples haven't been the same since. Aldo Tipolani runs it now, and they still do some of the usual stuff, drugs, gambling, so forth, but it's not a huge operation."

Surprise on top of surprise that morning. Maybe that's why Lucky Luciano doesn't bother with them, I thought. Chicken feed.

"GM and Ford want this town to be clean," Webb continued, "well, relatively clean, if possible." Good luck with that, I thought.

"Tripolani launders his money through some supposedly legit businesses. One of the biggest is called Stamping Products, over on the west side. They make bicycle frames, fasteners, window frames, metal plates and cups for camping, things like that."

"Maybe I should go and have a look at that place," I said, "say we're doing a story on small businesses, take one of your guys along."

Logan Webb's lips scrunched up doubtfully. "I don't think Tripolani would go along with that."

"What could they do, rough us up? That'd get in your paper and he couldn't have that."

"You're as reckless as that reputation of yours, huh, Jake? Okay, it's your funeral."

I wished I'd paid more heed to that.

TEN

I noticed for the first time a copy of our book, *Two Men at War: A Retrospective,* among the clutter on Webb's desk. He picked it up and said, "This is a fine book you fellas wrote. Would you sign this for me?"

"Glad to." I was a little surprised at the abrupt change of subject. He handed me the book, which I opened to the fly leaf, pulled out a pen and wrote, "For a good fellow newsman," and signed my name.

Webb then brought in his two investigative reporters, Matt Mason and Del Klesko. After he introduced me, he took the four of us to lunch at a place called Mister Mike's. "To get the ball rolling," he said.

Light snow drifted down like white feathers as we walked the two blocks to get there. The place was dark and smoky with a long bar along one of the wood-paneled walls.

When we'd settled in around a table, Webb recommended Stroh's as a good local beer so I ordered one, as did the others.

We chatted and got acquainted. Matt Mason and Del Klesko struck me as fairly solid reporters. Mason had been with the *Times* quite awhile and knew the city well, while Klesko had come from the *Toledo Blade* about a year before.

The Stroh's wasn't bad—and I'd downed most of it—when four platters piled with steak sandwiches arrived and were plunked down on our table. "House specialty," Webb explained. He began filling in the two reporters on what we'd talked about earlier. When a visit to Stamping Products was brought up some apprehension flittered across Klesko's face, but Matt Mason jumped in and said, "I'll go with you, Jake." So we arranged that I'd meet Mason at the paper at ten in the morning and drive out to the factory.

As we dug into our meals, Klesko asked about our L.A. anti-crime team and I described the Unholy Trinity, how we operated, and tossed out some ideas on what they could do here. They asked me a lot of good questions.

Webb asked if I'd like to go to the hockey game that night, the Detroit Red Wings and the Toronto Maple Leafs. I'd never seen a hockey game so I said sure, I'd like that.

That night he took me to the Olympia Stadium, northwest of downtown on Grand River Avenue, where I watched the Red Wings beat Toronto 3 to 2. This big arena was larger than any in L.A. I didn't understand terms like icing or the blue line, but the skating and skillful puck handling were impressive, and the body checks darn rough. A guy named Roy Conacher slammed home two of the Red Wings' three goals. I thoroughly enjoyed myself.

I couldn't say the same for the next day.

My thoughts went like this in the morning while Matt Mason drove us to Stamping Products: *The Detroit Times* isn't doing as badly as Hearst thought, and organized crime here has lost a lot of its punch. So after this interview I can tell Mason and Del Klesko a few more things about setting up an anti-crime campaign, and all this will be over. I can catch a plane out of here tomorrow and be home with Valerie and Ilse by Thursday night.

On Woodward Avenue, we passed a big stone church and an ornate movie theater with *The Best Years of Our Lives* on its marquee, then made several turns.

Stamping Products occupied a nondescript two-story brick building surrounded by a parking lot, about an inch of snow, and a chain-link fence. Inside, Mason and I met the guy who ran the joint, Gino Columbini. We introduced ourselves and told him we were doing a series of stories for the *Times* on successful small businesses, and we hoped to include his.

"Oh you do, hey?" Columbini said while leading us to his office, a dingy cubicle with a cheap little desk. The place resembled a sales room at a used-car lot. Cigar butts filled a glass ash tray, and framed photos hung on the wall. One pictured him posing proudly with Hank Greenburg and another Detroit Tiger ballplayer I couldn't name. Another caught my eye. This one was a little dark but it showed Columbini with a man who . . . well, there was something about him. The guy's hat shaded a lot of his face, but there was *something*.

I got distracted by Mason getting out a spiral-bound notebook and a pencil. We began asking questions. How long had they been in business, what were their best products, who were their top customers, how much did they gross in a month? Stuff like that.

Columbini answered with little enthusiasm and also deviously, I thought. He entirely danced around the question about his gross. "You're gonna run this stuff in the *Times*?" he said. "A Hearst paper?"

"Sure, if you don't mind," Mason answered. "It'll send some business your way."

After fifteen minutes of getting only a little from this guy, Mason asked if we could see the shop.

Columbini shrugged and said, "Not much to see." He led us into a big room where about twenty workers busied themselves around sundry machines labeled sheet-metal stamper, marking press, and power curver, contraptions I knew nothing about, except that they made a lot of noise. Long tubes of fluorescent lights hung from the rafters. As we moseyed about, I noticed some of the men sneaking furtive, uneasy glances at Columbini and curious ones at us.

Columbini left us for a minute, went to a wall phone and made a short call. When he returned, Mason, almost shouting to be heard, said, "We could get some good shots in here. Can we send a photographer out?"

"Well . . ." Columbini stopped himself right there. "Let's go out back," he said. "There's something I wanta show you." We followed him through a door into a small fenced lot filled with trash barrels and stacks of sheet metal. Two goons were standing there, guys right out of central casting. They wore what I would call lumberjacks' coats. Heavy plaid wool. I shivered, but not from the cold.

One stood in front of me and the other one moved around behind. That one suddenly grabbed me. Before I could do a damn thing, he jerked my hands together behind my back.

"What the hell!" I shouted. The other guy circled around and roughly lashed my wrists together with something sticky. Felt like electrical tape.

"We don't need no goddamn publicity," Columbini said, "and we're gonna take this outta-town guy for a little ride. I think Mr. Hearst will cough up around five grand for his safe return," he told Mason.

"Shouldn't you call Trip—" one of the goons tried to ask.

"Shut up!" Columbini snapped. "Me an' Ben know what we're doin'."

Turning back to Matt Mason: "We're gonna park this guy for awhile, but we ain't gonna hurt him if we don't hafta. You go and tell your boss that. If you try to do anything about this, go to the cops or somethin', I'll blow up your fucking newspaper. And don't think I won't."

I felt a blindfold being slapped over my eyes. Along with a ton of fear. God, this was really happening!

"You're out of your damn mind," Mason said.

"I don't think so." Columbini again. "Now you run along like a good boy, sonny, and tell your boss about the five grand. We'll be in touch."

Next thing I knew I was shoved into a car. The back seat, probably, because I felt—and smelled—one of the Lumberjacks beside me. He was pretty ripe.

The car drove for fifteen or twenty minutes. I heard traffic sounds, trucks running through their gears, horns honking. Several stops were made at what must have been red lights. Whoever was driving and the guy next to me didn't say much, just occasional things like "take a right here" and "how far to Telegraph Road?" I had no idea where Telegraph Road was.

Along the way I silently cursed Hearst for sending me to this damn town in the first place. Why couldn't the old man have got his facts straight on the *Detroit Times?*

When we finally stopped for good, I was hauled out of the car and led away. A strong hand gripped my arm. I stumbled on something that must've been doorsteps. The guy steadied me and I heard a door open. I was nudged inside, but inside what? A house? A warehouse? At least it was warmer here.

I must've passed through an archway or an open doorway because my shoulder brushed against a hard surface. Then my captor halted me and someone tore away the bindings from my wrists, which hurt like the devil—some hair departed with it, and maybe even some skin. It had been some kind of tape, for sure.

The instant that tape came off I tried to throw a blind punch, but I was grabbed by an arm stronger than mine. I felt a handcuff snap onto my left wrist. Only my left wrist. That was odd. I heard a metallic jangle of some kind, followed by a small tug on the manacled wrist.

Someone shoved me on the chest and I fell backward—onto what had to be a chair. A comfortable chair at that. The blindfold was yanked off. My eyes smarted with the sudden shock of light. When they adjusted, I found myself in a bedroom. A small single bed lay against one wall, a wooden chest of drawers stood along another, and a light fixture hung from the ceiling. One of the

Lumberjacks stood facing me and the other was leaving through a doorway with some wadded-up black tape in his hand.

"Where the hell am I?" I demanded.

"Ha. Wouldn't you like to know, Red?"

"Yeah, I would."

The guy gave a sadistic little grin and also walked off. I raised my left wrist and found the handcuff attached to a chain, explaining the jangling sound I'd heard. My eyes followed the chain to an O ring inserted in a wall about three feet up from a barren wooden floor. The chain looked about five feet long, so I would have some freedom of movement, but not much. I couldn't reach either the bed or the chest of drawers. My chain was too short for that.

The room was about ten by twelve with walls papered in light yellow with faint burgundy pinstripes. Nothing hung from them, no pictures or decorations of any kind. Weak daylight shone through the room's lone window, just above the cedar chest. My jail cell—for that's what it was—contained nothing but the bed and the chest I couldn't reach, my chair, that window, and this damned chain. My wrists were red and raw where the tape had been torn away.

I heard the Lumberjacks muttering somewhere else in the house but couldn't make out what they were saying. Man, I was scared.

I walked around awhile, as far as possible, and tried to think, but no brilliant ideas came to mind. *Why in hell had I ever gone to Stamping Products?*

I hadn't recalled being searched. With my free hand I checked myself and found my wallet still in my back pocket, and elsewhere my pen, small notebook, and hotel-room key. Good, even though the pen wouldn't make much of a weapon. I wished I'd had the Luger I'd acquired in Germany—and put to good use—but it was a couple of thousand miles away at home boxed up in a crawl space above a closet.

Although I couldn't reach that window, from my angle I could see some trees out there, wintry skeletal, shorn of their leaves, and just a small upper piece of a house beyond—a shingled roof and part of a dormer. This must be a residential neighborhood.

I sat and wondered if I would ever get out of here and if a ransom offer really was being made to Hearst or Logan Webb or to anyone. I figured Matt Mason or Webb would go to the police despite the warning not to, but the cops would have no idea where I was or even a clue where to start looking.

I leaned back in the chair and closed my eyes.

ELEVEN

I must have dozed off for when I opened my eyes weaker daylight seeped through that window. The short twilight of early winter was coming on. I noticed a roll of toilet paper next to the chair beside an old-fashioned clay chamber pot, just like the one I'd used at my cousin's farm at Opelousas when I was a kid. Thus vanished any hope that they'd unchain me so I could use a restroom.

I was thinking that Valerie would worry when I didn't call tonight as I'd assured her I would. I was also wondering what Logan Webb and Matt Mason were doing about all this when a door opened and a young woman came in carrying a paper plate and a bottle of Coca-Cola. Short brown hair, gray Michigan Wolverines sweatshirt, slacks, about five-foot-four. I figured she might be one of the Purple Gang's hookers.

"Hi hon," she said. "I'm your new babysitter. Here's a little supper for you." She knelt, reached forward and set the plate and the Coke on the floor where I could get to it, being careful to keep herself out of grabbing reach.

"My babysitter, huh? Where are the guys?"

"They went back to town, if it's any of your business. I drew the duty for tonight."

"Back to town" gave me a clue. Maybe I was outside Detroit. The ride here hadn't taken long so this was probably one of the suburbs.

"That's too bad," I said. "Everybody who's involved in this is in deep shit, and that includes you, baby."

She sat on the bed and looked at me, a little worry wrinkling her face. My words had hit home. "Look, mister, this wasn't my idea. I had nothing to do with bringing you out here."

"You could probably get off at that," I said, "if you unchain me and let me go. Instead of being an accessory you'd be a heroine."

"Heroin? I don't use none of that stuff."

I chuckled for the first time in hours. "No, not that, I meant you'd be a good guy, an angel of mercy."

"Huh uh, mister, I'd be in worse shit than you know if I let you go. Trip would break my knees."

"Trip?"

"Mr. Tripolani. You know him, don't you?"

"Nope, never had the pleasure."

"Then why did he . . . I don't figure this, mister."

"He wouldn't break your knees. I'd see to that. I'd tell Lucky you did a good deed, and he'd come down hard on Tripolani."

"Lucky Luciano? You're with *him*?" More anxiety creased her face and clouded her eyes, which were a pretty green.

I just gave her a little grin. Let her draw her own conclusions.

She got up and said, "Go ahead and eat. I made you a ham sandwich. I gotta go and do some thinking." She hurried from the room and pretty soon I heard a radio go on. It was playing some dance music. Sounded like Tommy Dorsey.

I sat on the floor in front of the paper plate. Along with the sandwich was a cup of potato salad and a wooden fork. I took a bite of the sandwich—it was good. I hoped the seed I'd planted was growing in her mind, that she'd let me go. But did she even have the key to my handcuff? Doubtful.

I finished off the meal and took a drink of Coke. I'd been hungry after all. Now the radio was playing some soap opera. *Just Plain Bill* or maybe *Ma Perkins*.

After awhile the gal returned to collect the plate and bottle. "No sir," she said. "Trip would crush me like a little flower before Luciano could get his boys in here . . . Say, you're kinda cute, you know that?"

"So are you," I said with a wink.

"You think so?" She put a hand to her cheek.

"I sure do. You're lovely. Let's hope you'll be able to stay that way."

More worry cloaked her face. She turned and scampered from the room. I'm getting to her, I thought. Nothing but darkness came from the window now and the overhead light was off, so I couldn't see much. I settled back in the chair. *Guess this is where I sleep tonight.*

The radio was silent now and the woman didn't return. I wondered what the cops were doing, if anything, and what Valerie was thinking. Was she worried? Probably not yet. It wasn't later than nine or so in California.

Before long I drifted off to sleep.

I woke up a time or two during the night. The first time I didn't know where I was, but when I stretched my arms the chain rattled and it all came rushing back.

In the morning, sunlight peeped through the window, I saw those barren trees, and I was stiff all over. I got up, stretched as best I could and walked the few feet available to me. Then I used the chamber pot, hoping my babysitter wouldn't come in as I did. But what did it really matter? She'd seen men's privates before, probably gobs of times. I'd begun to think of her as Trixie. As in turning tricks.

That done, I sat and thought about escape. I stared at that damn chain and suddenly wondered if the O ring had simply been screwed into the wall or if it was fastened by a toggle bolt. I tugged on the chain, drawing it taut. I didn't feel any give, but I tugged and tugged some more.

I heard the radio come on and also what sounded like the

clanging of a kitchen pan, so I let the chain fall limp. Maybe Trixie was out there making breakfast. A station break played on the radio: "You're tuned to station WXYZ in Detroit. The time is 7:45. Today will be clear and cold in the Motor City, with an expected high of 22 degrees."

Soon my babysitter came in carrying a ceramic mug and another paper plate. Both were steaming a little. She wore a pink blouse, black skirt and mid-heel black pumps. "Good morning, cutey. I'll bet you're hungry. I made you scrambled eggs and bacon. How'd you sleep?"

"Oh, just great, Trixie. It's such a delight to sleep sitting up."

"Trixie? Why'd you call me that?"

"Just guessing. What's your name then?"

"Maybe I shouldn't say, but what the hell. It's Tomasina, but everybody calls me Tommi."

"Okay, Tommi, nice name . . . Hey, this looks good."

"Darn right it does. I put some cheese and mushrooms in the eggs. I always do. I'm a waitress and part-time cook when I'm not babysitting gangsters."

"I thought you were a . . ." I stopped myself. It'd be stupid to insult her. ". . . a secretary," I finished.

"You know, I did take shorthand at Denby High, but never followed up on that."

"So, Tommi, have you been thinking? You going to unchain me?"

"Sorry, hon, no can do."

"That's too bad. It'll go hard with you when Lucky's boys show up . . . Well, let's see how good your eggs are." I picked up a fork and dug in, while she watched hopefully.

"Yep, they're good," I said. "Real tasty." She smiled the smile of a pleased cook, while I finished them off and drank some coffee from the mug. "Not bad, but I prefer mine black."

"Sorry, I had you figured for a cream and sugar guy. Let me get you some fresh black."

When she returned she put the mug on the floor, just within my reach. I picked it up, took a drink of black coffee—that was better—and said, "Thanks, good lookin'."

"Good looking? You mean that?"

"Course I do, Tommi, you're very attractive. Lovely face, pretty eyes. I hope nothing happens to change that. Luciano's boys, well, they have a temper, those guys do. Like I said, they won't be happy to find me chained up like this."

"Stop that, mister. You're starting to scare me."

That was the idea. "Just giving you the facts, Tommi." I finished the coffee and held out the mug to her. She forgot herself and reached for it. As she did, I made a quick grab for her wrist and got a slight hold, but not a firm grip—she jumped back too fast for that.

"Damn you!" she snarled. "Don't ever try somethin' like that again." Her face pinched with anger. "Here I was tryin' to be nice." She turned on her heel and stormed from the room.

The place was quiet for five or ten minutes, but then Tommi returned and said, "You're gonna be alone for awhile now, mister. I gotta go put in a shift at the diner. Be a good boy now, don't go anywhere. Ha ha."

"So long, good lookin'," I said.

She blew me a little kiss and left, her shoes clacking on the hardwood floor. I heard a door open and shut in the distance. Silence settled over the room. I stood, opened my fly, peed again in the chamber pot, and thought, okay, back to my chain.

I tugged and I pulled and I wrenched. That stubborn O ring didn't seem to budge a bit, but I kept at it. It dawned on me that I might have better luck if I walked over and simply tried to unscrew the ring, so I tried that. But no, that didn't work. I just couldn't get the damn thing to turn. So, back to my chair, where I would yank at it for about ten minutes at a time, rest my wrist a bit, and go at it again. This went on for a couple of hours or more.

All this effort must have been more tiring than I realized, for during one of my rest breaks I dozed off. Pretty soon I was dreaming about getting this thing out of the wall, bolting from the front door awkwardly dragging five feet of chain, and scaring the heck out of strangers who refused to let me use their phones. I ran around frantically trying to find a taxi but this was a residential neighborhood and I couldn't find a cab stand anywhere. It began to snow hard, a real blizzard. I got damn cold.

I woke up and found myself still stuck in that room with no snow on my head and little hope in my heart. I sighed and began tugging on the chain again. Minutes passed, maybe an hour. I thought it must be about time for Tommi to come back.

Then I remembered a cop friend telling me it really wasn't very hard to shim handcuffs. Dumb me, why hadn't I thought of that before? Wasted a whole damn day. It would be nice if I had a hairpin—the cop had told me those worked best. I pulled out my pen and began fussing with the cuff, using my right hand. Finally I stuck the pen's sharp end in the keyhole above the hinge, wiggled it around a bit, and—*voila*—the cuff popped open. I took the darn thing off my left wrist. The chain dropped to the floor. Damn, I could have done all this yesterday.

I was rubbing that wrist when I heard a door thrown open and heavy footfalls in the house. Three guys barged into the room, guys I'd never seen before. Geez, Tommi had called in the first string, must've been pretty pissed at me for grabbing at her. Two of these guys wore gray overcoats and the third, a leather jacket.

A swarthy guy—husky, maybe five-eight, black hair—said, "You shimmed that handcuff, hey? Ain't all that hard to do."

Now what, I thought, are you gonna drag me out back and shoot me? But the guy asked, "Are you Jim Weaver?"

"Jake Weaver."

"Oh, sorry, Jake Weaver then. I'm Aldo Tripolani. Sorry as hell about what happened here, Mr. Weaver. It was all a big mistake. Nobody was s'posed to nab you and haul you out here."

I had trouble catching my breath. Rescue by the Mob was the last thing I'd ever expected. One of his guys was coiling up the chain and dumping it beside that O ring. The other one took the handcuff from me and stuffed it in a coat pocket. I rubbed at my left wrist, trying to get some circulation going.

"You're with the *Times*, ain't that right?" Tripolani said.

"Consulting with them. I'm actually with a Hearst paper in California."

"Well, goddamn, as I say, Weaver, I'm sorry as hell. For chrissake, last thing I need is to get my tit in a wringer with William Fucking Randolph Hearst."

This Tripolani guy probably knew that besides the *Times*, Hearst owned a radio station and a couple of movie houses here. The old man had clout in this town.

"The guys who pulled this stupid stunt will pay for it, I promise you that."

"Not killed, I hope." Still rubbing my left wrist.

"Nah, but they'll be taught a lesson, a painful lesson, you can count on it. Columbini was a stupid ass to pull somethin' like this. Thought he'd score points with me. What he scored was a big pile of dog shit. What can I do to make it up to you, Weaver?"

I was still amazed at this sudden turn in my fortunes. "Just drive me back to the *Times* is all."

"Sure, but that ain't good enough." He reached into a pocket, pulled out a wad of bills and extended them to me. "There's a few hundred bucks here. Take 'em. Please."

"Hush money?" I said. "No thanks."

"It ain't hush money, no sir. I can't tell the *Times* what to print, though I'd be damn happy if they printed nothin'. I'd send Mr. Webb a case of champagne."

And Logan Webb would probably accept it, I thought. Actually,

I didn't want this to get in the papers, either. A story on getting myself abducted would embarrass the heck out of me, plus, it would be on the INS wire before I got home and Valerie would be frantic.

I put my hands up, palms out, and said, "No, Tripolani, no money."

"Please," he pleaded. "If you want more'n this, I can get it."

"No, no, no, with a capital N."

He reluctantly shoved the wad of bills back in a pocket.

I asked if I could use a phone. Tripolani said okay as long as I wasn't calling the cops. In a front room I was seeing for the first time I found a black telephone on an end table. I picked up the receiver and asked the operator to connect me with the *Detroit Times*. Before long I was telling a surprised Logan Webb to call off the dogs. "I'm okay, Logan. I'll see you pretty soon and tell you all about it."

I hung up and we went outside into some biting cold. On an icy-slick sidewalk I had to step carefully not to slip and fall. A long black Packard sat at the curb. Tripolani got in front with a driver and the other guys slipped in back with me.

When we turned onto Telegraph Road, I spotted a sign saying "Dearborn's Finest Dry Cleaners." Dearborn was a suburb I'd heard of. As we veered onto Michigan Avenue, I told Tripolani, "You don't need to punish Columbini for this, he just made a mistake. And for heaven's sake, please don't kill the guy."

"Nah, we ain't gonna dump him in the river, but he's gonna feel some pain."

"I hope you don't harm that girl back there named Tomasina. She was good to me."

"Glad to hear it. Tommi Kurowski's a sweet doll. Nah, we ain't gonna hurt her none."

The Packard rolled past a cluster of ball diamonds called Retreat Field, then Henry Ford's Greenfield Village, and a little later

Briggs Stadium, the Tigers' big gray ballpark close to downtown.

When I was finally dropped off at the paper, Tripolani again tried to hand me some money. Again I refused it. "Well," he said, "I'm damn sure sorry about all this." He patted my cheek, of all things, and added, "You take care now."

Once inside the *Times*, I called Valerie, apologized for not calling the night before, and said I'd be home late the next day. Didn't say a thing about the kidnapping.

"That's okay," she said. "Something came up, right? It always does."

"Yeah, I got a little tied up. This assignment's about over, Sweets. I'll see you tomorrow night."

After hanging up, I filled Logan Webb in, and then he took me to a late lunch at the Detroit Athletic Club, an imposing neo-Renaissance building on Madison Avenue, where he was a member. This time instead of a Stroh's beer, I had a martini, a double—man, I needed it! Webb said he'd called the cops, who hadn't got anywhere and were glad to call it off. I urged him not to print any of this.

"Yeah, okay," he said, "though it's the sort of stuff Hearst would love. It'd make the *Times* look pretty sloppy at that, though. Big embarrassment."

Later I called the airline and booked a flight home for the next day, then spent a couple of hours with Matt Mason and Del Klesko, throwing out suggestions about their planned anti-crime campaign. Mason said some contractors building the postwar suburbs that were starting to sprout in the sugar-beet fields outside Detroit were cheating their investors. He wanted to target that, plus investigate some shenanigans thought to be going on with the United Auto Workers' pension fund. He and Klesko would also go after the Purple Gang, though not writing anything about my "little ride."

87

I frankly thought they weren't likely to accomplish much, not that they weren't good reporters, but because Logan Webb's heart wasn't really in it.

It was snowing pretty hard Thursday morning and I was glad to get out of there. I wouldn't have to miss Ilse's soccer game.

I got home late that night. Although the westward flight chased the sun—and lost—the trip was completed in one long day, stopping en route at Chicago, Denver and Salt Lake City. During the flight I pondered whether to tell Valerie about the kidnapping fiasco, and finally decided not to. I'd already given her more than enough to worry about.

As I looked out the window at some Nebraska farmland I recalled that Columbini had said "Me an' Ben" when they rousted me. Who was Ben? I wondered.

After nine and a half hours, we put down at Mines Field, out by the coast, close to where Valerie worked at North American Aviation. City Council was considering changing the field's name to Los Angeles International Airport. After all, they had one whole flight a day to Mexicali, the capital of Baja California.

The next day I took Valerie and Ilse out to breakfast before the soccer game. Thinking of my babysitter Tommi, it would be good to have breakfast in a place with a real restroom. Also with her in mind, I ordered scrambled eggs with cheese and mushrooms. Valerie gave me a curious look and said she couldn't recall my having eggs that way. "You usually have them over easy."

"I've actually come to like them this way."

"Since when?"

"Since Detroit," I said vaguely.

Then came questions about my trip, and I told them what I'd

done to help them set up an anti-crime team, and also about the hockey game and the Detroit Athletic Club.

The rest of the weekend with my two lovelies was great—Ilse's Tigers won again and now had a 5 and 1 record. Again I was impressed by the coaches, the big German and the Hungarian woman. I somehow held at bay any thoughts of kidnapping as well as my Unholy Trinity.

All that changed on Monday when I was back at work.

TWELVE

Meetings with Aggie Underwood, Johnny Campbell, Marko Janicek and Richie Millsap filled my first day back. I also called Gretchen and told her about the peculiar death at Loma Linda Hospital. We arranged to go out there on Wednesday.

While I drove us there in my Chevy Ridemaster with the newly repaired front fender, Gretchen said she'd come up empty at surgical supply places and was getting discouraged. "MI-6 is giving me just two more weeks," she said, her voice heavy with disappointment. "I hope that we will learn something good here."

I told her about Ilse being on a girls soccer team. Gretchen, who'd played soccer in Germany as a teenager, was glad to hear that and said she would like to see one of Ilse's games.

"What are all those interesting buildings over there?" she asked, looking over to the left.

"That's a cluster of colleges, Gretchen. Claremont, Pomona, Scripps, maybe a couple of others. Big educational complex."

When we got to Loma Linda, the hospital administrator we talked to was uneasy about our looking into that poor girl's demise. "We were aggrieved that this got into the papers," he said, wringing his hands. "We would prefer not to have any follow-up stories."

"We're not going to write a thing," I assured him. "This is just background. Can we speak to the physician who was in charge of her?"

He reluctantly agreed and soon we met with that doctor. In his office this man, a stethoscope hanging from his neck, didn't want to talk about the incident either. After we gave him our assurances, though, he motioned for us to sit. Framed certificates and diplomas hung on a lime-green wall behind his desk. Taking his own seat, he admitted that, "We had a visiting physician, a Swiss doctor"— Swiss? I thought—"with impeccable credentials. He treated the patient for two days before the unfortunate death."

"What was this man's name?" I asked.

"Kristian Egger."

"I see. And how long was he here?" Knowing Kristian Egger could be a phony name.

"About three weeks, long enough for us to be satisfied that he had good medical skills and could tend to patients. However, as he was not officially a member of our staff, we could allow him only to do nursing duties. One day after the regrettable incident, he just left."

"He just left?" Gretchen said.

"Yes, without a word. It was very peculiar. He just failed to show up anymore. Didn't say where he was going or anything." *Otto Woolf,* I thought, and was sure Gretchen was thinking the same thing.

"Can you describe the man?" I asked.

"Well, he was slightly taller than average, maybe five-ten or eleven, brown hair, and blue eyes, I believe. Yes, blue I think. He wore glasses."

"Did he have any distinguishing features, a birthmark, a limp when he walked?"

"Now that you mention it, he had a small scar on one of his cheeks. I don't recall which one."

"What was his address?" I asked. "What kind of car did he drive? Can we see his employment form?"

"I never saw his car, if he had one. And as a volunteer he didn't fill out an actual employee form, just a questionnaire." The doctor began riffling through a card file. Let's see now, somewhere here

I have . . . yes, here we are. His address was 6446 Bolton Avenue, Redlands."

Time for some bluntness. "Did you suspect this guy murdered your patient," I asked, "especially when he vanished right afterward?"

"Not at first, he was so professional, but now, well, I must admit the thought has crossed my mind." He twisted the card in his hand nervously. "You really mustn't write this."

I assured him again that I wouldn't, shook his hand on it, thanked him for his time, and Gretchen and I left.

I drove to the *Redlands Facts*, the local newspaper, where we learned there was no Bolton Avenue in town. There was a Colton Avenue, so it could have been a simple typo, but it turned out that there was no 6446 on Colton. So the guy obviously had given a phony address.

Before heading back to L.A., Gretchen and I had lunch at Phil's Broiler alongside Highway 99. Our waiter told us this was a popular stop-off for Hollywood celebrities on their way to Palm Springs. "Edgar Bergen was in here just the other night," she said, sounding as if that should impress the heck out of us. I doubt Gretchen had any idea who Edgar Bergen was.

"Do you think this was really Woolf's work?" I asked as I held out a chair for her. "I thought he was more of a bizarre experimentation guy than thrill killer."

"*Ja*, I do. The 'impeccable credentials' that were mentioned sound just like the kind of counterfeits MI-6 has discovered with other Nazis who are—as you put it—on the lam. And he would surely give a false address as well as call himself a Swiss or something other than German."

I still wasn't convinced. "Why would your man come out here, take the time to win their confidence, kill a woman, and scram? That doesn't fit his MO."

"Perhaps it does, Jake. He is likely a misogynist. All of his victims at Buchenwald were women."

"All women? He only dealt with women? I didn't know that."

"*Ja*, strange, isn't it? And there is something else. One of the missing art treasures stolen by the Nazis is a special dagger, the blade six inches long, the hilt encrusted with diamonds. It was a gift in the last century from the King of Sweden to one of the Rothschilds. It was looted from Les Invalides in Paris during the occupation. It is worth a fortune. MI-6 thinks Woolf may have it in his possession."

"How could they know that?"

"MI-6 is very good at finding out things, you know. Perhaps Woolf was close to someone in one of those teams that confiscated such things."

"It's possible, I guess. Well, if you think this was Woolf out here, he's long gone now, but to where?"

Gretchen remained all business through the rest of our lunch, trying along with me to figure this thing out, until, that is, we finished our barbecue turkey sandwiches and paid the check. When I opened the car door for her, she kissed my cheek and gave me that smoky look she had. As we headed out of Redlands we passed a place called Hansen's Motor Court, and Gretchen said, "What a charming spot. They must have cozy rooms."

I said nothing to that and kept on driving, my eyes straight ahead. After awhile, she said, "I very much like your Valerie. She is an exceptional woman. You are fortunate to have her."

"I know," I said, wondering where this was going.

"But why are Americans so prudish? In Europe many men have both a wife and a mistress, and everyone is happy with the arrangement."

"Everyone? I doubt the wives are happy with the arrangement."

"You would be surprised. Most of them are glad to have their men go off somewhere for awhile. Too much togetherness can spoil the pie."

Mangled metaphor, I thought. Bad logic, too. Off somewhere hunting or fishing, sure, but not with another woman.

After a long, quiet moment, Gretchen said, "You Americans are so hypocritical. There is as much sexual activity outside of marriage here as anywhere, but you pretend it is not happening. You turn the blind eye. Other cultures do not kid themselves. They find it emotionally healthy to accept the facts."

I drove a mile or more before saying anything. Finally, though: "Let's get something straight, Gretchen, I'm very fond of you. I cherish your friendship. I might not be alive if you hadn't helped me leave Germany. But if you're auditioning for the role of my mistress, forget it. It wouldn't work. Besides, you say you'll be leaving here in a couple of weeks."

She crossed her arms tightly across her lovely chest and said nothing more for a long while. Tension filled the car like a mist.

"You are the only man I have loved since my Friedrich," she said at last. "If I cannot have you, even a part of you"—the words softer now, little more than a murmur—"and if I cannot find Otto Woolf, what good am I?"

I didn't know what to say. Wasn't good at cheering up people when they were depressed. So I kept mum.

I stopped for gas in Covina. The sixteen cents a gallon was two cents less than at my local Richfield station.

When I finally dropped Gretchen at her apartment, she touched my hand and said, "Thank you, Jake, for taking a day off to help me. I know you have other more important duties. You have been very kind."

I was about to say something sympathetic, but she hopped out of the car and scampered toward the building's front door before I could come up with the words.

* * *

When I got to the paper I found a business envelope from the First State Bank of Detroit in my mail slot. Inside was a certified check for eight-hundred dollars. I snapped my fingers. Tripolani! He'd sent me some conscience money after all. I was tempted to tear the check up, but didn't. Eight-hundred smackers was a lot of money.

I went to my desk and put in an hour of work before going home, where Valerie had prepared a dinner of roast chicken, salad, French bread, and of course Napa Valley wine. During the meal I described my day at Loma Linda, and Valerie asked if I thought Otto Woolf had killed the poor girl.

"Gretchen thinks so, but I'm not totally convinced," I said, and went on to tell what the doctor had told us about the volunteer and the phony address he gave.

"I think Gretchen is right," Valerie said. "I think so, too," Ilse put in. Maybe my clever women were right about that.

I then told Valerie about the check from Detroit. "What do you think, Sweets, should I tear it up, deposit the thing in our account, or return it to that bank? Sending it back would probably be best."

She put down her wine glass and rubbed her chin. "Why ever would this man send you money? Does he owe you something?"

I didn't want to tell her about the kidnapping. "Well, one of his guys said some pretty insulting stuff to me during an interview," I fibbed.

"Must have been *very* insulting," Valerie said, her voice dripping with sarcasm, "to be worth eight-hundred dollars. Well, in case there's ever any kind of legal proceeding between the paper and this Purple Gang, it would link you to them. But that's a remote possibility, isn't it?"

"Extremely remote. This guy Tripolani is scared to death of riling Hearst, and we have no reason at our end to bring suit against them."

Ilse, who'd been listening intently, spoke up. "*Vati*, I believe this man Tripolani has given himself—to use a term I have heard from you—an insurance policy. If he were to face criminal charges, he could show that he has a connection or linkage—what is the word?"

"A paper trail," I provided.

"Yes, a paper trail—to you. I think that you should not keep this."

Valerie and I flashed quick and identical smiles at Ilse. "Gosh, you're smart," I said. "You're exactly right. I was planning to send it back in the morning and that's just what I'll do." Valerie nodded her agreement. Shoot, I thought, eight-hundred bucks is about a tenth of what I make in a year. Dumb to keep it, though.

After dinner I helped that smart girl with her homework. Plane geometry, which somehow I was pretty good at. We spoke some German just to keep in practice. Then, before her bedtime, Ilse came up with one of her bright ideas. "*Vati*, Mr. Cohen has his finger on a lot of things, doesn't he? Knows a lot about Los Angeles?"

"Yes he does, *Liebchen*. He's been here forever, has a ton of contacts."

"Then do you think perhaps he could help you and Gretchen find this bad doctor man?"

"Mickey's an okay guy, as evil bastards go, pardon my language, but that's not a bad idea, Ilse. Maybe he could at that." The Mick didn't owe me any favors, but so far our anti-crime drive had gone easy on him, my main target being Jack Dragna, and I intended to keep it that way. It might be worth a try.

In bed that night, Valerie said, "Something worse than being insulted happened to you back in Detroit, didn't it?"

I kissed my perceptive wife and said, "Go to sleep, hon."

* * *

Next morning, after mailing that certified check back to the First State Bank of Detroit, I called Mickey Cohen and said I'd like to see him. "Sure," he said, "meet me for lunch at Musso & Frank—12:30 okay?"

I said that was fine and two hours later I battled noontime traffic on Hollywood Boulevard and parked behind Musso & Frank, one of the movie crowd's hangouts. Musso's had been here for years. Inside, I found The Mick in one of the front booths with a gorgeous blonde. They were having martinis.

When he saw me approach, he said, "Have a seat, Jakester. Say hello to Lana Turner." The gorgeous blonde extended an elegant hand, nails painted a bright red, which I took and said, "A pleasure to meet you, Miss Turner. You were excellent in *The Postman Always Rings Twice*, excellently evil I might add."

"Well, thanks, and please call me Lana," she said as I slid into the booth. She was all a-glitter with gold: necklace, earrings, bracelet. "Yes, I loved that role. It gave me a chance to show some depth, be really *bad*," she said with a cunning smile displaying a row of white teeth that were anything but bad.

We chatted awhile about that film and her costar, John Garfield. A waiter came by and I ordered a Falstaff beer.

When the waiter left, Mickey said, "The Chicago Stags beat the New York Knickerbockers last night."

"The who did what?" I asked.

"That basketball league they started back east, Scribbler. You think pro basketball will catch on?"

"I doubt it, Mick."

"Don't be too sure. It'd be somethin' else for suckers to bet on."

"With your bookies, of course," I said, putting a grin on it. I figured it was time to tell him why I'd wanted to see him, so I explained about Gretchen and the fugitive Nazi surgeon and our efforts to find him. Could he maybe help?

"My, that's fascinating," Lana Turner said.

"Well," Mickey said, "I guess I could do some nosing around"—a steely glint in his eye—"that is, if you . . ."

"I know, Mick, I'll go easy on you. Dragna's the guy I'm after." The waiter came by again and we all ordered the crab Louis for which Musso & Frank was famous.

Mickey asked a number of questions, like what had Gretchen and I done so far. I filled him in on Sachsen Haus, the probable murder at Loma Linda and so on.

When that topic had played out, he asked how it had gone in Detroit.

"It was damn cold there. And it turns out the Purple Gang are small potatoes these days. No wonder Luciano leaves 'em alone." I didn't mention the kidnapping. The Mick didn't need to know about that.

He asked if I'd met Aldo Tripolani and I said, "Yeah. He didn't impress me."

Then, feeling mischievous, I asked Lana, "What are you doing hanging out with a guy like Mickey Cohen?"

She touched Mickey's hand and said with a coy grin, "I love gangsters, God help me."

"She refuses to be in one of my B movies," Mickey said. "Can you imagine that?"

Recalling the tip I'd got from Lenny Navarro, I said, "Mick, is Bugsy having trouble getting his hotel built on the Vegas Strip?"

"You're one hell of a snoop, ain't you, Scribbler? He might be, I don't know, but Siegel's business is Siegel's business. That's all I can tell you."

Which I translated to, "I could tell you plenty but I won't. Bugsy's my business, not yours." I took the hint and changed the subject to things like Artie Aragon's next fight.

After our meals and a second round of drinks were polished off, Mickey said he'd be in touch. Over my protest—this lunch was my idea—he picked up the tab. I thanked him and exchanged nice-to-meet-you's with Miss Turner.

When I drove off, I thought, wait'll I tell Valerie and Ilse who I had lunch with. They'll shoot a ton of questions at me.

THIRTEEN

I wondered if I'd ever hear from Gretchen Siedler again after telling her I wasn't in the market for a mistress, but hear from her I did.

She called me at the office that afternoon and spoke as if the mistress conversation had never taken place. She said she'd gone to Sachsen Haus and asked a lot of questions. "In hindsight, that was foolish. I got a very chilly reception there. I spoke with a woman receptionist and also a man from the office whose demeanor was most defensive and suspicious. He glared at me in a way that frightened me. After I left I had a most strong sense that I was being followed. I looked behind me several times and saw no one on the sidewalk who looked suspicious. But I could not rid myself of that scary feeling. I was relieved to find a taxi and get away from there."

"Gretchen," I said needlessly, "you've got to be very careful. Maybe you should go to the FBI. Do they know anything about this?"

"I do not know for certain. The MI-6 may have made my presence known to them as a courtesy. I will have to ask the Pope about that."

I sure didn't want Gretchen to get hurt—or worse—and concern about her shadowed me the rest of the day. Maybe I should go see her again.

Soon I would have something to see her *about*. I got a big surprise the next day—Lana Turner called.

"Maybe you can't tell," she said, "but I've had some plastic surgery done. Just a little tuck around the eyes. Please don't tell anyone. There's a clinic in Beverly Hills that does very nice work. I went there today to have a little something done."

"But your face is perfect, Miss Turner," and I meant it.

"It's Lana, please, and thanks, you're very sweet. Anyway, my regular doctor was not in and I was examined by someone else, a European gentleman. Although he seemed to be very good at his work, he frightened me."

"European? Did he get more specific, like Swiss or German?"

"No, I don't think so."

"What was his name, Lana?"

"Doctor something or other. I don't remember."

"Was it Kristian Egger?"

"I can't really say."

"How did he frighten you?"

"The way he looked at me, Jake. Something in his eyes, something about his touch when he made his measurements. I can't tell you exactly, but I remembered what you told Mickey about this Nazi doctor. This man looked sort of, well . . . avid?"

"Predatory?" I offered.

"Yes, maybe that's the word. After his examination he made some recommendations. When he picked up a scalpel, I almost froze. I just thanked him and rushed out of there. I didn't ever want that man's hands on me again. Am I being silly?"

"Not a bit, Lana. Please give me the name of that clinic." After she did and I wrote it down, I said, "Don't go back there. Believe me, you don't need anything done to that lovely face of yours."

"Oh, thank you, but—"

"Don't go back," I repeated.

After we hung up, I put my feet up on the desk. I did some of my best thinking that way. Okay, I told myself, that may be Gretchen's Otto Woolf in that plastic surgery place. The guy who only killed women. We can't barge in there and start asking questions as we'd done at Loma Linda. That wouldn't work. We need to nab this guy, haul him off somewhere and grill him. How to do that? We couldn't get a search or arrest warrant. I didn't know or trust any L.A. cops who could help with that, and we didn't have enough to make a warrant feasible anyway. Did Gretchen have any backup? Some tough, experienced MI-6 operative she could call on?

Marko Janicek came by at that moment, putting an end to my musings. "That's some foot stool you got there, Jake," he said. I pulled my feet down and said, "What's up, Marko?"

"I tailed Judge Bonadio," he said. "He had lunch at Clifton's Cafeteria, never went to a bank. I followed him home after work. Lives in a nice house in Westwood. Got his address."

"Good. Who'd he have lunch with?"

"Nobody. He ate alone. Had a sandwich and a glass of 7-Up. Poured something into it from a flask."

That didn't give me much but at least we knew where the judge lived and that he liked to take a snort.

Richie Millsap came over and joined us. We spent a few minutes talking about what the Unholy Trinity would do next.

That night Valerie, Ilse and I had a tuna casserole and scalloped potatoes for dinner. I told them about meeting Lana Turner at lunch, but not about her experience at the plastic surgeon's. As expected, they asked lots of questions. Was she prettier in real life than on-screen? How was her hair done? Did it look peroxided? What did you talk about? Why was she with Mickey Cohen?

I related that Lana had said she enjoyed the company of gangsters. Valerie put her wine glass down and said, "What a fool."

* * *

The Mick called the next day. Lana Turner had told him the same thing she'd told me about her bad experience at the plastic surgeon's. "I don't like foreign freaks scaring hell outta my friends. I can have a couple of my people strong-arm him when he comes outta that place after work," he said. "We'll haul him off to a warehouse I use and get to the bottom of this."

"No, Mick, bad idea. The MI-6 has people who can do that." But did they? I had no idea.

"Don't be telling me my business, Scribbler. We can do this."

Oh shit, I thought as Cohen hung up.

I got up and went to John Campbell's office and asked if he had a minute.

"Sure. Come on in."

I dropped into a chair and said, "Johnny, I'm not going after Cohen anymore. Siegel and Dragna, sure, but not Cohen, not unless he gets way far out of bounds. I thought you should know."

My managing editor clenched his fists. "Why the hell not, Jake? W.R. wouldn't like that a bit."

"Mickey's done me some favors, Johnny. Besides, nothing we write will really stop any of his illegal doings. The cops sure aren't going to stop him, you know that, and neither will our stories."

"But—"

"As to Hearst," I interrupted, "he's a little froggy nowadays, pretty much in his dotage. He didn't even have the *Detroit Times'* circulation numbers right. As long as we keep printing good stuff about Siegel and Dragna he won't even notice about Cohen."

"But Cohen's as big a crook as those two."

"I know, but those guys who gamble on Mickey's race wire and hump his whores, they do it 'cause' they want to. It's their choice. These are basically victimless crimes."

Campbell picked up a coffee mug, stared into it, and put it down again. "What kind of favors he doing you?"

"Tips on this and that. Info on the Purple Gang, that maroon

Buick of Dragna's, stuff like that."

"He a friend of yours then?"

"Hell no, no friend, just a useful tool sometimes."

"I still don't like it, Jake," Campbell said, a resigned look on his face, "but I guess the Unholy Trinity is yours to do with as you see fit. I won't say anything to the old man about this."

As our most senior reporter and coauthor of an acclaimed book about the war, I knew I was sort of a fair-haired boy, a role I didn't relish. I just wanted to be one of the guys.

"Thanks, Johnny," I said.

"Okay, haul your butt out of here. You've got work to do."

I walked away knowing I'd pissed off my boss, a boss who'd always been good to me. I never kept anything from him and wasn't going to start now.

I turned back, stuck my head in the door and said, "Johnny, if Cohen starts bumping people off, anything like that, way beyond his current rackets, all bets are off. I'll be after his ass in a heartbeat."

The man just frowned at me and said, "Go away."

Cohen called on Wednesday and said, "I'm sorry, Scribbler. We button-holed that guy and took him for a little ride. Scared hell out of him. Turns out he's some Hungarian, name of Laszlo Pentele. Showed us his ID and passport. He's got a work permit and everything. He looks legit. I had one of my people check with the Hungarian consulate and it all added up. He ain't your German guy."

"Jesus, Mick, I wish you hadn't done that, but thanks anyway. Does he know who you are?"

"Give me some credit, Jakester. I flashed him some phony tin and told him I was FBI—special agent Miller. We dropped him back at the clinic and told him we were sorry to've troubled him, but keep his hands off movie stars."

"Mickey, you're a real piece of work."

"Course I am, Scribbler. See you in church, kid."

So the Loma Linda business was inconclusive and the Lana Turner thing was off base—or was it? Gretchen's guy had to be *somewhere*.

FOURTEEN

To my surprise, Gretchen showed up about halfway through Ilse's soccer game on Saturday. I must have told her about this playground. After she and Valerie hugged, Gretchen said she'd been eager to see a game ever since I'd told her about Ilse's Tigers.

I gave Gretchen my camp stool, saying, "I should get on my feet and move these old muscles a bit."

While I walked the sidelines the rest of the game, Gretchen and Valerie sat side by side. When not clapping and cheering, they chatted animatedly. What the devil were they talking about? Sharing confidences?

Gretchen occasionally pointed out a good or bad play. "*Die Linke, die Linke, aufpassen,*" she called to Ilse at one point, meaning, "The left, watch that girl on your left." The coach, Schäfer, the German one, heard that and shot a curious look at Gretchen.

When the game ended—the Tigers lost 3 to 2, darn it— Gretchen gave Ilse some kind words and then drew the coach into conversation. I didn't listen in, but I was disturbed by a kind of shifty look I saw on his face.

I was busy consoling Ilse and making sure she drank some water. My daughter hated to lose. "Hey, *Liebchen*, it's only your second loss. You guys are 7 and 2, and you scored one of your team's two goals. Nothing to be ashamed of." Still unhappy, she managed a weak smile.

When Gretchen finished chatting up the coach—they'd been speaking German—we thanked her for showing up. She'd come by cab, so after getting a prodding look from Valerie, I said we'd drive her home. Along the way, Valerie said, "Gretchen, we'll have to have you over for dinner again soon."

When we reached her apartment, Ilse and Valerie hugged her goodbye, Ilse saying, "Thank you so much for coming. I am sorry we could not have won the game."

I couldn't say why, but somehow I felt uneasy about that coach, *Herr* Schäfer.

I had lunch the following Monday with Raymond Chandler at a little joint he suggested in Manhattan Beach. The famous mystery writer said he'd enjoyed the book Kenny Nielsen and I had written about the war. Fiddling with his unlit pipe, he said, "Corralling that German rocket scientist and his crew was excellent."

I thanked him and we ordered, Chandler asking for a martini and me for a Falstaff beer. We each chose the abalone plate. The place had barnwood wall paneling and light fixtures that were imitation ship's lanterns. Sunlight from a big window overlooking the ocean reflected on Chandler's gold-rimmed glasses. He grumbled awhile about his marital troubles—he was often having those—and also about the film *The Big Sleep*, which he said butchered his book. "I got a screenwriter credit, big deal, but they swept most of my suggestions under the rug."

A young guy was playing a piano in the corner, tinkling out some nice jazz riffs.

"That's Dave somebody," Chandler said. "Brubaker or Brubeck, something like that. I think he's going places."

"Yeah, he's good." I then asked Chandler what he was working on these days. "Still fiddling with the damn script for *The Blue Dahlia*. Paramount says I've gotta change the ending."

Reaching up and sweeping an unruly shock of black hair off his forehead, Chandler said he and his wife were planning to move to La Jolla, down by San Diego. Our conversation finally turned to Bugsy Siegel, and I told him I'd heard Siegel was having financial problems with the Flamingo Hotel he was building in Las Vegas.

"I didn't know that," he said. "You going to write about it?"

"Not till I know more. Don't have any hard facts yet."

"An Arizona builder named Del Webb is his contractor," Chandler said. "Big construction fellow, has projects going all over the West. He's also part owner of the New York Yankees." I knew that. "There's this bloke," he went on, "who handles a good bit of his L.A. work. I could ask him some questions." *Bloke?* Then I remembered that Chandler had lived in England for several years.

"Any chance I could meet this fella?" I asked. "Could you arrange that?"

"Shouldn't be a problem." Chandler drank some of his martini, got up and went to a wall telephone and made a call. When he came back, he said, "He's at a construction site in El Segundo. He said come on out."

"Today?" I said. "Great." I took a bite of grilled abalone. It was darn good.

After we polished off our meals and drinks, I laid a half-dollar on the piano and gave a thumbs-up to Dave Brubeck, Brubaker or whatever. He grinned at me and kept on playing.

I followed Chandler's 1941 Dodge Deluxe over to El Segundo, which was just a couple of miles away. The Webb company was putting up a warehouse there, close to Standard Oil's big refinery. We pulled our cars into a dirt lot beside some trucks and went to a construction trailer.

Chandler's contact was a big burly guy named Wally Spradling, the construction manager. We found him in the trailer wearing a hard hat and smoking a cigarette.

"Wally, meet Jake Weaver of the *Herald-Express*. He's got a few questions for you." Spradling and I shook hands and swapped nice-to-meet-you's. After I declined his offer of coffee, he said, "Can't blame you, it's pretty awful stuff. Well, what can I do for ya, Jake?"

"I'd like to know something about the Flamingo Hotel you guys are building on the Vegas strip. I hear Bugsy Siegel's having some trouble up there."

"That's what *he* says. That guy knows jack shit about construction. Keeps wanting to change things and add stuff that's not in the architect's drawings. Wants to double the size of the cocktail lounge. Now? At this point? After all the walls are up? The thing's ninety percent finished. Sure glad I ain't the crew boss out there. Hey, I seen some of your stories on Siegel. I don't wanta be quoted on this."

"You won't be, Wally. This is just background."

Chandler gave him a little trust-this-guy nod.

"Okay then. Well, these changes cost money. He owes us a helluva lot more than our original bid."

"How much more?"

"You sure you'll keep my name out of this?"

"Absolutely, cross my heart."

"Okay then, a million and a half so far."

"And are all your over-charges legit? Are you pumping up the numbers some?"

Spradling snuffed out his cigarette in a tin ashtray. "Well..." He said no more, but he didn't have to. I gave him what I hoped was a disarming smile.

The man reached up and adjusted his hard hat. "The Webb company's not a charity, Jake. We have to turn a profit. We got huge expenses. Insurance, union wages to pay, so forth."

I tossed out a few more questions. What was the pay scale for carpenters and cement masons? How many craps and roulette tables at the Flamingo? Finally I said, "Well, thanks, Wally, we've taken up enough of your time."

"No, look," he said, "I changed my mind. Don't use this. This could put me right in Siegel's gunsights."

"Relax," I told him. "I'm not using your name, plus you're not the only guy with the Webb company who could've told me this." Trying to sound convincing. "Bugsy couldn't pin this on you."

I shook his hand and got out of there before Spradling could backpedal any more. In the parking lot I thanked Chandler, who called me a piece of work.

A million and a half, I thought as I battled Venice Boulevard traffic. Yeah, Lucky Luciano can't be happy with Bugsy Siegel, not a bit.

I had to detour around a big construction site where bulldozers were slashing a wide path through an old neighborhood to make room for a new freeway. Looked like one of the shattered towns I'd seen in Germany during the war.

Back at the paper I told Aggie Underwood what I'd learned and my city editor said, "Good. Go for it."

I rolled some paper into my trusty old upright typewriter and started working the keys. The lead on my story soon read:

Ben "Bugsy" Siegel, the New York and Los Angeles hoodlum who is building a hotel in Las Vegas, is in hock to his contractor for some $1.5 million, the *Herald-Express* has learned from reliable sources.

I went on to tell about the changes he was demanding of the builder and that the hotel was along Highway 91 outside of town so he could dodge city taxes. When I finished fifteen minutes later, Aggie read it. Never one to over-praise, she said, "Not bad, Jake. Above the fold, second edition."

She also said, "Johnny tells me you're going to go light on Cohen."

"Yeah, I've been able to use him some. I owe the guy, a little bit anyway."

"It's your call, Mr. Untouchable."

"Aw, Aggie, don't say that. Please. I'm nobody special."

I'd always known this anti-crime push of ours involved a lot of risk, but this was our hardest-hitting story yet and I was more worried than usual. This would be on the INS wire and Meyer Lansky would see it in New York and pass it on to Lucky Luciano in Italy. The whole underworld would soon know that Siegel's problems—of which they were already aware—were now out there in the public media.

I hoped I'd done the right thing. Earlier I had dinged him on giving funds to his madam girlfriend—now this. *Jesus*, if Siegel ever bought me another beer, I thought, there'd probably be some cyanide in it. What worried me more, though, was the possible danger I might be putting my family into.

Not forty-five minutes after our late edition, the Night Final, hit the streets, Bugsy himself called, not exactly a surprise.

"God damn you, you son of a bitch," he stormed. The receiver in my hand seemed to turn hot. "I told you to go easy on me. And you go and do this."

"Well, Mr. Siegel—"

"I told you before to watch your step. Now you better watch your *every* step. You haven't heard the last of me, you slimy bastard."

I started to say I'd just been doing my job but I heard a sharp click. I was talking to a dial tone.

I drove home in a heavy December rain. Yes, L.A. actually had a rainy season. Sometimes. After shaking out my umbrella, I went inside where Valerie told me she'd seen the story. She said she was worried—for me, for Ilse, and for herself. I tried to assure her it would be okay but, hell, I was anxious too. Instead of Jack Dragna trying to kill her—or me—it could be Bugsy Siegel next time.

"He's too smart to hurt us now," I told Valerie. "With this story out there, everyone would know it was him if any harm came to us." There was some logic to that, and yet I knew I was trying to persuade myself as well as her.

The following day the paper got a lot of response. Ninety percent of the callers backed us big time, saying things like great work and keep them coming. Surprisingly, though, a few took Siegel's side. I got a call from somebody at Temple Emanuel saying Siegel was a big supporter and how dare I embarrass such a good member of the community. He added that others were upset too, including the lyricist Ira Gershwin.

Ira Gershwin? Really? Hmm, well, he and Siegel both came from Jewish neighborhoods in New York. "You don't mind taking dirty money, rabbi?" I said. And wished I hadn't.

Johnny Campbell was ecstatic: "We sold more than two-thousand copies of the Night Final yesterday, ran completely out. Marion Davies called and said congrats. Hearst is happy as a sailor in a whorehouse."

"Maybe W.R. will come to my funeral," I said.

Gretchen Siedler had seen the story too. She called, said she had enjoyed the soccer game, then, "That story, Jake, that was most brave of you. How did you ever obtain that information?"

"Journalistic secret," I told her.

"My, Colonial Four, you are still a good spy."

I laughed at her use of my old MI-6 code name and asked if she'd learned anything new.

"*Nein*, nothing new, I am sorry to say. And now I have only seven days left or I must leave." This made me a little sad. I'd miss her. "Oh, by the way," she went on, "the FBI does know that I am here. MI-6 has informed them. Colonel Freeborn says I must not be stepping on their toes."

I asked if she'd had more bad feelings about Sachsen Haus.

"*Nein*, not so much. No one has approached or bothered me."

"Nevertheless, there's something queer about that place, Gretchen. It might still be the key to your *Herr* Woolf. I'll give some thought to how we could look into that and let you know."

And I would. I wished I had some other ideas to give her right then but I didn't. Bugsy Siegel and Jack Dragna remained first and foremost on my mind.

I thought about telling her there were plenty of plastic surgeons in L.A. where she could get her nose fixed, though not at the Beverly Hills place Lana Turner had frequented. But I discarded that thought as a dumb one, none of my business.

After Gretchen rang off, something that had been lurking in the back of my mind since Loma Linda surfaced. She'd told me that day about a stolen dagger with a diamond-studded handle that Freeborn believed Woolf had in his possession. It was worth a fortune, she'd said. That put a whole new light on things.

FIFTEEN

Ilse, a sophomore now, was on the school paper, "following in my *Vati's* footsteps," as she liked to say. While we set the table for dinner that evening she excitedly told me she'd covered a student council meeting, a rare assignment for a sophomore.

"The council president got into a bit of a quarrel with one of the council members. It was about raising the fee for a school play. I did not know if I should include that in my story, but in the end I did because I thought it was important. I think that is what you would have done."

"Good, but always use your own news judgment, *Liebchen*. You don't need to be thinking about what I would do. You have a good sense of what's important."

"Thank you, *Vati*." As we arranged the silverware we then talked awile about our anti-crime series. Ilse had a strong interest in that.

Later that evening Valerie and I chatted awhile over a nightcap about her work at North American. She mentioned some of her fellow workers in Tool Design. "We have a new guy, a Czech war refugee with a heavy accent, who claims he was a tool and die man at the Skoda Works in Pilsen, but I have my doubts about that. He doesn't even read blueprints very well." She also brought up a guy named Harry Monahan who'd come on to her, "but I put a definite stop to that!"

"Can't blame him," I said, though I resented the nerve of the guy. "You're a very desirable woman, Sweets, but good for you.

Save yourself for me." She gave me that warm, reassuring smile of hers, and I reached out and put my hand on her arm.

I called Gretchen the next day and asked if she knew what Otto Woolf looked like. "Yes, I have a photograph," she said. "It is black and white and not very clear. He wears glasses and has a full head of hair that appears to be blond or light brown."

"Good, there's a suspicious fellow at North American we need to have a look at."

"We shall have to do that quite soon then," she said, sounding gloomy. "I must go to London in less than a week, you know. I am to report to Colonel Freeborn before returning to Berlin."

Although I was uneasy about her being here, close to Valerie, I had to admit I was a little disappointed she'd be leaving.

"Okay, I'll get back to you right away," I said. I called Valerie at work, explained what I had in mind, and asked if Gretchen and I could get inside the plant and go to Tool Design.

"You know better than that," she said. "That's absolutely not permitted, but if you want to look at this guy, be outside Gate Two any afternoon at five. We clock out then, as you know, and we all leave through that gate around five minutes after."

I explained that this would have to be done tomorrow or the next day because Gretchen had to leave in less than a week.

"In that case, Jake, let's have her over for dinner tonight. It's the least we can do for her, and Ilse and I would like to say our goodbyes in person."

"Aw, Sweets, do you really—"

"Yes I do, hon. We need to be nice to her."

I reluctantly told her okay, that I'd pick up Gretchen if she was available and get her to the house by six.

* * *

She was available, darn it. "It would give me much pleasure," she said when I called.

As I drove to her apartment building at Wilshire and Union, I dreaded another face-to-face between the wife I dearly loved and the woman I'd slept with four years ago in Berlin, the woman who wanted to be my mistress. And whom—stupid me—I was still fond of. Hell's bells, I'd be walking on eggshells again. But since our Thanksgiving dinner had come off with no embarrassing moments, maybe tonight's would too. One could hope.

It surprised me that Gretchen wasn't on the sidewalk waiting for me as we'd arranged. The woman was the picture of punctuality, unlike a lot of American women I knew. I went to the door and buzzed her. No answer. I buzzed again and again. Still no answer. Through the window in the door I could see the concierge seated at his desk. I rattled the door, got his attention, and waved him over. When he opened the door I said, "I'm a friend of Gretchen Siedler. She was expecting me but didn't answer my ring. Do you know—"

"Miss Siedler isn't here. She left about half an hour ago, sir."

"Really? Was she alone?"

"No sir, with a man."

"A man? What did he look like?"

"I don't know if I should—" He put a hand to his chin. "You say you're a friend?"

"Sure am." I got out my wallet, slipped him a buck, showed my press pass, and said, "I'm with the *Herald-Express,* and Miss Siedler's welfare is a special interest of ours."

"I see. Well then, he was a fairly big fellow, sir. He had a good grip on her arm. Miss Siedler glanced back at me over her shoulder, like she was about to say something."

"Like she was scared, like she wanted to say 'help?' "

"Can't really say scared, maybe like she forgot to tell me something."

"Did they get into a car?"

"Don't know. They went down the steps pretty fast and off to the right, beyond my line of sight. It was after dark, you know."

"Don't suppose you called the cops?"

"No. What could I possibly tell them?"

"Not much, I guess. Well, thanks."

I didn't like this a bit. Was she with an MI-6 operative, or had she been kidnapped? With a black foreboding I thought I knew the answer.

What could I do? I couldn't think of a thing, except to put in a call to Colonel Freeborn at MI-6. It would be about three a.m. in London, but this couldn't wait.

When I got home, Valerie said, "Where's Gretchen?"

She looked as worried as me after I told her what had happened. "That's terrible, Jake. What can you do?"

"I have no idea, Sweets, except to call the Pope in London. There's a big time difference, you know, but someone's got to be there."

"The Pope?" Valerie asked. I explained that was what some of his agents had nicknamed him.

I went to the phone and asked the operator to place a transatlantic call to the Military Intelligence office in London. She said she'd try and would call me back. When I hung up, Valerie said, "Let me fix you a drink, Jake. You could use one."

"I'll do that." I went to the sideboard, poured myself a glass of straight Scotch, and took a gulp before pouring one for her, adding some water and ice.

Valerie had gone all out for dinner. She'd stopped at a German deli we knew and picked up sausages, porkchops, cheeses, coleslaw and potato salad, as well as some Pilsner beer. A thoughtfully prepared German meal for our farewell to Gretchen, a farewell meal my spy friend wouldn't get to eat.

After about ten minutes, the phone rang and I jumped to it.

"I have your call, sir."

The connection was a little staticky, but a voice said, "I am Lieutenant Baker, the duty officer tonight. Who are you, sir, and what may I do for you?"

"I'm Jake Weaver, known to Colonel Freeborn as Colonial Four. This is urgent. I think Gretchen Siedler, code-named Tapestry, has been kidnapped. Freeborn should be told right away."

"Very good, sir. Colonial Four, you say? Please stay near your phone."

I said I would, hung up, and told Valerie what he'd said. I took another drink.

Ilse came in from her room, where she'd been doing homework, and asked what was going on. I explained it all.

"*Mein Gott,*" she uttered, throwing a hand to her chest. "*Gretchen? Die Vermisste?*" Ilse often reverted to her native tongue when she was upset.

Valerie motioned us to the table, where dinner was waiting.

I didn't eat much—didn't have much appetite. Valerie didn't either. The bite of sausage I took seemed to form a knot in my stomach. We had the radio on to the news in the background. Lowell Thomas was talking about Juan Peron becoming president of Argentina.

"I know you don't feel like talking about Christmas," Valerie said, "but it's less than two weeks away and we haven't done much."

I appreciated her steering the conversation away from Gretchen. "Right," I said. "Let's get a tree this weekend. Ilse, you can pick it out." My daughter smiled at that.

When we finished, Valerie and Ilse put the leftovers—there were quite a few—in the fridge. I went to the phone and called Gretchen's apartment again. Still no answer. I hadn't expected one.

Later, I sat on the couch reading the *Mirror*. I always liked to see what the competition was printing. Valerie came over and sat next to me. "Are you still going out to Gate Two tomorrow to sneak a look at our new designer?"

"No point in it now, Sweets. Gretchen had a picture of her German guy but I haven't seen it. I wouldn't know who I'd be looking for."

The phone rang. It was Colonel Freeborn in London. I skipped the usual pleasantries and told him what had happened.

"Most alarming, Weaver. I daresay Tapestry is clever, and likely is all right. But it's out of character for her not to keep your appointment. I have an agent at Muroc." This was a hundred miles from here in the desert where U.S. jet and rocket planes were being tested. "I'll have him get to Los Angeles straightaway and work on this with our friends in the FBI. Have you any leads to go on?"

"Afraid not, sir."

"Well, do what you can. Please give me your phone numbers and I shall be in touch. My chap may contact you as well. His name is Virgil Travis, code-named Cromwell." I gave Freeborn my home and newspaper numbers, told him I was sorry to have brought bad news, and hung up.

Valerie had been standing nearby, listening. "Well, hon," I said, "let's hit the hay and try to get some sleep."

We didn't get much. At least I didn't.

I went back to Gretchen's building in the morning and asked the concierge if she'd returned. She hadn't. I spent half an hour out in front asking passers-by if they'd seen a woman, attractive though with a crooked nose, leave with a man around 5:30 the evening before. Some of them frowned and rushed off as if I were a weirdo, others were cooperative, but none of them had seen her.

I was about to leave when a little old woman crossed Union

Street using a cane. She'd come out of a coffee shop on the opposite side. She approached and demanded, "What are you up to, young man? If you're begging, shame on you."

I gave her my best smile, said, "No, ma'am, I'm not panhandling." I showed her my press pass and told her what I was doing.

She looked me up and down real good before saying, "I believe I know the young woman. You see, I live here. We've spoken a few times at the mailboxes. She has a foreign accent, doesn't she?"

"Yes ma'am, she's German."

"A refugee from those horrid Nazis, I suppose. Yes, I saw her leave yesterday. She got into a car down the street a ways." The woman pointed her cane in the direction. "The man she was with put her into the car."

"Did he shove her in?"

"I wouldn't say shove, but he was holding her arm firmly."

"I see. What kind of car was it?"

"Oh, goodness, let me think. Oh, yes, it was a black Hudson Commodore Eight, four-door."

"How can you be so precise, ma'am?"

"You see, my late husband used to drive one."

This would help some, I thought. There probably weren't a lot of Hudson Commodores in L.A. Good thing it wasn't a Ford or Chevy. "I couldn't make out the license number in the dark," she went on, "but it was not a black California plate. It was a white plate." That helped even more.

I asked if she could describe the man. "Not well. He was tall, wore a dark suit and hat. I'm afraid I can't tell you any more than that."

"Was anyone else in the car? Maybe a driver besides the man you saw?"

"I think so. The man I saw got in back with the woman, so someone else had to be driving. I didn't see him."

I thanked her and told her she was very observant and a good neighbor.

How could I find out about black Hudsons with out-of-state plates? Maybe the FBI guys supposedly cooperating with MI-6 had a way. I knew an FBI agent, Warren Grimsby. We'd worked together back in '42 on a matter involving an ex-Navy man who'd been spying for the Japanese. Maybe I should call Grimsby. I also knew the police had what they called the hotsheet, a daily listing of stolen or otherwise wanted cars. It was a longshot that our Hudson would be on the hotsheet but it would be worth a try. I still had a friend or two on the force.

"Let's ask our readers to help," Aggie Underwood said when I was back at the paper and had filled her in on Gretchen's disappearance. "Write a story," she said. "British official believed abducted by man in black Hudson Commodore with white out-of-state plates. Let us know if you see such a car. Get license number if possible."

"You just wrote my story," I told my city editor. "You haven't lost your touch, Ag."

The piece was too late for the first edition but it ran in all the others, front page with heavy box rules around it.

Minutes later, the editor of our book, *Two Men at War: A Retrospective,* called from the University of California Press. He said a book signing and discussion was being arranged. It would be held at UCLA in about a month. My coauthor, Lt. Colonel Kenny Nielsen, would be there.

The timing wasn't great—I had so much else on my plate at the moment—but it would be nice to see Kenny again. Maybe a little break from Bugsy Siegel and Jack Dragna would do me some good at that.

Meanwhile I had work to do. The Unholy Trinity met again

around my desk, Marko Janicek and Richie Millsap pulling up some chairs. Janicek's face wore a cat-that-ate-the-canary look and I asked what was up.

"Guess what, Jake," he gushed. "I had a look at Judge Bonadio's bank account."

"How the devil did you pull that off?"

"I followed him Monday. He went into the Mercantile Bank. After he left I went in and opened an account. Fifteen bucks. A sweet young thing called Gloria set it up for me. I laid on my famous charm and sweet-talked her for awhile. Told her I was an important reporter chasing a big story. Talked her into having dinner with me that night."

"Way to go, Don Juan," I said.

"You haven't heard the best part yet, Jake."

"So you scored?"

"Well, that too"—a self-satisfied grin—"but yesterday she gave me a look at Bonadio's account. She was pretty nervous about it but I assured her it was important."

"And?" I prompted.

"He deposited five-hundred bucks the same day he found you guilty of trespassing. He's got about seven grand in the account."

"Five bills the same day? Great work, Marko. Let's write it."

The story we soon penned said a judge believed to be on the payroll of the Mob made a big deposit the same day he found a *Herald-Express* reporter guilty of trespassing at gangster Jack Dragna's home despite no hard evidence, only the word of two known mobsters. "There is no proof that this was a payoff from Dragna, but the timing is highly suspicious," the story went on. "The *Herald-Express* has reason to believe that Pasqual Bonadio is a crooked judge, a disgrace to the solemn robe he wears." So on and so forth.

Johnny Campbell and Agness Underwood gave their okay and ran it on Page One that day. We'd nailed the schmuck. Maybe the bar would take action.

There would be repercussions of course, but so what? There always were when the Unholy Trinity broke a big story.

We'd kept Gloria's name out of it to protect her and we also didn't name the bank. That wasn't good journalism, but it covered our ass from a lawsuit by the bank. It was the Hearst way.

Jack Dragna would be furious, and Bonadio might sue for defamation of character, but Hearst had a battalion of lawyers to fight it, and the old man would relish the headlines.

"You going to see Gloria again?" I asked Janicek.

"Sure I am. She's a honey." Sounding like me a few years ago before I met Valerie.

SIXTEEN

Bugsy Siegel opened his Flamingo Hotel—and the big event flopped. The *Las Vegas Review-Journal* reported that few people attended and that Siegel closed it the next day.

That AP wire story had just come in. I'd previously met the guy who wrote it, so I called him in Vegas. "The place just wasn't ready, Jake. Some of the paint was still wet and a few scaffolds were still up. Two of the roulette wheels didn't work. Siegel was furious. He tried to pass if off a just a soft opening, a trial run. Said he'd reopen after the first of the year when everything would be perfect."

Lucky Luciano would be furious too, I thought. Bugsy, Bugsy, you really screwed up.

Virgil Travis, the MI-6 man code-named Cromwell, called later that day, said he was now in L.A. and wanted to meet as soon as possible. I gave him the paper's address and told him to come by.

When he showed up, I introduced myself and motioned him to a chair opposite my desk. Travis was a small man but stocky and tough looking. He resembled Tony Zale, the middleweight prizefighter, and he even looked as if he could give Zale a run for his money. He glanced around curiously at the busy city room, the aging wooden desks, clattering typewriters, men and women working the phones, the fat load-bearing pillars.

He fixed a brown-eyed gaze on me and said, "So Tapestry is missing, Weaver? Tell me about it."

I filled him in with everything I knew about Gretchen's futile search for Otto Woolf, our dead ends at the Loma Linda hospital, the Beverly Hills plastic-surgery clinic, all of it.

"And she was seen being placed into a black Hudson automobile by a big fellow?"

"Right." I told him about the cops' hotsheet and that I'd check it, though a black Hudson Commodore with out-of-state plates wasn't likely to be on it. "But maybe the FBI can help us identify that car."

"Doubtful, but I will speak to them about it. I suggest we go and pay a call on this Sachsen Haus you mentioned. Tomorrow morning suit you?"

"Sure."

"I am staying at the Mayfair Hotel on West Seventh Street. Collect me at half nine if you would. Come armed."

"Armed?"

"Certainly. You're a spy, are you not?"

"Not really, Travis. I've never taken one brass farthing from MI-6. Whatever I've done for Freeborn was on the house."

"I see. Didn't know that. Nevertheless, come armed," he said.

I swallowed the lump in my throat.

That evening, Valerie, Ilse and I went to a Christmas tree lot. I let Ilse pick out the tree and she did a good job, selecting a nice full spruce. It cost me two-fifty. We roped it down on top of Valerie's Plymouth and brought it home, where my wife chose a corner of the front room where she said it would look best.

I brought in our boxes of decorations and the Christmas-tree holder from the garage and when I had the tree set up, Valerie said, "Ilse and I will do the decorating. You usually get the tinsel all wrong." I didn't argue—that had been my plan.

While they sorted out the strings of lights, glass balls and other stuff, I told Valerie I'd met with the MI-6 guy and that we'd be looking for Gretchen the next day.

"I do hope you find her and that she's all right. I'm pretty worried."

So was I.

While they decorated the tree, I went to our bedroom closet, reached up to the overhead crawl space and got down the box holding my Luger, the Luger with which I'd killed a couple of Germans two years before.

Our story asking readers to help generated a lot of cockamamie responses. The black Hudson had been driven off the Santa Monica pier and was under thirty feet of water, depending on the tides. It was owned by Betty Grable. Hudson doesn't make black cars. It was tooling around East L.A., driven by zoot suiters. Or maybe a mariachi band. It was at Citrus College, where Illinois was practicing for the Rose Bowl game against UCLA.

We actually checked out the Betty Grable and Citrus College tips. Neither was true. The others were too obviously worthless to bother with.

In the morning I picked up Virgil Travis at the Mayfair Hotel and drove over to 17th Street. What was this guy called Cromwell planning to do? Burst in there like the mighty British lion and play the big conqueror who'd just trounced these guys in the war?

He asked me to park half a block away from Sachsen Haus. December in L.A. is seldom cold but it was a little chilly so I'd worn an overcoat to conceal the Luger tucked under my belt. It bothered me that I didn't have a carry permit. Sure didn't want to encounter any cops. Several were on Jack Dragna's pad.

I parked and we got out. "We shall have a look in back before going in," Travis said. We'd noticed a driveway running alongside the building. "If there is a car park, let us see what's in it."

"Okay, Virg."

"Please, I prefer *not* to be called Virg."

With that out of the way, we walked to the rear and found a small concrete parking lot back there. It contained three cars, an old Mercedes and two Chevys. No black Hudson. A rear door opened and the woman I'd met before at the reception desk came out carrying a cigarette, about to take a smoke break. She shuddered when she saw us and dropped the cigarette. "Who—"

"We are British agents," Travis said, and showed her a wallet badge. "We are authorized by the FBI to search this place. Take us inside, please."

The woman collected herself and said, "You will have to show me your authorization papers."

Travis grabbed her arm and said, "Cooperate, madam, or you shall be placed under arrest." Playing the British lion. I didn't like that. He wouldn't get any traction with this woman that way.

"*Ach!* On what charge?"

Travis let go of her arm. "For impeding the performance of official duty." And opened the door himself.

I followed him into a storage room, the *Frau* following behind us. Floor-to-ceiling shelves filled with cardboard boxes and stacks of maps, brochures and flyers. A water cooler with paper-cup dispenser, beside a hotplate and a coffee pot.

The woman blurting, "You are trespassing."

"Madam, we are not," Travis said. "We are in search of a man named Otto Woolf." I checked her face for any sign of recognition. Saw none. "There is no one here by that name," she said.

"How about Gretchen Siedler?" I put in. "Do you know that name?" Now a small glimmer of something in her eyes.

Those eyes locked closely on my face. "Do I not know you? *Ja,* you were here before, asking about river cruises."

"I'm still interested in those," I said. "Germany is a beautiful country. Right now, though, I'm more interested in finding Gretchen Siedler. I think you know who I mean."

"You are mistaken, sir."

I switched to speaking German. Maybe that would shock her, maybe startle her into revealing something. "*Wo ist Gretchen?*" I asked. "*Frau Siedler.*"

Surprise on her face. Travis's too.

"I know nothing of this person you mention." Also speaking German.

"I think you do."

An inner door opened and the man I'd seen before came in carrying a coffee mug. Seeing us, he almost dropped it. Same gray suit, same rimless eyeglasses.

"Who are you?" he demanded in English. "What is going on here?"

Travis again showed his wallet badge. "An official investigation," he said.

"That appears to be an English badge. What authority could you have here?" A good question, I thought. "And what is it you wish to investigate?"

"These offices," Travis said, "and as to authority, Great Britain is one of the four occupying powers in Germany and has legal control of its institutions and facilities."

"This is not a German facility. It is an American one, a not-for-profit organization registered with the State of California and run by modestly-paid volunteers, such as we two. Well, come on then, we have nothing to hide." He opened the door to an inner hallway.

We looked into the three offices along the corridor, and a bathroom. One of the offices belonged to this gray-suited guy, one was vacant, and in the third a young woman stopped typing and looked at us with what I'd call startled curiosity.

We checked everything, a closet that held a vacuum cleaner

and brooms, and the front reception area. No sign of Gretchen anywhere. I felt stupid, especially with that Luger under my coat.

"What was it that you were hoping to find?" Gray Suit asked when we'd seen everything.

Before Travis or I could answer, the woman said, "A *Frau* Siedler, Nikki."

"Siedler? Never heard of her." Did the man's face register anything—a fleck of recognition? I wasn't sure, but I didn't think so.

But the woman said, "You remember, Nikki, that tall one with the bent nose." The man shot her a look that could only mean, "Shut up, you fool."

"Give him your card," Travis said to me. "If your memory improves on Gretchen Siedler, or if she should turn up," he told the guy called Nikki, "contact this man."

I pulled a card from my wallet and handed it over. The man read it closely, then slipped it into a coat pocket, looking surprised to see I was a newspaperman.

We thanked him and left. I was tempted to tell Travis he'd been dumb in there, but let it go. What had he accomplished with his strong-arm tactics? While I drove back to his hotel, I said, "Gretchen was put into that black Hudson by a big man. That guy who the woman called Nikki isn't huge but he's kind of big."

Travis said little to that. In fact, he didn't say much at all, nothing about his next steps. When we arrived, he told me he'd be in touch. *Oh, joy.*

"Okay, Virg," I said, trying to contain a grin.

He gave me a frosty look, got out of the car, and still didn't say what his next move would be.

I drove away wondering how MI-6 could have such an oddball on its payroll. I also recalled that Gretchen had been spooked after going to Sachsen Haus, had sensed that she was being followed. So where the hell was she?

SEVENTEEN

At my desk the next day, my mind for some reason drifted back to the pictures Gino Columbini had on the office wall at his factory in Detroit, especially the photo that had caught my eye. There'd been something about the man standing beside Columbini. The shot was a little dark and the guy's hat partially shaded his face but now that I concentrated, I recalled that the nose and jaw had looked familiar. A nose and jaw that looked a lot like Bugsy Siegel's. Could that have been Siegel? Could Siegel and Columbini be friends? It was a possibility. Siegel had contacts galore in the underworld. And he hated my guts.

I pondered those possibilities. Mickey Cohen had known I was going to Detroit. Had he mentioned that to Siegel? Could be. If so, then maybe Bugsy was behind my kidnapping. Back then, he was already sore at me, even though our story about his owing big money to the Del Webb company hadn't run yet. Aw gee, this is pretty farfetched, I thought, and yet . . .

I picked up my phone and placed a call to Matt Mason at the *Detroit Times*. In my opinion he was the better of their two investigative reporters. When I got Mason on the line I asked how their anti-crime push was going. He filled me in. They'd run two stories he'd thought were pretty strong. Then I laid out my suspicion about Siegel possibly being behind my kidnapping. "What do you think?" I asked.

"Could be, Jake. I'll look into that for you. I'll see what Tripolani says. He's been pretty contrite lately, still really embarrassed about that, and sore as hell at Columbini. Pretty cooperative with us too if you can imagine that."

"I know I'm asking a lot, but yeah, please do check with Tripolani if you would. By the way, he sent me a check for eight-hundred dollars, which I didn't keep, so, yeah, he's definitely embarrassed. Tell him I said thanks but no thanks on that money."

"Wow, eight-hundred bucks? Sure, Jake, I'll follow up and get back to you."

When Mason called back two days later, he said, "Yep, Tripolani claims it was all Siegel's idea. I had Tripolani tell Columbini if he didn't come clean on all this, we'd run the kidnap story and ruin the guy. Columbini was scared Tripolani would dump him in the river, so he spilled his guts out. He said Siegel wanted him to make you disappear."

"Disappear? *Jesus!* Siegel wanted to waste me?"

"So Columbini says. Doing it in Detroit would keep Siegel's fingerprints off it. But Columbini got the bright idea of going for some ransom money from Hearst instead, the ignoramus. Tripolani is really pissed off. He's pulled Columbini out of that factory and has him driving a garbage truck or something. Columbini really broke his pick on this one."

"Do you actually buy all that, Matt?'

"Yeah, Jake, 'cause Tripolani really wants to keep the lid on your kidnapping. He made Columbini spill it all out."

"Okay, thanks a million then, Matt. I owe you big."

"You going to send me a check for eight-hundred bucks?" he said with a laugh.

"No, but how about a bottle of fine Scotch?"

"Good enough."

I felt sick the rest of the day. Bugsy Siegel wants to whack me? And now that we'd put him in the soup with our story on the big bucks he owes, I was in his crosshairs more than ever.

I was worried for myself but more so for Valerie and Ilse. Maybe I should get them out of the house for awhile, move them up to Big Bear, have our Christmas in the mountains.

No, that wouldn't work. Valerie couldn't get away from her job for two weeks and neither could I.

Maybe, as I'd tried to assure Valerie, Siegel wouldn't harm us now, because it would be obvious he'd done it, thanks to the story we'd printed about the debts he'd run up on his Vegas hotel. The thought didn't give me much comfort.

Suddenly I wondered if Siegel could have some connection with Otto Woolf. Both were of German descent, both had relatives in New York—and Woolf was out here in Bugsy's stomping grounds. Was that a coincidence? Probably. And yet, that dagger Woolf supposedly had could bail Bugsy out of his money problems if it really was worth a fortune. Woolf must have a powerful friend *somewhere*. Maybe in Beverly Hills?

All this Siegel rumination had been blocking out my concern for Gretchen. Where was she? I guessed I'd have to call Virgil Travis, darn it, and see if he'd learned anything. Was this bullying oaf cooperating with the FBI as Colonel Freeborn had said he would?

On my way home I stopped at a liquor store and bought a bottle of Chivas Regal. I got to the post office just before closing time, packaged it up and added a note saying, "Thanks for everything, Matt. Have one for me." I mailed it to Mason at the *Detroit Times*.

Following dinner and after Ilse went to bed I filled two snifters with brandy and beckoned Valerie to the living room. "What's up, Sailor?" she asked as she sometimes did, knowing I'd had a hitch in the Navy. "A little romance?"

"I wish. That'd be more fun, but there's something you need to know."

"Oh-oh," she said as we seated ourselves on the sofa. "Is Gretchen dead, is that it?"

"No, at least I hope not. Here's the thing, hon." I proceeded to tell her everything. Me getting kidnapped in Detroit. Siegel's role in that. How he'd wanted me to "disappear." The danger I'd put her and Ilse in.

Valerie sat silent for a long while, her face lovely even when scrunched in dark thought. Finally: "You bastard. Why didn't you tell me this before?"

"I didn't want to worry you. I hadn't known all this at first, not the Siegel part." I sipped some brandy. "But you're right, I should have leveled with you right away about getting kidnapped."

"Okay, okay, I guess I understand that. But what now? What'll we do?"

"I thought about having you and Ilse go away for awhile, but that wouldn't work. You couldn't leave your job, so—"

"I want a gun, Jake! Get me a pistol."

"A gun, Val? Really?"

"Sure. I'll defend Ilse and myself if it comes to that."

God, I loved this woman, her determination and her strength. I watched her take a gulp from her snifter. "I know you got out your Luger and took it with you the other day."

Clever, sneaky old Valerie. How had she known that?

"Okay, if that's what you want," I said. "I'll take you to a shooting range and have you practice with it. Handling a gun is a tricky thing, you've got to know what you're doing." I tried for a little grin. "But of course you'll never really have to use it." I hoped. Fervently hoped.

On Wednesday I got a call from Kenny Nielsen, my coauthor friend in Galesburg, Illinois. Now a reserve officer in the Marine Corps, Kenny had been a hero in the Pacific during the war. At age twenty-seven, he was about to enter his junior year at Knox College, his education having been delayed by the war. He said his wife Claudia was fine and old man winter was starting to get a grip on Galesburg. He thanked me again for helping him get out of a scrape he'd had with the War Department's judge advocate general.

I told him about our anti-crime crusade and mentioned Bugsy Siegel, but nothing about my being kidnapped.

"Bugsy Siegel? I've heard of him. I hear he's a bad hombre. You be real careful, Jake."

"I will, Kenny, don't worry." As we wrapped up our conversation, I said, "You'll enjoy some California sun. Stay with us when you get out here for the signing. Valerie and Ilse will be glad to see you."

Next day I told Agness Underwood what I'd learned from Matt Mason and that I wanted to buy a gun for Valerie. Aggie had been our police reporter for several years, still had great contacts in the cop shop.

"Siegel's not going to do anything," she said. "If he couldn't get it done in Detroit, half a continent away, he's too smart to try anything here. Everybody would know it was him."

I'd been trying to persuade myself of that too. "I hope you're right, Aggie, but maybe he could do something and make it look like an accident." *Like forcing Valerie's car down a canyon.*

"Hmm, be hard for him to do, Jake, but if you really want to get the wifey a gun, don't waste your money, I can get you a police special, a .38. I've got one myself."

So next day my ever-efficient city editor brought me a police special and a box of ammunition. The .38-caliber revolver was oiled and ready to go. My wife, a latter-day Annie Oakley, I thought. Kind of a gloomy thought.

I thanked Aggie and put the revolver in my briefcase. My thoughts went elsewhere.

The best defense is a good offense, USC's legendary football coach Howard Jones used to say, according to Mel Durslag, one of our sportswriters. That gave me one of my brilliant ideas. I would confront Bugsy Siegel. Why wait around to see what would happen? I'd go to his house, walk right up to the front door and ring the bell.

EIGHTEEN

That night I showed Valerie the revolver Aggie had brought me. "We'll go to a pistol range one of these days," I said, "and get you checked out with this little cannon. Meanwhile, you can handle it, get a feel for it, and dry-fire it a time or two. Do not load it! Not until we go to the range."

"Aw, Sailor, you're no fun," she said with that grin of hers that said don't worry, I won't.

Changing the subject, Valerie said Ilse had been asked out on a date. My daughter was sixteen. I'd known this moment would come, but I still wasn't prepared for it. "A date?" I said. "Who's the boy?"

"He's seventeen, a junior, on the school paper with her. She says he's a good guy."

"Sounds all right, Sweets, I guess. Let's meet him first. Have him stop in here to pick her up, 'stead of meeting her someplace. Does he have a car?"

"I think he drives his dad's."

"Geez, my little girl's growing up," I said with a sigh.

Valerie gave me a reassuring hug. Clever woman, my wife. She knew I was a little uneasy about Ilse starting to date.

My head was spinning. How could I cope with this jumble of stuff? My friend Gretchen missing, almost certainly kidnapped. The Buchenwald Butcher she'd been trying to find still on the loose. That bull-in-a-china-shop agent Travis MI-6 had sent. Jack Dragna's boys trying to kill Valerie. Bugsy Siegel wanting to bump me off. My work at the paper suffering. Ilse starting to date.

Okay Jake, get organized, I told myself. I decided to deal with Siegel first. Go right out there and confront the bastard.

Bugsy lived in one of those two-story Beverly Hills jobs a few blocks north of Sunset. Not as elegant as the palaces built by movie stars in the Twenties, but way above my standards. Rumor had it that his girlfriend, Virginia Hill, leased this place from some millionaire. I'd told Aggie Underwood where I was going, in case I didn't come back.

Stately palms lined the street like soldiers at attention. Bugsy probably had a bodyguard or two around here somewhere, I thought as I got out of my Chevy. I wondered if Virginia Hill was in there as I marched up to the front door, hoping a forceful stride masked the nervousness crawling in my gut.

Why was I even doing this reckless thing? Was I going to say "Here I am, Bugs, if you want to kill me here's your chance, plug me right now?"

Siegel himself opened the door moments after I rang the bell. "Well, hell, if it isn't ace reporter Jake Weaver himself. Come on in." He stood aside and gestured me in. He wore gray slacks, a white tennis sweater with maroon detailing along the V-neck, and was in stocking feet. "I guess it's a little early for a drink, Weaver. Like some coffee?" It was about ten a.m.

I said sure and he called out, "Hildie, some coffee in the study, okay?" He led me into a richly paneled room with sofa, love seat and upholstered chairs. Parquet floor, huge rock fireplace, no fire going. A couple of cigar butts in an ash tray on an end table.

"To what do I owe this pleasure?" Siegel said, waving me to a seat on a cream-colored sofa imprinted with colorful little tree leaves.

"I know you're pissed off at me," I began.

"Not at all, Weaver. You really kicked me in the nuts with that last piece, but I understand. A little character assassination can sell a lotta papers. You got a job to do, I know that. Sorry about that angry call I made. I was a little hot under the collar when I saw your story. My dumb temper got the best of me." All charm. *Phony* charm.

A saucy young thing looking more like a Daisy or a Bunny than a Hilda came in with a tray containing cups, saucers, spoons, cream and sugar. "Thanks, Sweetie," Bugsy said as she set it on the end table. He reached over and patted her lovely fanny. How's she in bed, Bugsy? I wondered.

Hildie sashayed off and I poured myself a cup.

"I've got nothing against you personally, Ben." No way would I call him Bugsy—he hated that. "It's just business, Hearst's orders."

"I know that, Jake. I like you, pal."

"I like you too, Ben, you and Mickey both. Don't much care for Dragna, though."

"I don't have any use for Fat Jack either."

After we exchanged a few more cordialities, I took a shot. "Do you know Gino Columbini?" I asked.

"No, don't think so." Recognition in Siegel's eyes, though. "Who's that?"

"A guy with the Purple Gang in Detroit."

"Never heard of him," he lied. "We don't have anything to do with the Purples."

After I took a drink of coffee—it was excellent—I said, "I had a nasty experience with him a couple weeks ago back there."

"Sorry to hear that. Anything I can do?"

"Nah, Aldo Tripolani's setting him straight. Do you know Tripolani?"

"I've heard of him but don't know him." Fiddling with his coffee cup. "They say he runs a pretty crappy little outfit."

"I've heard that," I said.

If Siegel really didn't know Columbini or that I'd been to Detroit, he would've been curious, would've asked why I'd gone.

He didn't, and that told me Matt Mason's information was on the money. Bugsy had known all about it. Instead, he did a one-eighty in the other direction.

"I saw your story on that wop judge, Bonadio. Great piece of work. I hear the bar is looking into him, or the grand jury, something like that. He's probably finished." Siegel laughed. "Fat Jack will have to buy himself a new judge." He produced a pack of Old Golds and offered me one.

"No thanks, I don't smoke."

"I do." Siegel pulled out a gold-plated lighter and fired up. He took a deep drag, drove blue plumes from his nostrils, gave me a direct look, and said, "You're so damn good at digging up stuff, finding out things, how'd you like to work for me? I could use a good investigator."

If you can't kill me, buy me, hey? "As they say in the military, Ben, you've achieved surprise. Thanks, but I'll stick with newspapering. It's in my blood."

"I could pay you a lot more than the *Express* does."

"I'm sure you could, but no, definitely no. By the way, have you heard of Otto Woolf or Klaus Schäfer?"

"No, who are they?"

"One of them coaches my daughter's soccer team. Has relatives in New York like you do. You both having German backgrounds, I just . . . well, it was a longshot. Idle curiosity." *Curiosity about that dagger with a diamond-studded handle that could bail this guy out of his money woes.*

Bugsy tossed me a quizzical look, leaned back in his chair, took another hit on his fag, and said, "I guess you heard my soft opening of the Flamingo didn't go so well. I rushed the damn thing. Hell, the paint wasn't even dry. That's all being fixed, though. I'll have a gala reopening in February and it'll come off great. You'll be invited. Bring the missus along. I'll comp you a nice room."

"Maybe so, maybe so. She might like that."

After a few more minutes of chit-chat, I took my leave. "So long, Ben," I said at the door. "I'm glad you don't hate my guts." Though I knew he did.

"Course I don't, pal." He shook my hand. "Come by anytime."

As I left, one of his toughs sat on the porch, casually smoking, and throwing me a steely look he must have regarded as the evil eye. I tried not to laugh.

Siegel is one shifty bastard, I thought while I got in the car. But smooth, I'll give him that, he's smooth. I had a sense that the names Woolf and Schäfer, or one of them, had registered with him.

A gruesome thought occurred as I drove away. Maybe Mr. Smooth had in mind that Valerie and I would "disappear" during his grand reopening of the Flamingo. Bumping us off there would be a simpler matter than doing it here in L.A. Highway 91 was a lonely stretch of road up in those parts, surrounded by miles and miles of nothing but bleak desert. After the buzzards and coyotes had feasted on our flesh, our bones would bleach in the sun out there forever.

First thing I did back at the paper was call a gun club I'd been to in Glendale. I made an appointment for some shooting-range time there for Valerie and me. Aggie Underwood came by and said she was glad to see she hadn't had to call out the cavalry.

On my way home that evening I saw a Hertz sign on a low building along Wilshire. Hertz was one of those companies that rented cars. This had been going on awhile, but the business really began to boom after the war. Passenger cars, limousines, station wagons, people were renting those nowadays. That gave me an idea. A longshot of an idea.

I pulled in, hopped out and went inside. A young man with an Arne Bengtsson nameplate pinned on his blue blazer asked what he could do for me. Did they have any Hudsons for rent, I inquired.

"At this location, no," he said. "Only Chevys, Fords, Caddies and Packards. I can set you up with something very nice."

"No, somebody I know rented a black Hudson Commodore Eight. Said it was real good. I'm interested in that one."

"My, the gentleman certainly knows what he wants. Our Alhambra office may have one. I'll check for you." Bengtsson picked up a phone and made a call. He asked some questions, said, "Okay, thanks, Linda," and hung up.

"Alhambra doesn't have one, sir, but Pasadena might. I'll check." In the middle of his second call, he cupped his hand over the receiver and told me, "Well, Pasadena *had* one, sir, but it's rented out. It was dropped here by a gentleman who'd rented it in Las Vegas, a one-way dropoff."

"Ask if it's black and if so, get the license number."

"The license number, sir?" Starting to look cautious and skeptical.

"Yes, please, and the name of the customer. It's important. You see, I'm a cop," I lied, hoping he wouldn't ask for ID. If he did, I'd open and close my wallet fast—I had a toy police badge in there. Bought it at Woolworth's.

He didn't ask. Bengtsson removed his hand and spoke some more. He wrote something on a notepad, said, "Thanks, Harvey," and hung up. He handed me the note. It said: NIKOLAUS EICHEL. NEVADA 2884.

Nikolaus Eichel. I'd half expected it to be Kristian Egger, the name given by the so-called doctor at Loma Linda who'd vanished after that girl was killed out there. And who might be Otto Woolf, the Nazi surgeon. And probably now had Gretchen.

At last I had something to go on, but it was probably too late. He'd already had plenty of time to kill her, I thought with a cold quiver in my stomach. God, I hoped that hadn't happened.

I didn't know any cops well enough to see if they'd put out an all-points bulletin on the Hudson. I'd have to turn to the MI-6's Virgil Travis, even though he struck me as a jackass. He supposedly was coordinating with the FBI. Maybe the FBI could find that car, or get the L.A. police looking for it.

I called Travis's hotel as soon as I got home. Damn, he wasn't in and hadn't left any word. I gave the operator my name and number and told her to have him call the minute he showed up, that it was of the highest urgency. "And tell him I've tracked down the Hudson . . . that's right, ma'am, the Hudson. Thanks."

Ilse stood in the archway leading to the kitchen. She'd heard. She knew about Gretchen's disappearance and was as worried as me, so I told her what I'd found out at Hertz. We talked about that awhile, Ilse wringing her hands and saying "poor Gretchen."

For both of our sakes I needed to change the subject, so I asked how school and soccer practice had gone that day.

"Practice was fine, *Vati*, but Coach Schäfer did not show up. Only Miss Kardos was there." A Hungarian, Miss Kardos was the assistant coach.

"Did she say why Schäfer wasn't there?"

"She did not know, *Vati*. She was surprised also."

This didn't bother me at first, but after a moment or two it did. Klaus Schäfer was a German. Gretchen had talked with him after the Tigers' last game. Why did he miss a practice now, at this particular time? Just a coincidence? I didn't much believe in coincidences.

NINETEEN

Travis finally called at nine p.m. His words were a little slurred. Sounded like he'd been drinking.

After I told him what I'd learned and given him the Nevada license number, he said, "Fine work. I shall contact the FBI straightaway."

"See if they can get the L.A. police looking for it."

"I shall, Colonial Four, never fear. I'll keep you informed."

The line went dead. *You'd better, you dumb ass.*

At work the next day—three days before Christmas—I thought again about the police hotsheet listing cars they were on the lookout for. Since I didn't know or trust any L.A. cops well enough to ask, and had little faith in "Cromwell," I turned to Aggie Underwood. She'd been our police reporter before moving up, so she knew a lot of cops, including Police Commissioner Clem Horrall himself.

I told her I now had a Nevada license number for what might well be our black Hudson and the name of the man who'd rented it. Could she get someone to put that car on the hotsheet? She said she might be able to. I jotted down Nikolaus Eichel's name and the tag number for her, and she made a call.

I didn't listen in. Went to my desk and tried to re-read some notes I had for a story. Found it hard to concentrate. Aggie came over a few minutes later and said, "It's already on the hotsheet. The FBI asked 'em to do it this morning. What aren't you telling me, Jake?"

I'd sold Virgil Travis short. He'd jumped on this right away.

"Aggie, there's a British agent in town who's also looking for Gretchen Siedler. He says he's coordinating with the feds. Guess he's got more on the ball than I realized. Thanks anyway."

"If the British government and the FBI are on this, Jake, there's not much for you to do. The feds wouldn't like you tracking your footprints over this anyway. So how about doing some work for *us* today?"

I could've told her the feds wouldn't even know about this car if it hadn't been for me but I saved my breath. She was right of course. I called a meeting of the Unholy Trinity and we went over several leads and a couple of story ideas.

After work, I drove Valerie and Ilse to the shooting range in Glendale. Along the way I brought them up to date on the Hertz rental and the FBI's involvement.

At the range, we picked a spot along an extended hardwood surface facing a line of target positions several yards away, backed by rough-cut, bullet-pocked slabs of wood I'd been told were several feet thick.

I showed Valerie how to load the .38 and coached her on gripping the revolver with both hands. We each put on heavy ear covers to deaden the sound. I also handed a pair to Ilse, who'd been intently watching all this.

I called for a target, which was levered up into place by a target boy safely below in a deep dugout. The white paper target displayed round rings with ascending numbers, eight, nine, ten and so forth, then a small center ring marked with an X.

"Okay, Sweets," I said, "grip it like I showed you and aim for the X. Remember, squeeze the trigger, don't jerk it."

She fired and a black hole appeared in the three ring. She shook her head, steadied her hands, and fired again. This shot missed the target altogether. Valerie muttered and shook her head even more. Her lips pinched. The next shot pierced the five ring. The last of her six shots were a four and two sixes. Not great shooting.

"Good going, Val," I managed to say.

Ilse said she wanted to try now. I was about to say no but Valerie beat me to it. "Not today, dear, maybe another time." Ilse was disappointed but didn't push it.

I pulled out my Luger and called for a fresh target. I squeezed off a six, then an eight, and finally an X, dead center. I put the gun down. Three shots were enough. A creepy feeling had come over me while firing that Luger for the first time since Germany.

We removed our ear protectors. "Hey, you showoff," Valerie said, "pretty darn good. I guess I need more practice."

"Not bad for your first time," I said, though I wasn't sure more practice would help—she hadn't shown much aptitude for marksmanship.

I kept to myself that when I was firing I had flashed on the German men I'd shot during the war. I'd always been haunted by that, and I wasn't going to break my vow that I would never divulge that to anyone. Two of them had claimed to be SS men who were going to execute me as a German deserter. It was my life or theirs. Sometimes I saw their faces in my sleep. I'd sort of blacked out for awhile after that shooting. About an hour had passed before it all came back to me. My mind must have thrown up some kind of a psychological roadblock.

"What is it, Jake?" Valerie asked. "You look kind of upset."

"Guess it's just that I'm not real comfortable with the idea of my wife firing a handgun," I fibbed. The look on her face said she didn't believe that.

On the drive home I said, "Nice going back there, Sweets, but you'll never actually have to use that little cannon to defend yourself."

"I hope you're right," she murmured.

We made plans to see the Christmas Eve parade on Hollywood Boulevard, both of us glad to stop talking about firing handguns.

In the morning I called the Hertz office in Pasadena to ask about the rented Hudson. The woman there told me it had been turned in that morning. "Who by?" I asked.

"Mr. Eichel, the man who rented it, of course. Say, who are you, mister?"

I told her I was with the *Herald-Express* and that we were concerned about a woman who may have been in the car.

"You and the FBI both, sir. They just called too. The man sounded upset when I told him the car was here, safe and sound. They also asked about a woman. Yes, a woman was with Mr. Eichel. Two men also. After he paid us, the four of them left in a cab."

I thanked her and hung up. My mind swirled. If that woman was Gretchen, I was damn glad to hear she was alive. But I wondered what the hell was going on. Yeah, the FBI would be pissed, figuring Virgil Travis had wasted a lot of their time. I contemplated my coffee mug but it had nothing to suggest about all this. Nor did my fat yellow copy pencil.

I was set to call Gretchen's apartment when Marko Janicek came by and told me about a story he was working on. The grand jury had subpoenaed some people at the Mercantile Bank and was going to look into the Judge Bonadio matter. We were still talking about that when my phone rang. It was Gretchen!

"Gretchen, thank God. Are you all right?"

"Yes, dear Jake, I am. So much has happened the last two days it will take some time to explain it all, but first I must apologize for not meeting you that night. I am most sorry for that. Things happened so quickly that I was in a bit of a daze. What must you think of me for standing you up? I must have worried you terribly."

"That's all right, Gretchen. The important thing is, are you okay?"

"Yes, I am fine. Can you come over and let me explain about all this?"

"Sure, how about that coffee shop across the street from your building? I can meet you there in an hour."

"Why not come up to my apartment? I can make coffee."

I didn't like the sound of that. Why her apartment? I hadn't been alone with her in an apartment since Berlin.

She must have sensed my reluctance. "Please, Jake, there is much to tell. I would not want to be overheard. My apartment would be best."

Despite a lot of uneasiness, I said okay.

Fifty minutes later, the concierge, who knew me by now, let me in and I climbed the stairs to Gretchen's second-floor unit. After opening the door to my knock, she gave me a rather embarrassed hug and led me to her sofa. She wore a lavender silk blouse and black skirt. The coffee table was set with cups, saucers, croissants and napkins.

"I will only be a moment," she said, and went into the little kitchen. I glanced around the room, furnished in a neutral manner, neither masculine nor feminine. Cream-colored sofa, two armchairs, a radio console, stand-up lamps, and an oak secretary desk. On an end table stood the same framed photo of her late husband Friedrich that I'd seen four years ago in Germany. On the desk's flip-down surface were two or three envelopes and a *Life* magazine with the atomic bomb test at Bikini Atoll on the cover, a monstrous, watery mushroom cloud rising out of the ocean. Odd to see this here now, because that test was five months ago.

I plopped down on the sofa, and Gretchen returned with a coffee pot. She filled the two cups, and sat a couple of feet away from me. She gave me an apologetic look, picked up her cup, and said, "Jake, here is what happened."

The man at Sachsen Haus—I recalled the woman there had called him Nikki—had somehow tracked Gretchen down. She couldn't remember for certain but apparently she'd carelessly given her name there. He'd come into a café on Wilshire where Gretchen was having lunch and sat uninvited at her table. Not in a threatening manner—he was polite and apologetic for intruding. He introduced himself as Nikolaus Eichel and said he recalled her visit to Sachsen Haus. He said he needed some help from Germans, which he assumed Gretchen was.

There was a big issue with German prisoners of war at an alfalfa and lettuce farm in the Coachella Valley where they'd been working. Most of them wanted to go home now that the war had been over for more than a year. A few wanted to stay and settle in the U.S., though. They knew most POWs had now been released, but figured the farm's greedy owner wanted to hang onto his free labor as long as he could. They went on strike and the farmer had called out the Riverside County sheriff. It became a dangerous situation.

Since there was no German government yet, Eichel was looking for responsible Germans who could go out there and stand up for the prisoners, insist that their rights be respected. He'd found a man who'd worked in the pre-war German consulate in L.A. and a retired colonel from World War I who'd emigrated. Eichel had gathered from Gretchen's demeanor that she was well-spoken, honorable, and probably employed. Would she go out to the farm with them and see what they could do? A woman's presence might help.

Gretchen sipped from her cup, set it down, and said, "I was skeptical at first, though he seemed sincere enough."

I was skeptical too. This didn't sound like the behavior of the man I'd encountered at Sachsen Haus.

"He went to the pay phone there," Gretchen went on, "called the former consulate man, and had me speak with him. This man struck me as intelligent and honest, so I agreed to go. We left that night."

"In a rented Hudson?" I asked.

"Yes, Jake. How could you possibly know?"

I told her about her sharp-eyed neighbor woman and the sleuthing I'd done at Hertz.

"You are still a remarkable spy, Jake. Well then, it all happened so quickly. We were twenty miles away when I remembered our appointment. You can imagine my anger at myself. When we reached the valley, we took rooms—separate rooms of course—at a motel in a town called Indio. I called from there to apologize, left you a message at the paper. Did you not receive it?"

"No, Gretchen, I never did. I guess one of the copyboys screwed up." This wasn't adding up for me. Messages for reporters were taken by either copyboys or the city desk clerk, and they were usually reliable. I drank some coffee and asked how it went out there.

"We met the farmer and two sheriff's deputies the next morning and insisted on their release, firmly but politely. Most of the talking was done by the former consulate man."

"And?"

"The farmer had to admit he'd kept the workers too long and finally agreed to so inform the War Department. He also would inquire how those who preferred to stay could apply for immigration, so it ended well."

"Have you told Freeborn?" I asked. "He sent an agent here on this, a guy named Travis."

"Yes, I called the colonel just a bit ago. He was none too happy. Oh, the fuss I created. But at least we helped those poor young soldiers."

I was having trouble buying this. If this Eichel person was on the level about aiding these prisoners of war, why would he ask the help of a woman he'd barely met and wasn't even sure was German?

"The four of you," I said, "had a lot of time to talk in that car. I suppose they asked about your background and so on?"

"Yes, I told them that my husband, a flier, was killed in the Battle of Britain and that I hated Hitler. I gave them a story that I stole off to Switzerland, where I stayed till the war ended, then emigrated to here. They think I teach German and Italian at a night school."

"Good cover, Gretchen."

"*Danke*. Oh, by the way, since Christmas is in two days, Colonel Freeborn extended my stay until the 27th. I must leave the day after Boxing Day."

She slid close to me on the sofa, gave me that look she had, and said, "I so regret having put you to so much trouble, dear Jake. Can you forgive me?"

Before I could answer, this beautiful woman kissed me. A nice big warm kiss. Our time in Berlin swam in my memory. I'd had what my old Navy buddies called "unauthorized ass" only once since becoming engaged to Valerie and that had been with this woman. I put my arms around her and kissed her back. We started fooling around. Before long, like a couple of hot-to-trot teenagers, we were involved in some heavy making out.

I kissed the crooked and yet appealing bridge of her nose, then lightly brushed her neck just below the ear with the tip of my tongue. "Aah," she murmured, her breath warm on my cheek.

I began to unbutton her blouse, exposing a black lace bra. I put a hand on one of her breasts. It rose and fell with her quickened breathing. More memories.

"Oh, I do love you, my sweet Jake," she whispered.

I almost said I loved her too. Damn, I *wanted* this woman. A few more moments of this and I would find myself making a terrible mistake. Somehow, fighting against my revved-up libido, I found the will to stop. I pulled back and slid away from her. "This would be swell, Gretchen, but no, we mustn't."

She reached over and slapped my face hard. Man, that stung! I guess I deserved that. "You are making me a frustrated woman, Jake," she snarled. I was frustrated too, you bet, but. . .

"It wouldn't be fair to Valerie," I said needlessly. "I'm very sorry, Gretchen."

She began buttoning her blouse as I got to my feet. "Thanks for explaining what happened out there," I said. "Maybe I'd better go now."

"*Ja*, I suppose you had better."

I wanted to say that if Nikolaus Eichel wasn't the Nazi surgeon we'd been looking for, who was? But she'd probably throw a vase at me if I stayed any longer. I went to the door, looked back and saw her face puckered with anguish, tears in her eyes.

TWENTY

I got home before Valerie and quickly changed, hanging my shirt and jacket in a far corner of my closet in case Gretchen's perfume happened to linger on them.

I talked with Ilse awhile about her day at school, then took a beer from our Kelvinator, which we'd bought as soon as refrigerators became available again after the war, and sank onto my favorite living-room chair. I sat there and tried to sort it all out in my mind.

Besides my friendship for Gretchen—probably ruptured for good—why should I concern myself with that Nazi surgeon sadist? Although finding Otto Woolf so he could be punished for his crimes would be a good thing for peace-loving people everywhere, that was MI-6's business, not mine.

I should focus one hundred percent on Jack Dragna and Bugsy Siegel. They'd both tried to kill me! Siegel pretended otherwise with that bogus cordiality when I called on him, but I'd learned he tried to have me bumped off in Detroit. Why would that fool Columbini lie about that?

And when you really got down to it, how much did I truly know about Gretchen? We'd only been acquainted for a few days in Berlin back in '42, and now four years later for a couple of weeks here. She'd seduced me—yes, she'd instigated it—on our very second meeting back in '42, and was trying hard to do it again. Besides me, how many guys had she fooled around with since her husband was killed? And how much good did she really do for MI-6?

On the other hand, Ilse and I couldn't have escaped from Nazi Germany without her help. I owed her a lot for that. Gosh, wouldn't my life be simple and rosy if I'd never met that woman and if Old Man Hearst hadn't decided on an anti-crime crusade?

I heard Valerie's car pull into the driveway. After she came in and hung up her coat and hat—a salmon-colored felt cloche—we hugged and she said, "Any news on Gretchen?"

Gulp! What should I say? I told her what had transpired, except of course nothing about our clinching in sexual arousal in her apartment. I even hedged with a white lie that we'd met in a coffee shop.

"Wow," Valerie said, "what a surprise. That's not like her to forget your meeting, and think of all the trouble she gave you and your Colonel Freeborn. But I'm sure relieved that she's okay, thank goodness for that."

I told her Gretchen had claimed to call from Riverside County but that I never got the message.

Later, after Ilse went to bed, we sat in the living room, made cheery by the Christmas tree lights, and wrapped gifts for Christmas morning. "Ilse's really looking forward to the parade," Valerie said, "and me too. Let's try to forget these other things for awhile and just enjoy a fine Christmas."

"Absolutely," I agreed.

"But let's have Gretchen over Christmas afternoon," she added. "It'll be nice to say goodbye before she leaves."

She caught the look on my face. "What? Is there something I should know? Something else about Gretchen?"

I leaned over and kissed her. "No, I don't think so, hon."

I couldn't decipher the look she gave me. Could she sense that I'd told her a half-truth? Could she detect a trace of scent that wasn't hers?

Outside, rain started to fall. Rivulets of water began squiggling down our windows.

* * *

At the *Express* on Christmas Eve day, only half the staff was on duty. The other half would work tomorrow on Christmas. Holiday or no, we had a paper to put out. The rain had moved on. The sun shone brightly and it would be a fine night for the parade.

First off, I called a stringer in Palm Springs who covered that area for us and asked if some German prisoner-of-war farm laborers had gone on strike against a farmer south of there. He didn't know, so I asked him to look into it, check with the sheriff's office, and send us a story if they had. It wasn't that I hadn't believed Gretchen, but I always liked independent confirmation on such things.

That done, I filled my coffee mug and put my feet up on the desk to think. It was strangely quiet. The few reporters on hand didn't have many people to call, just the Weather Bureau to get the forecast, the harbor to tally up ship movements, and so on.

I had told Valerie I didn't think having Gretchen over was a good idea, and with a hard look she'd asked why ever not. I lamely said Gretchen would have lots to do, a final report to Freeborn to prepare, bags to pack, so forth. Not buying that, Valerie prevailed. Of course. And what else had she been thinking?

I pulled my feet off the desk, drank some coffee, and picked up the phone. Dialed half the numbers to Gretchen's apartment, hesitated, said "What the hell," and finished dialing.

I apologized for disappointing her and rushing off, and said we'd like her to come over the next afternoon if she was willing.

Gretchen was as gracious as she'd been after I told her on our drive back from Loma Linda that I didn't want her as my mistress. "Of course," she said. "I would like to see Valerie and Ilse once more before I leave. It is most nice of you. As to yesterday, you were right, Jake. Going to bed would have been wrong, unfair to your good Valerie. We will say no more about it." The mysteries of womanhood eluding me yet again.

I told her she was swell and that I'd pick her up the next day at three.

That night Valerie, Ilse and I enjoyed the parade on Hollywood Boulevard. Colorful floats, clowns, lavishly costumed men and women on horseback, the Occidental College and USC bands, and of course Santa Claus at the end.

In the morning we sat around the tree and opened gifts. Kris Kringle must have come during the night, for Ilse made out like a bandit: two sweaters, a suede jacket, the makeup kit she'd been wanting, and a new soccer ball. Valerie got a sweater, scarf, kid gloves and a gift certificate from Buffum's. Me: socks, ties, a belt and, of all things, an electric coffee percolator.

"You're usually up first to make the coffee," Valerie said, "and you never liked that old one."

"Let's see how it works," I said. Went to the kitchen—stepping over piles of crumpled ribbons and wrapping paper—and plugged it in. Instead of sitting on a gas burner, this baby would perk electrically. Weren't we getting modern?

During the morning Valerie called her mother in Illinois to wish her a Merry Christmas and I got holiday calls from my father in Baton Rouge and my coauthor Kenny Nielsen. He said snow was falling and Galesburg had a white Christmas.

At lunchtime we just had sandwiches because Valerie was baking a ham for Christmas dinner with Gretchen.

I took Ilse along when I drove over to get our guest. Didn't want to be alone in the car with Gretchen. Along the way I asked Ilse about her upcoming date, which would take place in two days. The boy's name was Dave Honeycutt.

Ilse assured me that Dave would come in before they left. "You can inspect him and see that he has only two legs and one head," she said with a chuckle. They would go to a malt shop, have a burger or something, and just talk. "He suggested a movie but I did not want that. I want just to visit and to better get to know each other."

Clever girl, my Ilse. "Good idea," I said, still a little uneasy about it all. But I realized she was growing up and that boys would become a part of her life. I trusted her.

"Make sure he does the driving," I said. I'd given Ilse a couple of driving lessons. Now that she was sixteen, she wanted to get a learner's permit.

"Oh, *Vati*." She punched me affectionately on the arm.

When we pulled up in front of her apartment, Gretchen came out carrying a bouquet of yellow roses. She hugged each of us in turn and said, "*Frohe Weihnachten*"—Merry Christmas—"I thought that you and your *Mutter* would like these."

Ilse took the flowers, said, "*Danke schön*," and put them in back. While she was doing that, Gretchen slipped into the front passenger seat. Darn, I'd wanted her in back. Despite my being uneasy, though, we had nothing but pleasant small talk on the drive home. At one point I caught Gretchen looking at me oddly, maybe wistfully—but no affectionate touching of my leg, no little kisses on the cheek. Thank goodness.

The rest of the day went well. Valerie thanked Gretchen for the roses, put them in a vase, and poured champagne. I even let Ilse have a little.

The conversation was congenial, the dinner delicious, and Gretchen, oohing and aahing about our Christmas tree, was full of compliments. The ham, sweet potatoes and salad were supplemented by the sauerkraut that'd been in the fridge since that earlier aborted dinner the night Gretchen had disappeared.

Later, while Valerie and Gretchen chatted in the living room, Ilse and I were alone in the kitchen doing the dishes. My daughter said, "That woman is in love with you, *Vati*."

"I hope so, she's a wonderful wife."

"No, silly, it is about Gretchen I am talking."

I looked at her, put down the plate I'd just rinsed, turned off the faucet and said, "No, *Liebchen*, I don't think so."

"I do, *Vati*. I saw her kissing you at her place back in Berlin—do you recall?—and I have seen how she peeks at you, quick but adoring glimpses when *Mutter* she is not looking."

"I still think you're wrong, Ilse, but even if Gretchen does feel some affection for me it's not a problem. We won't see her again after tonight."

After we all had dessert in the front room near the tree—peach cobbler—Gretchen went to the front window, looked out and said, "My ride is here."

"Your ride?" Valerie asked, surprised. "Jake will drive you back."

"No, it is all arranged. I have bothered you enough."

Surprised too, I got to my feet as did Valerie and Ilse. Hugs all around. Best of luck, don't be a stranger, hope to see you again someday, all of that expressed by Valerie. From Gretchen, "*Danke schön* for a wonderful Christmas. Be well, all of you."

I stood in the open doorway and watched Gretchen scamper down the walk and climb into a black four-door Chevy. I couldn't see the driver clearly, but it was a man. They drove off.

Back inside, Valerie said, "That woman is up to something."

"Yeah, Val, she sure is, but up to *what?*"

That's when I remembered seeing two Chevys in the parking lot behind Sachsen Haus. One of them had been a black four-door.

TWENTY-ONE

Our stringer in Palm Springs called me at the office the next day. The Riverside County sheriff had said there was no POW farm-worker strike and that the last of them had left the Coachella Valley months ago.

Well, now.

I drove to Sachsen Haus, which wasn't far, wondering why Gretchen had cooked up that big lie about her two-day disappearance. I planned to confront Nikolaus Eichel and demand some answers. But a notice on the door said CLOSED FOR CHRISTMAS. WILL RE-OPEN DEC. 28. Which was two days from now.

Frustrated, I drove back to South Trenton Street and went to the Continental, our watering hole across from the paper, to have some lunch. I sat at the bar, ordered a Falstaff beer and a ham sandwich, and fell into conversation with Shaker, the jovial bartender.

He asked how my Christmas had been, and talked about the NFL championship game. The Chicago Bears had beaten the New York Giants, 24 to 14. "That Sid Luckman's a hell of a quarterback, isn't he?"

I agreed that he was and took a bite of my sandwich. On the jukebox, Bing Crosby and the Andrews Sisters were warbling their up-tempo "Pistol Packin' Mama." I smiled, thinking of Valerie's performance at the gun range.

"Haven't seen that lady friend of yours lately," Shaker said. "That looker with the foreign accent."

"She was just here for a short visit," I said. "Going back to

Europe tomorrow." But was she?

I wondered if I should call Colonel Freeborn in London and tell him about these strange new developments. Maybe that would be out of line, though. Should I really be telling Freeborn about the woman's trickery? Tapestry, her code name, had been with MI-6 much longer than my recent and totally unofficial connection with them. He might dismiss my account as out of place, possibly the result of some petty grudge I'd developed.

If Gretchen had gone rogue, would it have been because of frustration at my refusal of her affections? No, probably not. Or that she didn't want to return to a Germany which faced hard years of rebuilding, its shattered cities just piles of rubble? Or—darkest thought of all—because the communists had offered her more than MI-6 could? It was hatred of Hitler, not love of England that had brought her into Freeborn's camp in the first place.

"You're pretty deep in thought, Red," said Shaker, who was wiping a highball glass with a towel. "Something about that babe?"

"Nah, I was thinking about the Rose Bowl," I fibbed. "Maybe I'll take Illinois and the points. Whatta you think?" The oddsmakers had UCLA down as a six-point favorite in the New Year's Day game.

"Yeah, take Illinois," he said.

I finished my meal and the beer. The bill was fifty-five cents, thirty for the beer, two bits for the sandwich. I plunked down a dollar, said so long to Shaker and crossed the street.

Gretchen was scheduled to leave the next day, would probably fly out from Mines Field. I was pretty sure only TWA and United had flights to the East from here. Maybe MI-6's Virgil Travis could see if she was booked on one of those.

I called the Mayfair Hotel, but was told he was gone, had checked out on Christmas Day. Good riddance to that oaf, I thought, so I called the airlines myself. Made up a tale that Gretchen Siedler was famous, that we wanted to interview her before she left, and get a picture of her boarding the plane.

My clever ploy was wasted, as it turned out. She wasn't booked on any of their flights. I could think of three other possibilities: She would leave by train, or by bus, or she wasn't going at all.

Why don't I leave this alone and earn my newspaper pay for awhile? I called a meeting of the Unholy Trinity, except it would have to be the Unholy Duo because Richie Millsap had the day off. Marko Janicek came over and we updated each other on what we were working on. One of Janicek's snitches had told him a Mexican truck full of cocaine had unloaded at a warehouse owned by Jack Dragna. He said he couldn't write it without blowing the snitch's cover.

"Let it go," I said. "A lot of coke's coming into L.A. these days and the cops always look the other way anyhow."

We went over two or three other things. The grand jury would hold a hearing on Judge Bonadio on Friday. Our guy who covered the courts would handle that, not us.

I couldn't quite let go of the Gretchen business, though, so after Janicek left, I called her apartment. Let the phone ring at least a dozen times. No answer.

I remembered the name of her apartment building so I looked up the number in the directory and called. The concierge said he hadn't seen her all day.

"Did she close out the lease?" I asked.

"She couldn't do that, sir. The British government holds that lease. Before Miss Siedler moved in they used that apartment for visiting diplomats, so forth." I guess I should have known that.

Ilse's date came the next night. Dave Honeycutt showed up at exactly the time they'd settled on. Dressed nicely in slacks and a gray V-neck sweater, standing about five-nine, he looked like a nice enough kid. He greeted us politely and shook my hand.

Ilse came in from her room, looking swell in a black skirt, one of her new Christmas sweaters, and saddle shoes. She said, "Hello, Dave," and gave him a chaste little hug, their faces not very close.

"You're on the school paper with Ilse, I understand," Valerie said.

"Yes, ma'am. I'm the features editor. Ilse is our best reporter." Which made my daughter blush.

"What other school activities do you have?" I asked.

"Football, sir. I'm a tailback."

"He scored two touchdowns this year," Ilse put in proudly.

"Well, are you ready, Ilse?" Dave asked.

She said she was and when they went to the door he promised he'd have her back by 9:30.

They drove off in his father's black Dodge. No peeling of rubber, no showing off, but then he wouldn't, not right in front of our house. I let out a big sigh and told Valerie, "Well, our girl is growing up. I hope all they do is go to that malt shop."

"Don't worry, Jake, they will. Ilse won't let him take her to lover's lane, wherever that is these days."

I hoped she was right.

"But you can take *me* to lover's lane one of these days," Valerie said, giving me that look she had.

Ilse was back at 9:35. Close enough. Valerie said I'd been watching the clock like a nervous hen. I'd been tempted to look out the window and see if he walked her to the door and if he tried to kiss her, but didn't. It'd be a big embarrassment for them if they saw me.

Ilse was all smiles. She said they'd had a nice time and that Dave had been a gentleman.

* * *

The next few days passed rapidly. I'd almost put Gretchen out of my mind—almost, but not completely.

The mail brought an elegant invitation to Bugsy Siegel's grand reopening of the Flamingo Hotel in February. Valerie said we ought to go, it would be fun. She got her way as she often did.

She also got her way regarding New Year's Eve. She dragged me to a party at the home of one of her fellow workers at North American. At midnight we had champagne, wore funny hats, sang "Auld Lang Syne," all that. The "old acquaintance" part made me think of Gretchen.

The next day the Illini battered UCLA in the 1947 Rose Bowl game, 45 to 14, even though Mel Durslag had assured me the Bruins would win. What did he know? I should have listened to Shaker and taken Illinois and the points. I heard some of it on the radio, Bill Stern calling the play-by-play.

I decided I really should call Colonel Freeborn and tell him about Gretchen's disappearance, even though I might end up being embarrassed. He might say she showed up in London as scheduled, and you got worried over nothing, Weaver.

I got up early on January 2nd, tried to be quiet and not disturb Valerie and Ilse, and placed the call. It was just after five a.m., which would make it early afternoon in London. Freeborn came on the line and said, "Mr. Weaver, thank you for calling. I was about to contact you. Do you know anything of Tapestry's whereabouts?" Damn, she hadn't shown up. I'd been afraid of that.

"No I don't, that's why I called. My wife and I had her over on Christmas but haven't seen her since."

"She was to have flown to New York," he said, "but didn't turn up. Nor have we heard from her. The people at our Los Angeles flat say she left that morning without a word."

"I know, Colonel. I asked about her there, too."

"I'm most concerned, Weaver. Is there anything else you can tell me? Anything you've observed?"

With some reluctance I told him about Gretchen vanishing for two days and then giving me a story about trying to help some German war prisoners out in Riverside County and that the story turned out to be false.

He wanted to know how I knew that, so I explained what our Palm Springs man had found.

"Mm, most disconcerting," he said. "We'd not known Tapestry to be deceitful before. I can think of a few possibilities. She has been snatched by the communists . . . she's done a bunk . . . she's had a bad accident . . . or she just got tired of all this and dropped out. It wouldn't be the first time an agent became burned out and just quit on us. Everyone has the right to resign, but it must be done using the proper procedures. The worst possibility of all, I daresay, is that she's been killed by the very Nazi she was searching for. I shall have my people and the FBI get on this straightaway."

"Colonel, will that Cromwell guy be looking into it?"

"No, he's been recalled. I have a better man for this." That ham-fisted Cromwell was muscle; the new man would be brains, I thought. Before Freeborn rang off he said to let him know if I learned anything else about Gretchen, anything at all. I assured him I would.

Ilse's Tigers played their last soccer game of the season on Saturday. As I glanced around just before the halftime break, I caught sight of a woman watching from among some trees on a grassy slope at least 150 yards away. I wondered why she didn't come closer for a better view. She wore a bulky coat, a wide-brim black hat, and dark glasses even though it was a cloudy day. I saw her shift her balance and cock her hip—just the way Gretchen did!

I took off running, heard Valerie's voice behind me calling,

"Hey, what—"

Gretchen, if it was Gretchen, saw me coming, turned and began to run. I quickened my pace. When I reached the slope, breathing hard, I saw Wilshire Boulevard, just beyond the trees, bustling with pedestrians and cars. I reached the sidewalk, bumped into an old woman, apologized, and scanned in both directions. Saw lots of people but not the one I was looking for. Which way should I go, left or right? It didn't really matter. I'd taken several steps to the right when I saw a yellow taxi heading in the opposite direction. The passenger in back wore dark glasses and a big black hat. And looked over at me.

When I got back to the soccer field Valerie asked what the heck I'd been doing. I explained.

"Gosh, how strange. I wonder if it really was Gretchen. If it was, whatever's gotten into that woman?"

"I wish I knew, Val, I wish I knew."

The Tigers eventually won, 4 to 2. Great finish to a winning season. Afterward, the team celebrated at Tommy's, a malt shop at Rampart and Beverly. Burgers, sodas and ice cream for everyone.

The coaches congratulated each girl in turn with kind words, although the assistant coach, Miss Kardos, did most of the talking. She praised Ilse for being the team's leading scorer. The head coach, Schäfer, smiled at the girls, patted a few backs, but didn't say much. I caught him once glancing through his thick glasses at Ilse and one other pretty player with a look I didn't like. For just a moment he put a hand on the other girl's shoulder and gave it a squeeze that was not only unsuitable but creepy. It made me shiver.

I didn't mention this to Valerie until later. On the ride home we told Ilse how proud we were of her. My girl beamed with delight.

I was glad she was through with Klaus Schäfer. She was, wasn't she?

TWENTY-TWO

MI-6's new man phoned Monday to introduce himself. His name was Tom Doyle, code-named Scoutmaster. I told him everything I knew about Gretchen, including that I was almost certain I'd seen her at a distance Saturday, so she was probably still in town.

Doyle asked a lot of questions, which I answered as best I could. He said he would go to Sachsen Haus and do a few other things he had in mind. He was staying in the same British-leased flat Gretchen had occupied. I should call if I learned anything new. He would keep in touch. This man sounded sharper and more even-keeled than Cromwell.

He called again two days later and asked that we meet for coffee, which we did at a café on Olympic. He was small, blond-haired, and had inquisitive blue eyes. Somewhat resembled the actor Alan Ladd. It was a fruitless meeting in that neither of us had come up with anything new. It was good to meet him face to face, though, and get better acquainted. I liked the man.

That evening Ilse told Valerie and me about a new boy at school. He was shy and withdrawn and his name was Aaron Epstein.

"He sits across from me In English class. He speaks English well, but with more accent than I, although he does not actually speak much at all. He always wears a sweater or a long-sleeve shirt, but one day as he reached forward to his ink well, the sleeve, it rode up a little. I saw numbers tattooed on his forearm. I think he caught me looking. I averted my eyes quickly. When again I looked, he was blushing and his eyes looked terribly ashamed."

"The poor kid," Valerie said. "He was in one of those awful death camps. He was lucky to survive."

"I am going to ask Aaron to have lunch with me in the cafeteria one of these days," Ilse said.

"Good," I put in.

"When I was in the *Bund Deutscher Maedel*, we sometimes saw those people being put on trains. Each one had a suitcase. They looked most sad. We were told they were being transported to nice new settlements in the east, but I should have known better. I should have been angry that Jews from their homes were being taken, but I was not. That is just the way things were. Germany was to be all Aryan. I should have spoken up."

"You've no need to feel guilty," Valerie said, resting a loving hand on her shoulder. "No need at all. What could one girl have done?"

"You'd only have gotten in trouble if you spoke out," I said.

"Perhaps, but at least I should have been upset. What must God think of me?"

"That you're a swell young woman with a good heart," I said, "that's what He thinks of you. God will be happy that you ask Aaron to have lunch with you."

After Ilse went to bed, Valerie and I agreed that we had quite a girl. A former member of the girls' section of the Hitler Youth befriending a Jewish survivor of a concentration camp.

I sat at my desk the next day, thumbing through the second edition. We had a local-section story on Robert Oppenheimer giving a talk at Caltech on his proposal to the Atomic Energy Commission that nuclear control be placed under the United Nations. That proposal had made him very unpopular with political conservatives. I'd heard somewhere that the famous atomic scientist was teaching principles of quantum mechanics at the Pasadena institute.

A couple of photos accompanied the story. One showed Dr. Oppenheimer at the lectern, gesturing with an outstretched hand. The other was taken from partly behind him, facing out toward the audience. I glanced at these shots and went on. A few seconds later something clicked and I went back to the second photo and looked closely. Sitting side by side in the audience, about four rows back, were two people who looked quite a bit like Gretchen Siedler and Nikolaus Eichel, the guy from Sachsen Haus.

No, it couldn't be, I told myself, though not convincingly. I rummaged about in one of my desk drawers till I found my big magnifying glass. I studied the picture closely. The dot pattern created by the photo-engraving process made my enlarged view a little unclear, but it looked very much like Gretchen and Eichel. Both were wearing glasses—I'd never seen glasses on either of them before, but that could be because they wanted to be less recognizable. I kept staring closely. One of the overhead lights, though cropped out of the photo, must have been a little to the woman's right, because that side of her face—as well as the bridge of a nose that looked uneven—was splashed with white light, while the left side was darker.

I went to the photo lab, found the photog who'd taken the shot, and asked him to make a blowup from his negative, centering more on the audience than Oppenheimer. Without the engraver's dot pattern, this print would be sharper.

When I got the blowup fifteen minutes later, I felt a surge of excitement. I was sure it was Gretchen's face behind those glasses. Well, ninety-five percent sure.

What the devil was she doing with this Eichel character? And listening to a lecture on atomic energy, of all things?

I called MI-6 agent Tom Doyle, aka Scoutmaster, and told

him what I'd concluded. What was Gretchen's interest in Robert Oppenheimer? Neither of us could think of a reason why she and Nikolaus Eichel would attend a talk on atomic energy.

Doyle said he would do some poking around at Caltech, and went on to say he'd been to Sachsen Haus and talked to the woman there. "I didn't want her to know that I was aware of Nikolaus Eichel, so I asked who was in charge. She gave me Eichel's name and said he was away for awhile. I didn't want to raise suspicions, so I didn't pursue it further. I subsequently asked London to find out what they could about the man. It turns out that in prewar Germany he was a policeman in Düsseldorf."

"He was a cop?" I said, surprised. Last thing I would have expected.

"Yes, he was in the Catholic Center Party, never joined the Nazis. When war broke out he got himself to Switzerland. After the war he emigrated to the States."

"Wow, your MI-6 is sure thorough, finding out all that stuff."

"Right, most thorough. Intelligence is our business, don't you know."

I asked him to let me know what he found out at Caltech.

My coauthor Kenny Nielsen came out from Illinois a week later, along with his wife Claudia, for our big book signing at UCLA. Kenny had been wounded after almost three years of combat in the Pacific and was now a Marine Corps reserve officer. Although *Two Men at War: A Retrospective* had been published five months before, it was our first joint signing.

The couple stayed in our guest room as they had the previous May after their war-delayed honeymoon at Carmel.

UCLA had publicized the event well and it turned out to be a success. The Hearst papers of course had plugged it harder than the *Times* group, being big rivals of ours. About ninety people attended, plus newspaper and radio reporters. Kenny and I each spoke, answered questions, and signed books, fifty-one of them to be exact. Very satisfying.

Later that night, after the three gals chatted a long while getting reacquainted, Kenny and I sat up drinking beer and doing the same. He said he was busy with his studies at Knox College and was the assisting the high school basketball coach as a volunteer. Claudia enjoyed her nursing job at Cottage Hospital.

I told him about our anti-crime crusade, the Unholy Trinity, and the strange Gretchen Siedler goings-on. Her disappearance, that Eichel guy from Sachsen Haus, all of it.

Kenny digested all of that and asked lots of good, probing questions as if studying a tactical problem on a battlefield. "This Eichel fella was a cop and never a Nazi, huh?" He put down his glass of beer and gave me a serious look. "You know what I think then, Jake? They're trying to steal atomic secrets."

"Really? Who for?" I asked. "The Russians?"

"No, the Germans. Eichel was never a Nazi, you say. He and Miss Siedler are patriots. They would like to see Germany get strong again and regain their place as a leading European nation. A nation with an atomic bomb!"

TWENTY-THREE

Climbing the steep grade out of San Bernardino on Saturday my trusty Chevy Ridemaster began to overheat, so I stopped for water at the little filling station at the top of Cajon Pass. Valerie and I were on our way to Las Vegas for the grand reopening of Bugsy Siegel's Flamingo Hotel. She had talked me into it, insisting it would be fun—and safe. I wasn't so sure.

I topped off the radiator and splashed water over the surface of its air-intake. It was windy and chilly up here at the summit and it felt good to hop back in the car. We wore casual clothes, but our suitcase in the back held an evening dress and my black suit. We'd change after checking in.

Ilse was spending the night with my fellow reporter Richie Millsap and his wife and daughter, who was about Ilse's age. Under normal circumstances we'd trust Ilse to stay home alone. She was a level-headed and responsible young woman. But with all the unusual goings-on recently, Valerie and I didn't consider these normal times.

As we rolled downhill toward Victorville and Barstow, I reflected on my long-ago childhood worries about mountains. The only ones that had spooked me since then were the Harz Mountains in Germany, and that was only because of the grisly concentration camp I'd found there. What concerned me now was much lower: the barren flatland we were heading toward and what Bugsy might have planned for us out there. I remembered the phony good-guy charm he'd showered on me when I was at his house, and the desert was an ideal place to dump a couple of bodies.

I kept looking in the rear-view mirror for suspicious cars that might be tailing us. When a big truck approached from the opposite direction I was ready to dive off the road if it tried to ram us. Valerie caught my nervousness. "Relax, Jake," she said.

Somewhere beyond Barstow, she glanced over and said, "Penny for your thoughts."

"I guess I was thinking about Kenny Nielsen's take on Gretchen and Eichel, that they might be trying to steal atomic secrets. An atomic bomb for Germany? I wonder if he could be right. Kenny's got good instincts—his tactical and strategic successes during the war proved that."

Fortunately we weren't ambushed along the road by any gun-toting thugs and finally reached the Flamingo in midafternoon. I could see the buildings of downtown Las Vegas in the distance but there wasn't much out here. Siegel's low-slung but sprawling hotel dwarfed a couple of places called El Rancho Vegas and The Last Frontier. On the opposite side of the highway lay nothing but a vast spread of rocky desert. The only sign of life over there among the cacti and creosote bushes was a skinny little coyote trotting along, probably in search of a lizard for his dinner.

A chill wind whipped at us when we got out. Most people think the desert is always hot. News flash: not in midwinter, folks. While I retrieved our suitcase and turned the car over to a valet, fine grains of sand whisked at my face. I saw several big Caddies and Packards in the parking lot—my Chevy would look like a poor cousin over there.

Inside, the walls and columns were blindingly flamingo pink. As we walked to the check-in desk I caught sight of Carlo Gambino standing near a tall pillar. The New York hood was smoking a cigar and talking to somebody I didn't recognize. Welcome to the Mob, I thought.

The man at the desk took my name, checked his list, and said he was expecting us. "Your room is ready, Mr. Weaver . . . Boy!"

At which a bellhop trotted up and took our bag. The ching-ching-ching of busy slot machines could be heard nearby.

Later, dressed in our finery, Valerie in her black suede heels was a little taller than me but I didn't mind. We had a drink at the bar before going to the sumptuous dining room. Fine linen tablecloth, sparkling glasses and silverware, a small table lamp. "This is fun," Valerie said, looking terrific in her green, sleeveless evening dress. "I'm glad we came."

Siegel came over, a tall woman in a sequined gown on his arm. "Jake," he said, "glad you came. This must be your lovely wife. Meet my good friend, Virginia. Miss Hill, this is one of L.A.'s best reporters." Nodding of heads, smiles all around. "Enjoy yourselves and, Jake, keep your wallet in your pocket. Everything's on the house tonight."

I thanked him and they strolled off, stopping at table after table, working the room.

I ordered a bottle of pinot noir the sommelier recommended. Later while we ate—filet mignon for me, Fontina rosetta with chicken for Valerie—we played a game of identifying diners. At Siegel's table near the stage I spotted Meyer Lansky, a serious-looking little man in black-rimmed glasses. He didn't look very happy. L.A. Mayor Bowron was at the next table. Valerie spotted that skinny Italian singer the girls all loved, Frankie Sinatra, and the actor George Raft.

I didn't see Jack Dragna anywhere but before long Mickey Cohen, sitting at Siegel's table, caught my eye. He got up and came over. Said he was charmed to meet Valerie and made small talk for a couple of minutes. Before long he leaned down and whispered in my ear. "Take a good look at the parking lot, Scribbler."

"What did he say?" Valerie asked when The Mick was gone. I told her and she said, "That sounds ominous. I wonder what could be out there . . . Say, isn't that Rita Hayworth?"

"Yeah, I think so, Margarita Cansino herself. And over here's

L.A.'s police chief."

"And there's Hedda Hopper," Valerie said.

During dessert, Mayor Bowron went to Siegel's table, reached out and grasped both of Bugsy's hands like they were old pals. Man, I wished I could take a picture of that. We'd splash it on the front page and Hearst would be ecstatic.

Siegel stood, clinked a glass with a fork to quiet the room and made some welcoming remarks. Meyer Lansky gazed up at him with a dour look on his face, probably thinking all this was costing the Mob too much money. Siegel pointed to the big curtained stage behind him and told everyone to be sure to stick around for a spectacular show.

Minutes later the lights dimmed and the curtains parted to reveal a brightly-lit stage and a line of lavishly costumed young women. Huge headdresses, spangled dresses, high heels. Valerie gasped at the sight of two tall beauties in the center, bare-chested with sparkling necklaces dangling between their breasts. "Don't get too worked up, Sailor," she said with that coy look of hers. The band played and the showgirls did some dance steps. Their performance was followed by a magician's act, making things disappear, sawing a lovely girl in half, so on. Then came a singer I didn't recognize, but he had a fine baritone voice. He sang several show tunes, including Cole Porter's "Anything Goes."

The show closed with a reprise by the strutting showgirls and then the whole cast took their bows to a big ovation.

Afterward, Valerie and I went to the parking lot to look around. Valerie clung close to me against the cold—or in anxiety—clutching my arm. She kept nervously looking over her shoulder.

Shivering in the desert wind, I had no idea what we were looking for, or who might be looking for us. Lots of Lincolns and Caddies, even a Rolls Royce. Then, in the front row, I saw a maroon Buick Super. It bore black California plates. I went over for a closer look, bent down at the right front fender and saw what appeared in the dim light to be some newer, fresher paint!

This had to be Jack Dragna's car, the one that forced Valerie off the road a month ago. But I hadn't seen Dragna here. Puzzling, to say the least. I asked Valerie if this looked like the car that forced her off the road and she said, "It sure the heck does. Now let's get back inside."

In our room, she handed me her purse as she began to undress. It felt too heavy. I opened it and saw her .38 revolver in there with her other things. Valerie noticed and said, "Yeah, yeah, I brought along my gun. I also know your Luger is locked in the glove compartment." How had she known that? You couldn't put much over on this wife of mine.

Later she said, "How do you think I'd look in one of those topless showgirl outfits, Sailor?"

"Fantastic," I said. Our lovemaking that followed was fantastic too.

TWENTY-FOUR

As we drove out of town in the morning we passed the little Las Vegas airport. Several airliners were parked there. TWA, United. Smaller planes, too.

I thought about that maroon Buick and the fact that Jack Dragna hadn't been at the Flamingo. Could I have been mistaken? Could somebody else own that car? Somebody like Bugsy Siegel?

Five and a half hours later—I'd gassed up the buggy at a Sunoco station in Victorville—we reached Richie Millsap's to collect Ilse. "She was no trouble at all," Richie's wife said. "Such a fine girl."

When we drove off, Ilse said, "I cannot stand their daughter. She is a brat."

"Well, *Liebchen*," I said, "thanks for putting up with her. It was best that you spent the night with people we trust."

"I *know*," Ilse said, sounding peeved that we'd had her do this.

Although MI-6's Tom Doyle said he would do some checking at Caltech, I decided I would do the same. On Monday I went out to Pasadena to nose around.

I found Robert Oppenheimer's office and went in unannounced. The scientist was at a cluttered desk, talking on the phone. He had a thin face, smooth complexion, prominent cheekbones, pale blues eyes, black hair. A chart of the periodic table hung on the wall along with framed certificates and a picture of President Truman. Oppenheimer gave me an annoyed look that said who the hell are you?

When he hung up I said, "Dr. Oppenheimer, I'm Jake Weaver of the *Herald-Express*. Sorry to intrude. May I ask a few questions?"

"I've no time for an interview. My office hours are over. I have a class in ten minutes."

"Not an interview, sir, I'm not doing a story. Just a few quick questions."

He made a show of looking at his watch, emphasizing his shortage of time, and, frowning, motioned me to the one chair facing his desk.

I sat, took off my hat, and said, "Was your recent address about international control of atomic energy open to the public?"

"No, it was by invitation. Students, faculty, scientists, so forth. Why do you ask?"

"I happen to know that two people from Sachsen Haus attended. They showed up in one of our photographer's shots."

"What is this Sachsen Haus?" He was impatiently twirling a yellow pencil with the fingers of his right hand. "I haven't heard of it."

"A nonprofit that puts a friendly face on Germany, promotes tourism and the like. They started operating here before the Hitler period."

Oppenheimer's brows arched. "What's your interest in that place?"

"Just something I'm following up on. How do you suppose these two got in to hear you?"

"I've no idea. Maybe they stole or forged an invitation, something like that. A lot of people try to talk with me, often people I don't know." He put the pencil down. "Two German men, you say?"

"No, a man and a woman."

"I haven't been approached by a man and woman I don't know since that talk."

"Have you been contacted by anyone in the British government?"

Oppenheimer gave me quite a look. "Strange that you ask that. Oddly enough"—shaking his head—"I received a message from someone in British Intelligence the other day. I haven't returned the call. I'm quite busy, you know." Another glance at his watch. "I wish you could tell me what the devil this is all about, but not now. I really must go."

I stood, handed him my card and said, "Please contact me, sir, if this man and woman try to reach you or if anything unusual happens. It's important. Oh, and if you talk with that British fella, it's okay to tell him I was here."

Also getting up, Oppenheimer took the card, gave me a wintry look, and picked up a file folder. "I hate mysteries," he said. Scientists like facts and I hadn't given him any. He practically shooed me out the door and followed close behind.

"I understand, doctor," I said, and we walked off in opposite directions.

I drove back toward downtown on what I still thought of as the Arroyo Seco Parkway, though it was recently renamed the Pasadena Freeway. My thoughts turned to that maroon Buick out at the opening of the Flamingo—which Jack Dragna had not attended.

If that was Bugsy Siegel's car and not Dragna's, what had it been doing in Fat Jack's garage?

Time to find out, time to dare the devil. Instead of going to the paper, I got on Wilshire to make the long drive across town to Dragna's house in Brentwood. I'd have to run the gauntlet of Dragna's goons again but, hell or high water, I was going to see Fat Jack himself. My Luger was still locked in the glove box. I'd stick it in my jacket before going in.

I parked one house away so Dragna's muscle wouldn't see me getting out the pistol. But I got smart and changed my mind. I realized I'd be searched and if they found a gun on me they'd think I was here to shoot Dragna. Should have thought of that. I left it in the glove box.

No one was in sight as I approached, not even the Chinese gardener. When I got halfway up the walk, though, the front door flew open and out came the big-shouldered goon, the one I'd punched out a couple of weeks ago.

"You!" he snarled. "You ain't wanted here. Get the hell outta here, 'less you want your face busted up."

"Look pal, I'm sorry I hit you that time. I was a little rattled. Temper got the best of me. I just need to see Jack for a minute. Won't take long at all. Mickey sent me." I was telling lie after lie these days.

"Cohen sent you?"

"Yep."

"Stay right there. I'll be right back." Big Shoulders went inside.

I shifted my weight from foot to foot for a couple of minutes before he came back. "Gonna frisk you," he said. "You know the drill, hold your arms out."

I complied and got a thorough pat down. "Okay," he said, satisfied, and I followed him inside to a lavish living room. Expensive leather sofa, plush chairs, fancy lamps, all that. Dragna stood there in rumpled gray trousers and a USC sweatshirt that didn't hide his considerable paunch.

"Jake Weaver, ain't it?" I nodded. "The guy who's making me look bad in the papers. You gotta lotta nerve comin' here. It's open season on nosy reporters, you know."

"I hope you don't bag one today, Mr. Dragna. I just have a quick question for you."

"Shoot," he said, a word I wished he hadn't used.

The Unholy Trinity had run a story about one of Dragna's numbers runners pocketing a few grand for himself, the result of some great sleuthing by Marko Janicek following up on a tip. Maybe this was why the gangster standing here was less hostile than I'd expected.

"Here's the question," I said. "When I was here before, I saw a maroon Buick in your garage with a fender getting repaired. Is that your car?"

"What the hell business is that of yours?"

"It's my business," I said, "because I think it's the car that forced my wife off the road awhile back. Tried to kill her."

"No kiddin'? Didn't know that. Well, that car ain't mine. If you hafta know, it's Ben Siegel's. If it was me, Weaver—no offense—your old lady woulda been dead. I guess Bugs has a bad driver. He didn't want that car fixed up in no public garage. Wanted to do it quiet like."

"So you're sure it was Siegel's?" I asked.

"Course I am, I ain't lying to you. I had nothin' to do with it. Bugs sent out his own auto-body guys. All I did was loan him the space . . . So that's it, then?"

"Yep, that's all I wanted to know."

"You got guts showin' up here again, I'll say that for ya. You guys sure cut my judge pal off at the knees. And you did a nice job on that punk who skimmed me running numbers. I don't s'pose you'll tell me how you got that?" I shook my head no. "Anyway, he's been taken care of."

"Do yourself a favor," I said, "and don't tell me how." If that guy was at the bottom of Santa Monica Bay wearing concrete brogans, I'd have to write that, and right now I didn't want to blow the small rapport I had going here.

"Then do me a favor too," he said. "Don't tell Bugs I told you this."

"No problem. He and I aren't exactly close pals. Well, thanks,

Dragna, I'll be on my way then."

I passed Big Shoulders on my way out. "Nice to see you again," I said.

His right hand became a fist and he started to cock his arm. "Ah, ah, ah," I said, wagging a finger at him. "Mickey wouldn't like that."

As I drove away I told myself I wanted to kill Bugsy Siegel. Just take him right off the board. He tried to kill *me*—twice—once when it was Valerie driving my car and once in Detroit. Revenge is sweet, somebody once said.

Halfway back to the paper, though, I cooled it. Those Germans back in '44 were the only people I ever wanted to kill. Saw them in my sleep sometimes. Murder's never the answer. I'd think of another way to cook Mr. Siegel's goose.

TWENTY-FIVE

Hedda Hopper of the *Times* devoted her whole gossip column to Siegel's big shindig at the Flamingo, oohing and aahing at the celebrities who were there. We didn't touch it. Johnny Campbell, Aggie Underwood and I agreed that'd be inconsistent with our stance on L.A. crime.

Robert Oppenheimer called the next day, sounding agitated and upset. "You asked me to call if something unusual happened. Something certainly did. My office was burglarized last night. My file drawers were rifled. Some things were taken."

Kenny Nielsen apparently had pegged that right, Eichel hoping to steal atomic secrets. Smart man, that Kenny.

"Anything of great value?" I asked. "Something irreplaceable?"

"I don't know yet. Still trying to inventory all that. Mostly lesson plans, position papers and lecture notes, I should think."

"Have you called the police?"

"Of course. Pasadena PD came out here, looked around, and dusted for fingerprints."

I asked if his office door had been locked. "No, I wasn't in the habit of doing that, but I certainly will from now on." Locking the barn door after the horse had been stolen, I thought, and I also thought about Nikolaus Eichel and Gretchen Siedler. I still found it hard to believe the woman who'd saved my skin four years ago in Nazi Germany apparently had changed sides.

"Call the MI-6 man, Tom Doyle," I said.

"Why?"

"Because he's a good man, and he needs to know about this break-in. I think that man and woman we talked about are trying to steal atomic secrets."

"Oh, Lord," Oppenheimer said. "But if that is so, they didn't get any. Everything I have on explosive nuclear fission is locked in a safe at . . . well, I mustn't say, but it's not here. Yes, I will call the man. What is your connection with him?"

"It's complicated, but I've done some very unofficial work for MI-6. We have to find those people."

"Yes. All right, I will call. Thank you, Mr. Weaver."

That evening while Valerie was busy in the kitchen, Ilse came to me, her face wrinkled with worry. I'd been in my easy chair listening to the news on KFI. Something about John L. Lewis and the United Mineworkers.

"*Vater*, Ilse said, "I must tell you something." She seldom called me father, usually daddy. I went to our radio-phonograph console and turned it off.

"What is it, *Liebchen*?" Boy trouble, I guessed. Maybe a problem with that Honeycutt kid she'd dated.

"When I was walking home this afternoon a car, it followed me. Only for the last two blocks, though. Moving slowly it was. When I got to our house, I took a good look. The driver wore a big hat and dark glasses, but I think it was *Herr* Schäfer."

"Klaus Schäfer, your soccer coach?"

"I think so. I am not certain but I think it was him. When he saw me looking, he turned his head and drove off quickly."

I'd had a real bad feeling about that guy ever since the soccer team's season-ending party. "How odd," I said inadequately. Trying not to alarm her, I added, "I doubt it's anything to worry about," and gave her a hug meant to be reassuring. But I vividly remembered how that man had leered at Ilse and grasped another girl's shoulder at that hamburger joint.

"I never much liked the man," Ilse went on. "Miss Kardos was much nicer. Mr. Schäfer was always a bit . . . I do not know, cold I think. I did not want to trouble you with this, but I thought you should know."

"Is there any reason he should be upset with you?" I asked. "Any little thing that may have occurred?"

Ilse scrunched her face in thought for a moment and then said, "Well, one time at practice I corrected him. It was a minor rule thing, but he had it wrong. A goalkeeper cannot touch the ball with her hands on a throw-in."

"Yeah, that would have embarrassed him. He probably won't forget it."

"I know, *Vati*. I would have said nothing but it could have hurt us in a game . . . Say, I know you are worried about Mr. Siegel these days. I wonder . . ."

I wondered too. Could Siegel, who wanted to kill me, have any connection with Klaus Schäfer? "But Bugsy Siegel is my problem, not yours, *Liebchen*. Just continue to be careful, as I know you always are. And possibly it wasn't Coach Schäfer after all. But let's get one of the parents to drive you home after school from now on." I kissed her cheek. "We'll talk to your mom and make a plan."

"Do we have to?" Shaking her head.

"Yes, *Liebchen*, we have to. We've got to keep you safe."

"Okay," she said reluctantly. "I will go and help *Muti* now," and she slunk off to the kitchen.

I sank onto my chair. All kinds of bad thoughts swirled, thoughts about Klaus Schäfer, about Bugsy Siegel, about Nikolaus Eichel, and about danger to my daughter.

After hearing about this, Valerie was as upset as me. Over dinner we talked about which parents might be able to drive Ilse home after school, Ilse protesting that it wasn't necessary.

* * *

It was time to try out my new steel-shaft golf clubs again. At the Griffith Park Golf Club the next day, I teamed up in a foursome with Richie Millsap, one of our assistant city editors, and a guy I hadn't met. I figured a round of golf would be a good distraction from my recent worries.

I had some trouble with my fairway woods and landed in a couple of sand traps, but I putted okay. Until the last hole, that is. The grip on my putter came loose right in my hand. I pulled the damn thing off and borrowed Richie's putter for my final shot, a five-footer which I managed to sink. I finished with a 93, not too bad for a guy who doesn't play often. When I got home I would put the putter in my bedroom closet to remind me to get it repaired one of these days.

After I showered and changed, I was sitting on a bench in the locker room putting on my shoes when a man I knew came in, toweling himself off. He was the psychologist I'd seen twice after returning from Europe. He'd helped me in regard to the black memories that kept persisting of the German men I'd killed, and he'd explained the fog of short-term amnesia I'd undergone for a few hours immediately afterward.

"Hey, doc," I said.

"It's Jake Weaver, isn't it? How are, my friend?"

After a brief updating, I asked what would motivate some psychopath to kill girls and women. He was taken aback, asking why I would ever ask such a question.

After I filled him in on the Buchenwald Butcher, he thought for a moment and said, "The causes of misogyny and pedophilia haven't been clearly pinpointed, Weaver, but my belief is that much of it stems from bad experiences as a child. Growing up in a harsh family environment, having a callous, abusive mother, for example. In extreme cases, when the recidivist does great physical harm to a female, he will often take a trophy, like one of the victim's shoes or perhaps some underwear."

I thanked him, said it was good to see him again, and left. Driving to the office, I felt pretty darn glum over what he'd said.

I'd been at my desk no more than fifteen minutes when agent Tom Doyle called. He said he'd spoken with Robert Oppenheimer and that he learned I'd done the same.

"Apparently nothing sensitive about the uranium bomb was taken. Now, with all respect, Weaver, you must leave this to us. The FBI or I will find Gretchen Siedler, you can count on it. I shall keep you informed of our progress."

Leave it to them? Stay out of it? Fat chance, Scoutmaster, I told myself after hanging up.

I drove to Sachsen Haus that afternoon. By now the woman at the desk and I were familiar faces to one another.

"Well, so it is you again," she said the moment I came in. "I see that your British government has another man on this now, a man with a better demeanor than that *dummkopf* who was with you before."

"It's not my British government ma'am, but like them I want to find Gretchen Siedler. Speaking with your *Herr* Eichel seems like a good place to start."

"As I told your Mr. Doyle yesterday, Nikolaus Eichel is not here. He is taking holiday, vacation I believe you say."

I switched to speaking German. Maybe I could do better with her that way. "*Fraulein*, you are a good person, I know that. *Frau* Siedler is an old friend and I think she's in some kind of trouble. I want to see that she gets out of it unharmed."

"Of course, *mein Herr*, and how is it that you speak German?"

I explained that my parents were German immigrants and that I learned from them as a kid. Getting back on subject, I said, "Your

Herr Eichel is up to something, something wrong. I think you realize that. *Bitte Schön,* tell me whatever you can about this."

The woman fidgeted, looked down at a pile of travel flyers on her desk for a moment, debating, then directly up at me.

"Nikolaus Eichel," she said at last, "is a good man. He loathed Hitler and the Nazis, as did I. He wants to see a responsible new Germany emerge from that horrible war. He is zealous about that, perhaps too much so. I have told him that he must be more patient, that it will all take time."

She stopped and wrung her hands. "I do not want trouble with Britain or the USA."

"You won't have any," I said. "*Herr* Doyle and I will see to that . . . if you help us."

"Well then, Nikolaus has come into contact with two German men who I think are not respectable. They were with him here, two times it was. They looked to me—what is your word, shady? Gestapo types. The second time they were here, he left with them."

"Where were they going?"

"I do not know. Nikolaus did not say."

"Did you hear their names?"

"Just one. Nikki called one of them Schäfer."

Although I'd half expected that, it gave me a shiver. Both Ilse and I were darn concerned about her soccer coach. "When will Eichel be back from his holiday?" I asked.

"I do not know. It was unlike him not to say."

"And you have no idea where these men went?"

"*Nein.* Nothing was said about that."

I said, "*Danke schön,*" and gave her my card. "*Bitte,* call me, ma'am, if he shows up or if you hear anything more about Gretchen Siedler."

She took my card and said she would.

What had I learned here? Not much. Just that this woman

knew Eichel was up to no good and that a man named Schäfer was involved. That might not be Ilse's coach but I was pretty convinced that it was. Schäfer was a common German name but I still had no faith in coincidences.

Would this woman call when she learned anything more? I wanted to believe she would, that she was sincere about not wanting to get in trouble.

My thoughts fastened again on Bugsy Siegel as I drove to the paper, Figueroa to Pico to South Trenton. The maroon Buick was *his*, Siegel's. He was the one who'd tried to kill me the day Valerie was using my car. Short of killing the bastard, what could I do?

TWENTY-SIX

Ilse was driven home from school by Doris Palmer, the mother of one of her classmates. That evening she complained to Valerie and me that it hadn't been necessary, that she could walk home alertly and carefully and be okay.

Ducking a counter argument we might mount, she went on to say that she'd had lunch in the cafeteria with Aaron Epstein as she'd planned. "He was nervous about it and even spilled some of his milk. He was most embarrassed, but I could tell he was pleased to sit with me."

"Of course he was," Valerie said. "That was awfully nice of you." A mercy lunch, I would have called it, but a nice one.

"Both his parents died in the concentration camp. He lives now with an aunt. I told him that my mother was dead also." Ilse's face turned glum. "We got a couple of nasty looks from some boys who were at the next table, the popular ones, the football players. They seemed to wonder why I was wasting time on such a . . . pantywaist, I suppose would be their word."

"It's too bad prejudice starts at a young age," I said. "Did anything else happen?"

"Aaron asked about my German accent, so I told him about myself. He said it was most ironic, a concentration camp survivor sitting there with a former member of the Hitler Youth. The school once had a German Club, but during the war it was discontinued. We are going to ask Mr. Erkenbeck, who teaches German and French class, if we can start it up again . . . Oh, and Dave Honeycutt was across the room, staring at us. He did not look happy."

"He was jealous," Valerie said.

"Oh, I hope not, *Muti*. Dave is a nice boy. He wants to date me again. I hope he does not change his mind."

"He won't," Valerie said.

"Not if he's smart," I added. "Don't worry about this at all, *Liebchen*."

At the paper that afternoon I had called Cohen and told him I used his name to get in and see Dragna, in case Fat Jack checked up on my story. Mickey said no problem, he'd back me up on that, but that he and Dragna rarely spoke these days. Then he said, "Was real nice meeting your wife up in Vegas. Hubba hubba. What pretty eyes your lady's got."

"They're like summer sky in the mountains," I said.

"Summer sky? You're quite the wordsmith, aren't ya, Scribbler?"

"I can wax poetic sometimes, Mick, when it's about Valerie."

"You'll be interested," he said, "to know that Siegel's been called to New York by Lansky and Genovese. I figure they're gonna rake him over the coals about his big cost overruns in Vegas. They think Ben's gettin' too big for those expensive britches of his."

Yes, I was interested. I found myself thinking I wouldn't be sorry if Siegel ended up in the East River.

Cohen asked what was going on with Gretchen Siedler.

I told him about her disappearance and that I was trying to find her, so far with no luck.

"Anything I can do to help?"

"I don't think so, Mick, but thanks for asking."

"Lemme know if you think of something. See you in church, kid."

What a day it had been. Finding that Oppenheimer's office had been broken into. That the Buick Super was Siegel's, not Dragna's.

My burning anger at Siegel. Ilse's coach likely connected to Gretchen's whereabouts. What I needed to kick the tension was a good roll in the hay with a beautiful woman.

And later that evening I had just that. "Wow, Sailor, you sure had some good moves tonight," Valerie murmured in the afterglow. Exhausted, I fell into a satisfied and needed sleep.

Several dreamless hours later, while I was waking up to kitchen noises and the smell of bacon frying, I had a brainstorm. Valerie had a roster of Ilse's soccer team, listing addresses and phone numbers of the players and their two coaches. I should have thought of that before. I dressed in a rush and went to the kitchen.

Valerie turned from the stove, planted a big kiss on me and said, "Good morning, you animal."

"You're quite a hunk of wildlife yourself," I said, then shifted gears. "I'll finish cooking the bacon and eggs, Sweets. Go and get me that soccer roster, would you?"

"Right now?"

"Yep, I just thought of something important," I said, and took the spatula from her.

Ilse came in, yawning, and wordlessly began setting the table.

When Valerie returned with the mimeographed roster I gave it a fast scan. And was disappointed. The sheet listed addresses and phone numbers for everyone but Schäfer. The lines after his name were blank. Damn! But maybe his assistant, Miss Kardos, knew where he lived. I'd call her after breakfast.

Valerie had been looking over my shoulder. "I see what you're up to," she said. "Nothing there for Schäfer. Maybe Miss Kardos knows how to reach him."

"Mind reader," I said. "Let's hope so. First, let's dig in," and the three of us sat down to breakfast. I took a drink of coffee, fresh from our new electric percolator. It was darn good.

After taking a bite of pancake, Ilse put her fork down and said Dave Honeycutt had asked her out again. A movie date this time.

"Fine," Valerie said, "as long as it's not to a drive-in. He seems like a nice kid."

"No drive-in, *Muti*. We're going to see *Blue Skies* at the Pantages. Fred Astaire and Bing Crosby." Which sounded okay to us.

After breakfast I got the Hungarian woman on the line and introduced myself as Ilse's father.

"Yes, Mr. Weaver, I remember you." Her accent guttural but not unpleasing.

I asked if she'd seen Schäfer recently.

"No, not since the party after our last game."

"Do you know here he lives?"

"Why do you ask?"

"I need to talk to him. Nothing important, just a minor matter."

"Well, it was some hotel in Maywood. He had not been in Los Angeles very long. Let me think, what was the name? Something about palms or regal palms. I cannot recall exactly."

"Take your time and try to remember," I urged.

But she couldn't come up with it. "Just something about palms. I am sorry, Mr. Weaver."

I told her that was okay.

I drove Ilse to school on my way to work. I'd been doing that since the day that car, probably driven by Schäfer, had tailed her.

Ilse, who could be as stubborn as her stepmom, flatly refused to be driven home from school anymore by Mrs. Palmer. It was only six blocks, no problem, she insisted.

I reluctantly gave in, but said, "Then take a different route every day, even if it takes you a little longer. And walk with someone.

I'm sure you know some classmates who live over this way." I dropped her in front of the school and kissed her cheek before she hopped out, toting her books.

First thing I did when I got to my desk was get out the Yellow Pages and look for hotels or motels in the small nearby city of Maywood. Bingo! One was named the Royal Palms Motel. Nothing else even close.

I took Marko Janicek with me. Marko had been an Army Ranger on D-Day. He was a little tougher and cleverer than Richie Millsap. My Luger wasn't going to stay in the glove compartment this time. It'd be stuck under my belt.

Marko had an Army .45 with him. I'd already told him what had been going on, but I filled him in even further, including the stalking of my daughter.

"I saw you put some handcuffs in your pocket," he said as I drove south along Downey Avenue. "Where'd you get those?"

"From a cop I knew way back when. I've had 'em forever. If we find this punk, we roust him. He might be dangerous, might even be the sadistic Nazi asshole the Brits are looking for."

"I'm surprised you didn't bring MI-6 in on this," Marko said.

He had a good point. I should have contacted Tom Doyle, but sometimes when I find out something important, I jump in and act right away, without looking at the picture from all sides.

"But I'm glad it's us," Marko went on. "I'm keyed up. Feel like I'm going behind enemy lines at Pont du Hoc again."

"If this is the right place and we find his room," I said, "I'll go in first. You stand to the side where he can't see you when the door opens, but be ready."

Maywood was only about three miles from the paper. The Royal Palms Motel turned out to be over named. It squatted along Slauson Avenue like a washed-up, punch-drunk boxer. Dating from the 1920s motor court era, the place consisted of low, wood-frame cabins arranged in a U-shape around a central space that could have been a nice courtyard but instead was a cracked-asphalt parking lot. Not a palm tree in sight, royal or otherwise.

I guessed the NO on the neon sign above VACANCY hadn't been lit in years. If Schäfer was staying here he sure wasn't spending much money on it.

An OFFICE sign hung on the door of the first cabin. I went in, found the room empty, and punched the bell on the counter. Soon a fiftyish man appeared. Brown cardigan over a blue denim shirt. "Help you?" he asked.

"We're looking for Klaus Schäfer. Is he staying here?"

"We got four guests at the moment. Nobody by that name."

"Let me see your register," I said, and grabbed the open book lying there before he could answer, turning it toward me.

"Hey! Who the hell are you? Whatta you want?"

I flashed the toy badge I'd bought at Woolworth's—let him glimpse it for about a tenth of a second, while an amused look crossed Marko's face. The manager backed off a step, looking worried. One of the four names on his register was Robert Jones. He'd signed in three months ago. "This Jones," I said, "what's he look like?"

"Well, officer, he's a husky fella, light-colored hair, wears thick glasses. Doesn't sound like a Jones. Talks with a foreign accent, so I figure Jones to be a phony name. Pays his bills regular, though."

"Is he here now?"

"Couldn't tell you. He comes and goes a lot. Think he works part-time somewhere. Don't see his car down there at Cabin Four," he said, pointing to his left. "That's his cabin, four, just down the line there."

I had a disturbing thought: What if he's out prowling around Ilse's school?

"What's he drive?" I asked.

"Some rat-trap little Ford, '37 or '38."

"Give me a key," I said.

"Ain't suppose to do that. You got a search warrant?"

"Give me a damn key, pal, unless you want the building inspectors out here." His face blanched.

Turning to Marko, I said, "Let's bust the door down."

"No, no, officer, them doors cost money. Here." He pulled a key from a wallboard behind him, numbered 2 through 12.

As Marko and I approached number four, I reached down and felt my Luger. Marko stood to the side and pulled out his .45. I started to slip the key in the lock. Felt my heart thumping in my chest. Was I about to face Schäfer with a gun leveled at me?

TWENTY-SEVEN

I pushed the door open. No man with a gun. Saw only a darkened room. I stepped in. Found a light switch on the wall just inside and flipped it on. Saw a bed, poorly made, a couple of wooden chairs, small table, and a bathroom beyond an open doorway. The place smelled of stale cigarette smoke. "Jones?" I called. "Schäfer?" No answer. "Come on in, Marko."

We proceeded to look around and found very little. A suitcase, a few clothes on hangers in an open closet, soccer ball on the floor beneath them, two empty beer bottles, some papers on a nightstand alongside a glass ash tray. Three or four butts in it.

The stuff on the nightstand included a Gulf Oil map of L.A. I unfolded it and saw that five red circles had been drawn. One was right here, this motel. Another was the West Los Angeles Playground, where the Tigers played soccer. Another encircled a spot on 17th Street, about where Sachsen Haus was. The fourth was just above downtown L.A., maybe Union Depot. Nothing near Ilse's school. The fifth was a spot near El Segundo. I was clueless about that one.

Some numbers were scrawled near the bottom of the map. 2767984. I jotted them down in my notebook, then said, "Well, Marko, this is definitely Schäfer's room."

"Sure enough, Jake, but no Schäfer."

The other items on the nightstand were a bus schedule, receipts from a Ralphs grocery and a used-car lot—he'd paid forty dollars for a '38 Ford coupe—and the mimeographed soccer roster, creased with folds. I half expected to see Ilse's name circled in red, but it wasn't. The paper bore a round coffee-cup stain, nothing else but names and addresses.

We continued to search. The suitcase held some underwear and socks. Razor, toothpaste, toothbrush and shampoo in the bathroom. A tub, no shower. The razor was a Parc Solingen, a German brand. No lipstick on a cigarette butt, although Gretchen didn't smoke. Not an earring, pair of hose, or anything to indicate a woman's presence.

I was starting to feel jittery. Schäfer could come back at any moment. "Let's get out of here," I said.

"Yeah, we've been in here long enough," Marko agreed.

I was tempted to leave Schäfer a message, maybe one German word soaped on the bathroom mirror. If he knew someone was on to him it might make Ilse safer. But I was getting nervous—we'd been in there quite awhile. Besides, seeing that might make him scram out of L.A. fast, and then he'd be even harder for MI-6 to find. If he was Otto Woolf, that is.

When I returned the key to the manager, I said, "Don't say a word about this to Jones. If I find out you told him, I'll have safety inspectors all over your ass."

"Where the hell'd you get that badge?" Marko asked as I drove off.

"Bought it at the five and dime."

Back at my desk, I figured I should inform agent Doyle. I called the apartment Gretchen had occupied but now was his. He wasn't in, so I left a message with the concierge.

Ninety minutes later, the call was returned. "Doyle," I said, "I know you told me to back off, but I found out something you need to know. My daughter's soccer coach—and he's been stalking her—is staying at the Royal Palms Motel on Slauson Avenue in Maywood. We know he was at Sachsen Haus and that he left there with Eichel. You and I know he's involved in all this somehow."

"And how did you learn this?"

I explained about picking the assistant coach's brain on where Schäfer was staying.

"And I suppose you went to this motel?"

"Well, yes, I did. He wasn't there."

"There's just no keeping you out of this, is there, Weaver? Well, thank you, I daresay this is useful. Did you learn anything else?"

"He signed in as Robert Jones. With his German accent, even the manager spotted that as a phony. The man says he drives a '37 or '38 Ford. There was very little in his room, mainly just clothes and his toiletry stuff."

Doyle asked me to repeat the motel's name and location so he could jot it down.

After I did, he said, "All right then, Weaver. The Pope speaks highly of you, so I suppose you will continue digging. In future, though, please inform me of these things *before* you jump in."

"Cross my heart," I said.

Ilse was usually home alone for about two hours before Valerie or I arrived from work. She was good about using that time wisely, doing homework or some domestic housekeeping. Sometimes she began preparing the evening meal. German efficiency. A good latch-key kid.

Looking at my watch, I saw it was about time for her to be there. Feeling a little nervous, probably because Klaus Schäfer had been out somewhere, I called.

A feeling of relief swept over me when Ilse answered. She had walked home with two other girls, had taken an indirect route, and nothing happened. Well, two seniors in a convertible honked and whistled, but that was it.

I told her I'd knock off early and be there in about an hour. "I love you, *Liebchen*."

"You too, *Vati*."

After hanging up, I tried to piece all this together. There was a spate of loose ends.

Gretchen had lied to me about trying to help some German POWs in the desert. She and Nikolaus Eichel may have broken into Robert Oppenheimer's office. Kenny Nielsen believed they want to steal atomic secrets for the new Germany.

Klaus Schäfer leering hungrily at Ilse at the team's party, then tailing her one day after school.

Otto Woolf, the Buchenwald Butcher, he was God knew where.

Bugsy Siegel trying to kill me—twice. I still had a score to settle there.

All this was too much for my little brain to compute. I couldn't connect the dots.

That L.A. map in Schäfer's room came back to mind. He'd circled five places in red. Three of them were fairly obvious. The fourth was probably Union Depot. The fifth was near El Segundo. What could that be?

Standard Oil had a big refinery there, and that also was where the Webb company was building a new warehouse. I'd been there and questioned the construction manager. What else? Nothing much, just an old army barracks that stood empty now. War surplus. I'd heard that the government was planning to sell that property.

An abandoned army barracks. *Hmm.*

Aggie Underwood broke that reverie. She came by, pulled a chair up to my desk, sat, and said, "We're shutting it down, Jake."

I had no idea what my city editor meant. I'd been thinking about an abandoned army barracks out near the coast.

"Shut down what, Aggie?"

"The anti-crime crusade. Your Unholy Trinity. Johnny and I talked it over with W.R. and he agrees. It's been a success, Jake. You got that crooked judge thrown off the bench, nailed Siegel good on a couple of big things, and exposed that numbers guy who was skimming on Dragna. Circulation's up. The old man's happy."

I was actually relieved. Valerie would be, too. I wasn't sure what else the Trinity could do anyway, except maybe get ourselves killed.

"You'll go back fulltime to being our military writer," she said. "Marko will remain an investigative reporter, and Richie goes to general assignment."

"Good. There's a lot I need to get back into, Aggie. Army and Navy reductions in force, atomic tests in the Pacific, closure of several bases around L.A., the probability that the air force will become its own separate branch of the military. I need to interview the secretary of war." There's the Gretchen Siedler/Klaus Schäfer business too, I thought but didn't say.

"Attaboy, Jake. Johnny and I want to take you and the fellas out for some drinks, have a little wrap-up party."

"That's swell, Aggie, but please not tonight. I just promised my daughter I'd get right home today."

Aggie got up and laid a hand on my shoulder. "Okay, champ, tomorrow then. The Biltmore. Five o'clock."

With that map I'd seen at Woolf's motel room still on my mind, I opened my notebook and looked at the numbers I'd copied down: 2767984. What could they mean? A phone number, maybe? I checked my phone book and saw that 27 was the Crestwood exchange. That was Beverly Hills. Bugsy Siegel's number was unlisted but I had a trusted contact at Ma Bell. I called him and said it was important that I get Siegel's number. "No one will ever know where I got it," I promised. "I'm not even going to call it.

Just need to know."

He said okay, hang on. A minute later he read Siegel's private number to me: Crestwood 6-7984. *Aha*. Woolf had Bugsy's phone number.

"I owe you one, Charlie," I said.

When I got home I gave Ilse my A Number One hug. "You should not worry so much about me, *Vati*. I can take care of myself. Besides, if it becomes necessary, I can run very fast, you know."

"You sure can, *Liebchen*, like the wind, but we can't take this lightly. Neither you nor I trust your coach, and he may be involved in Gretchen's disappearance. Say, when that car followed you and it looked like Schäfer was driving, was it a '38 Ford?"

"I do not know cars so well, but it was small, black and had only two doors."

"I'm not sure, but I think all Fords in the Thirties were black."

"Why do you ask, *Vati*?"

"Because I found out today that's the kind of car Schäfer's driving." I changed the subject and asked how school had gone.

"In journalism I covered a school assembly for the paper, and geography class was good. Did you know that Antarctica is a continent?"

After I said that I did, Ilse turned on the radio. It was time for *Captain Midnight*, her favorite serial.

It was Valerie's turn to provide dinner, and she came home with three big takeout sandwiches from a deli. Ham, Swiss cheese, lettuce and tomatoes on Kaiser rolls. "I had a hell of a day," she explained, "and just didn't feel like cooking. I hope this is okay."

I kissed her and said, "It's fine, Sweets. These look great."

I got some mustard from the fridge and put it on the table, which Ilse had already set. "How about a drink, Val?"

"You bet, Sailor."

Over glasses of Scotch and water, we filled each other in. Valerie'd been frustrated because a subcontract with Boeing had been canceled after she'd done a lot of drawings on it. She'd also had a big argument with her foreman. Then, "Remember that Czech fellow I told you about, the one who's not a very good designer? He was laid off today, along with one of our file clerks." She took a swallow of Scotch and said, "With no war on and fewer contracts, quite a number have been let go in several departments."

"But your job's safe, isn't it, Val?"

"I think so, but as I've said before, I'd like to get into missiles and rockets, even if that meant switching companies. But what about you, Jake? What happened today?"

I told her about searching Schäfer's motel room—which got her to frowning—and the shutdown of the anti-crime campaign. Frown turned to smile. "I'm so glad.to hear that," she said. "I never liked you prowling around with those hoodlums. Although I admit going to the opening of the Flamingo was kind of fun."

TWENTY-EIGHT

I went to the old army barracks at El Segundo the next day, suspecting I'd find nothing but rats, pigeons and cobwebs, maybe some hobos. On the other hand, Schäfer had marked that in red on his map, either that or something else close by.

The place had been closed for two years, since the last draftees had passed through there in 1944. It now looked sad and rundown, encircled by a less than formidable chain-link fence. A sign reading NO TRESPASSING – VIOLATORS WILL BE PROSECUTED was pitted in three or four places where bullets had been fired at it.

I drove on by and parked behind a small cluster of eucalyptus, western sycamores and valley oaks where my car couldn't be seen from the barracks, and approached on foot. The gate was locked but there were a couple of holes in the fence where somebody could easily slip through. Which I did, but after first studying the bare ground outside of it. Being close to the ocean, the ground was wet with dew. The soil bore tire tracks, recent ones, not yet blown away by the ocean breeze. Footprints too. Most of them were large, but one set was smaller, the kind a woman would make.

Six buildings were laid out in two rows of three each. They were typical clapboard rectangles, like all World War II barracks I'd seen. Some windows were broken. Inside the fence, what once had been a lawn was stippled by weeds and scraggly clumps of almost-dead Bermuda grass. I went to the nearest building, hopped up the six wooden, creaky steps and found the door unlocked. Got out the flashlight I'd brought and pulled the door open.

A sudden loud whirring sound scared the bejesus out of me. My flashlight beam caught a flock of pigeons beating their wings, as startled by me as I was of them. Some fluttered crazily around the low ceiling beams and others fled through a broken window. Rats with wings I called those scavengers.

Rows of bunks, stacked two high, lined each wall flanking a center aisle, typical army barracks style. Gobs of pigeon shit splotched the bare wooden floor here and there. Nothing else. The bunks were stripped, no tables or chairs in sight.

I closed the door behind me and went to the second building. When I opened the door, no pigeons. Cardboard covered two of the windows, which probably were broken, to keep the birds out.

Then, a hell of a shock! My flashlight beam showed the first two lower bunks on the right side were in use. New-looking blankets and pillows there, definitely not army issue. A coil of rope lay on the floor beside the second bunk. Used for what? I had no idea. A black satchel lay there too.

Swinging the light around, I saw some clothes hanging from a wire strung across the center aisle. My nerve endings began chattering in overdrive.

Three wooden folding chairs faced a card table in the aisle, on top of which sat a Coleman lantern. Also paper plates and cans of beans and chili and such. An orange crate containing what looked in the bad light like a loaf of bread and other foods. A latrine at the far end of the building.

I spotted another bunk, six down from the first two, which also was being slept in. A suitcase stood beside that bed. Why would someone want to bed down so far away from the others? I saw a frilly, power-blue pillow there, and something else. My light reflected off a small, round mirror—a woman's compact!

It was pretty obvious that Eichel and Schäfer were hiding out here. And Gretchen too. I felt the Luger tucked under my belt, glad I'd brought it. I felt goosebumps on my arms.

Shining the light here and there nervously, I looked around only a minute or two more, then got the hell out of there. Scurrying back through the fence and over to my car, I thought about a jacket that'd been hanging in there. A lemon-colored jacket I'd seen Gretchen wear.

I'd tell Tom Doyle about all this and come back again with him. I'd bring Marko Janicek too, with his trusty .45.

Back at the paper I dialed the Brits' apartment and found Doyle in. I told him about the barracks and what I'd seen there. Got the expected lecture about acting on my own.

"I didn't want to waste your time," I said by way of apology. "Thought it would amount to nothing. It was just a hunch I had after seeing Schäfer had marked that area on his map."

"A good hunch at that," Doyle admitted. "Let's go out there in the morning then."

"Armed?" I asked.

"Yes, Colonial Four, by all means bring a weapon. Just in case." I hadn't been sure he knew the code name Colonel Freeborn had given me.

I told him I wanted to bring Marko Janicek, explaining that he was tough and reliable and had been on a special ops team in the Army. Satisfied, he agreed that was a good idea.

We arranged that I'd pick him up at eight. We'd reach the barracks by eight-thirty.

I wondered if Bugsy Siegel was back from New York or if maybe he was part of the foundation of a skyscraper being built in Manhattan. I wouldn't call Siegel himself—he didn't know I was aware he'd been ordered back there. So I called Mickey Cohen. I couldn't reach him, which wasn't unusual, but he got back to me within the hour.

"You're sure as hell nosy, ain't you, Scribbler? But yeah, Bugsy's back. Brought the wife and kids with him. I hear Lansky told him to, on orders from Luciano himself. Wants Bugs to clean up his image out here." Mickey laughed. "This'll play hell with his shack-up with Ginny Hill."

"Anything else happen back there?" I asked.

"You better keep all this to yourself, Scribbler."

"I will, Mick, scout's honor."

"Okay then, Lansky read him the riot act about all the dough he poured into the Flamingo. Dough he didn't have. He was told to pay it back or else. I also hear the New York boys might take over that casino and run it themselves. Why the hell am I telling you all this? Mum's the word, Jake, and I mean it . . . Look, I gotta go. See you in church, kid."

Cohen was Lansky's key man in L.A. His job was to keep an eye on Dragna and Siegel, so what he'd said must have been right. I sure wanted to write this, but I never double-crossed a source. Besides, the Unholy Trinity was out of business.

That evening after work our unsacred trio met with Johnny Campbell and Aggie Underwood in the elegant old bar at the Biltmore. Perched just across the street from Pershing Square, the stately Biltmore was *the* hotel in downtown L.A. Darn nice of our editors to set up this little celebration.

Johnny ordered champagne and we toasted the success of our campaign. We hadn't cleaned up the city or ended bureaucratic corruption—we knew that was impossible—but we'd put quite a few satisfying dents in L.A.'s underworld.

"We did some good, no doubt about it," Johnny said. As we nibbled on appetizers, we told the usual newspaper tales, gossiped about this reporter and that columnist, told a lot of jokes. Aggie's were as coarse as any of mine or Johnny's.

At one point, I gave Janicek a little nod when I got up to visit the men's room. When he joined me I told him about the barracks at El Segundo and that I'd like him to go there with me. Marko, who had a great sense of adventure, said sure, count him in.

Valerie and I had asked Dave Honeycutt to have Ilse in from their movie date by ten. Later, I heard the car pull up in front of our house twenty minutes ahead of time. I went to the window and saw Ilse jump out, slam the door, and stalk up the walk. I opened the door and she slumped into my arms.

"The date wasn't so good, *Liebchen*?"

Ilse leaned back from my close hug, but my arms were still around her. I saw a tear or two. "What is it?" Valerie said from behind us.

"The movie was fine, but at first Dave seemed to be—I don't know—less friendly. Then, when we had an ice cream soda afterward, he said he did not like me having lunch with Aaron Epstein."

"Why ever not?" Valerie asked.

"Because he said Aaron was a 'kike.' I was stunned, *Muti*. I had not heard that word since I was in the *Bund Deutscher Maedel*. I asked if he was serious and he said yes he was. 'My father says we do not associate with that kind,' Dave said. I told him . . ." Ilse let that sentence die and began to sob. I led her to the sofa and sat beside her. Valerie fetched a glass of milk and sat on the other side of her.

Ilse took a drink of milk, put the glass down on our maple coffee table and said, "I told him his father was foolish, that Jewish people are as good as anyone else. He said do not insult his father and that he should take me home right then. I told him, 'Yes, you should.' "

I was about to say some consoling words, but Valerie was quicker. "You mustn't worry about this at all, dear. You've learned a lesson, a painful lesson, that bigotry exists here too. Not as much as in Europe perhaps, but it's here as well. Fortunately, though, it's not as prevalent in California as in the Southern states. You'll find many boys here who are open-minded on these things, I'm sure of it."

"So am I," I said. "Just forget about Dave and try to put this behind you."

Ilse slumped against me and managed a little smile. She reached over and grasped Valerie's hand. "Do not worry," she said, "Dave is behind me."

In bed that night I told Valerie that Ilse was strong enough to get over this bump in the road and . . .

"Get along fine," Valerie agreed, finishing my sentence.

In the morning, trying to shove aside bad thoughts about Dave Honeycutt, I was driving along Rosecrans Avenue. Tom Doyle sat beside me. Marko Janicek was in back; Doyle had been getting acquainted with him.

"Weaver tells me you were with the Yank Rangers on D-Day."

"Yeah, we're the guys who scrambled up rope ladders under fire at Pont du Hoc. We were fuckin' crazy."

"Bloody brave is what I would call it. I was at Sword Beach on D-Day plus three. Was not even fired upon. What weapon have you today?"

"My army .45."

"Excellent handgun. Much stopping power. I am carrying my favorite little Beretta Modello." Doyle pulled it from a pocket in his windbreaker, reached back across the seat, and showed it to Marko.

Just as we approached the army barracks, we saw a black

Chevy pulling away. That ended the handgun talk. It looked like the same car that had picked up Gretchen in front of my place on Christmas day.

The car was too far away to make out the two people who were in it, but I assumed they were Gretchen and Eichel. I saw no sign of a '38 Ford that would be Schäfer's. I thought maybe I should have followed them, but Doyle said, "Let's have a look inside." I waited till the car was well out of sight, then parked behind the trees as I'd done the day before.

"Be careful, fellas," I said. "Schäfer could be in there." Bringing grim nods from Marko and Doyle.

We slipped through the hole in the fence and scurried warily up to the second building. By hand single, Doyle indicated for Marko and me to stand on each side of the door, guns drawn, while he opened it.

That proved unnecessary. With a pistol in his right hand and flashlight in the left, Doyle slipped in. Half a minute later, he called out, "Come on in, gents, no one's at home."

I tucked my Luger beneath my belt, got out my flashlight and entered, wondering where Schäfer might be. The three of us began searching the place, and made a more thorough job of it than I had the day before.

Things looked pretty much the same, though with a few differences. Paper plates on the card table held the debris of a spartan breakfast. Cardboard cups of coffee, mostly empty, lipstick on the rim of one of them. The remains of doughnuts, pancakes and muffins. A half-empty five-gallon glass jug of water on the floor nearby.

Marko went down to inspect the latrine at the end of the aisle, while I checked more bunks. Only three of them bore mattresses, blankets and pillows, same as before.

"The shower down here was used this morning," Marko called out. I was surprised the water hadn't been shut off. "Some towels and soap in here. Razors and toothbrushes too," he added.

"Scoutmaster" meanwhile had been rummaging around with his torch—as he called it—near the front bunks. He picked up a satchel from beside the second bunk, popped it open, and shone his light in. "Well, well," he said. "Have a look at this."

I came over and peered in. Surgical tools! Strapped down in two neat rows. Scalpels, retractors, forceps, and even a small stainless-steel hand saw. Several pairs of cotton gloves.

Holy Christ. I hugged myself against the wave of dread that engulfed me. Schäfer was Otto Woolf! There was no doubt now. He'd been hiding in plain sight all this time, coaching Ilse's soccer team. More than ever, I feared for my daughter's life.

"We've found Otto Woolf." Doyle saying what I already knew.

"His hideout, at least." I guessed that Woolf figured Gretchen and Eichel couldn't possibly stay in his little motel room, so they'd found this out-of-the-way place. What were they planning when they were all together in here? And why in hell was Gretchen mixed up in this? She had hated this Woolf guy, had wanted to bring him to justice.

After further searching uncovered nothing more of interest, Doyle said, "Let's go back to your motorcar, wait awhile, and see if Woolf returns."

As I slipped through the hole in the fence, I stumbled on a rock and fell to one knee. Maybe that's why the gunshot missed me.

TWENTY-NINE

Hearing the sharp crack of the shot and feeling the pneumatic pulse of a bullet flashing past my ear, I flattened myself on the rough dirt and reached for my Luger.

Bam. Bam. Kneeling nearby, Marko Janicek was firing his .45 at a sedan that was squealing away, leaving behind a cloud of scorched rubber. I caught a glimpse of a rifle barrel being pulled into an open rear window. At this distance I couldn't tell what make of car it was, but it was maroon. *Maroon!*

"Jake, you okay? Marko said. "Are you hit? Some bastard tried to kill you."

"Nah, I'm okay. Scraped my hand a little when I hit the dirt is all." I realized I was beginning to shake as I got to my feet. I'd last been shot at two years ago in Germany. It still wasn't any fun. I tucked the Luger under my belt.

"I think I hit that car once," Marko said. "There's probably a bullet hole in the trunk."

"Bloody good reactions there, Janicek," Tom Doyle said. "The shell casing would have fallen inside the car, but perhaps we can find the bullet." He was already studying the ground beyond where I'd fallen.

The three of us searched for about ten minutes, during which Marko said the weapon had looked like a sniper rifle, maybe a .30-30. A little blood oozed from a small abrasion on my left hand, so I wrapped my handkerchief around it.

Just as we were about to give up, Doyle crouched down beside a dusty western sycamore about forty feet from where I'd fallen.

He began digging at a spot on the tree trunk about two feet above the ground. His pocket knife looked like one of those many-bladed knives the Swiss had. Before long he'd extracted a misshapen lead bullet. "Look here," he said, holding it up to the light.

"This appears to be about .30 caliber," Doyle said. "I'll take it to the FBI, although that likely will do us no good, not unless we can find that rifle."

Meanwhile, I wondered what had just happened. Had Siegel's boys followed us out here? I hadn't seen a car tailing us, but then I'd had no reason to be looking for one.

"Did that look like a Buick Super to either of you?" I asked.

Doyle shook his head, but Marko said, "Maybe. Couldn't really tell. A four-door sedan, anyway. Wine-colored."

"Maroon?" I said.

"Yeah, you could say maroon. Ah, I see where you're going." Marko knew about the car that tried to force Valerie down a canyon, but Doyle didn't, so I filled him in on that.

"If you indeed hit the car, Janicek," he said, "Siegel would not want it back at his place."

I told him that a fender had been repaired at Jack Dragna's after the attempt on Valerie, "but I doubt Bugsy would patch it up again. He'll probably have it dumped out in the Mojave somewhere."

"Most likely," Doyle said, "especially so if it does have a bullet hole . . . Please take me back to my lodgings, Weaver, if you will. I have a car there. I will take this bullet to the FBI."

"And then what?" I asked. "What's our next move?"

"The FBI will come here. When they learn that Germans have been squatting in these barracks and that a homicide was attempted, they are sure to come and make an inspection. I will also inform the Pope of this development."

I didn't like the idea of Gretchen being pulled in by the FBI for questioning—that is, if they found her—but I had no idea how to prevent it. This was probably out of my hands now.

* * *

When I reached the paper an hour later, I had a message from Robert Oppenheimer, asking me to call as soon as possible.

"Mr. Weaver," the scientist said when I reached him, "something most alarming happened here at Caltech this morning. As I was approaching my office, I caught a man and woman there fussing with the lock. It looked as if they were trying to pick it with some kind of little wire tool. 'What the devil do you think you're doing?' I demanded.

"The man started to say something but the woman grabbed his arm and pulled him away." Gretchen and Eichel, I was thinking. "They hurried down the hall to the rear exit. I followed, shouting for them to stop. They ran out into the parking lot, got into a car and drove off."

"Was it a black Chevy?"

"Yes, I think that it was. How did you know?"

I told him I believed they were the same two who'd come and listened to his lecture and that I'd seen them in a car like that.

"In that case, the Pasadena police will want to speak with you. I reported this and they came out and dusted for fingerprints and so forth. Please call them. A detective Robertson."

I thanked Oppenheimer and said I would. Ha, like hell I would. I didn't need to get involved with the Pasadena PD.

The little scrape on my hand had stopped bleeding. I went to the men's room, washed it, then got a bandage from a first-aid kit the women in Society had, and put it on. "What happened, Jakey boy? Get your hand caught in the cookie jar again?" one of them teased. I just grinned noncommittally, got a cup of coffee from the pot they always had going, and went back to my desk.

I leaned back in my chair, put my feet up on the desk and thought, Gretchen old girl, you've really got yourself in some serious shit, haven't you? And Bugsy Siegel, you bastard, I've sure as hell got to do something about you. My anger at that man was like a blowtorch burning my insides.

Since our anti-crime campaign was over and I was back to being our military writer, I decided to try and kill two birds with the same stone. I'd call the army's Western Defense Command's public information guy, ask about force reductions in this area, and write a story on that. I'd also bring up base closures and ask what they had in mind for those barracks at El Segundo. I wouldn't volunteer that one of them was not exactly unoccupied. That'd drag me into some government questioning I didn't need. Let the FBI tell them about that.

I pulled my feet down, slid my chair closer, and reached for the phone. It rang the second I touched it.

It was Mickey Cohen. "Hey Scribbler, we haven't talked in awhile. Anything interesting going on? You ever find that German broad of yours? And how the heck are you?"

"At the moment, Mick, I'm a little shook up. Somebody took a shot at me this morning. Just barely missed."

"Tell me about it, Jakester," he said, oddly not sounding very surprised.

I gave him a condensed version, omitting the location. He didn't need to know about the army barracks. I told him it was a rifle shot, fired from a maroon sedan, a sedan I suspected was Siegel's.

"Did they stick around and shoot some more?"

"No, 'cause a guy I was with returned fire. He may have hit that car. It hauled out of there in a damn hurry."

"Who was your shooter?"

I told him about Marko.

"Bugs is damn sore at you, Scribbler, getting his money mess out there in the open like you did. Yeah, it was probably his boys.

I'm gonna tell Lansky about this."

"I wish you wouldn't, Mick."

"Nah, he needs to know, pal."

"No, Mick, please—"

But he'd hung up. A dial tone rang in my ears like exclamation points. *Well, shit.*

THIRTY

That evening as I drove home along Olympic in early March twilight, the sun was a burnt-orange ball hanging low in a smoky haze Angelinos were calling smog. I lowered my sun visor and got a strong, morose feeling that something was ending, not just this day.

Valerie was already there when I got home. She and Ilse were in the kitchen working on dinner. Ilse was dicing an onion and Valerie was sprinkling curry powder on pieces of chicken arranged in a ceramic baking dish. I interrupted their work for a moment, giving each of them a kiss.

We exchanged a few words about our days at work and school, and I took a head of lettuce from the fridge and began making a salad. It was always a pleasant time for me when the three of us engaged in kitchen teamwork like this. It almost made me forget I'd been the target of a murder attempt that morning. Almost.

I got the feeling, though, that Valerie sensed something. She was seldom fooled by my forced cheerfulness.

Ilse put down her vegetable slicer and went to the front room to change radio stations, *Terry and the Pirates* giving way to some boogie-woogie. Valerie shot me a questioning look and I whispered, "Later."

Later came after about ninety minutes. Our dinner—the chicken had been delicious—was finished, the dishes washed, and Ilse was in her room attending to homework.

Agreeing that we'd had enough Scotch or brandy lately, Valerie and I settled on the sofa with cups of Sanka. I'd kept too much from my life partner the past few weeks so I proceeded to tell her everything: Oppenheimer's call, the barracks, Gretchen's things there, and the gunshot that nearly hit me.

Valerie's cup wobbled in her hand. "My God, Jake! Thank heavens they missed. Listen, all this has just gotten too damn dangerous. For you, for all of us. Let's get out of this creepy town. I can get a defense job in San Francisco or Fort Worth, someplace, and any paper in the country would jump at hiring you."

"Uproot Ilse and put her in a strange school? We can't do that. We can't run away from our problems, Val."

She seemed to look at a thought buried deep in her coffee cup. "No, I suppose not," she said at last.

"I'll handle this, Sweets. Please don't worry about me."

"Don't worry? That's a laugh. How can I possibly not worry? So what are we going to do then?"

"*We* aren't going to do anything. I am!"

"What? Kill Bugsy Siegel?"

"No, I've got a better idea than that." But of course I didn't.

Valerie leaned against me and rested her head on my shoulder. She took my hand in hers.

"You're right, love," she murmured. "I spoke out of turn. Leaving town would give you a sense of running away, quitting, that would dog you for a long time. I understand that. You know, when we first met in that hospital room four years ago," she said, "I knew you were the man for me. Crazy, reckless fool that you were—and still are . . . Okay, Sailor, I'm taking you at your word then. Handle this. Keep us safe."

I had a lot of bad dreams that night. In one of them, Ilse was screaming, "*Vati, Vati*, help me!" I tried to get to her but just couldn't. My feet were struggling in gooey mud, not getting anywhere.

* * *

I tried hard the next day to push Bugsy Siegel and Otto Woolf out of my mind. And that nightmare. I got around to calling the Western Defense Command. I learned the Army Air Force was turning Daugherty Field over to the City of Long Beach, which planned to make it a municipal airport. Same thing for the fighter airfield at Ontario. That growing town in San Bernardino County was happy to have the property. Uncle Sam tried to give the Marine Corps airfield at Miramar to San Diego for one dollar but the city fathers turned it down. Miramar, fourteen miles away, was deemed too remote to be of any use.

Personnel totals were down to thirty percent of their wartime peak. The old barracks at El Segundo? The Army was in negotiations with a developer. Still haggling over price.

I slipped two sheets of paper in my trusty Underwood upright, with a carbon in between, and banged out my story.

At lunchtime, Marko Janicek and I jaywalked over to the Continental for a sandwich and beer. We perched on stools at the bar and chatted about the Barracks Incident, as I'd begun calling it. Billie Holliday coming from the jukebox.

"I kind of enjoyed that," Marko said. "Felt like I was back in action with the Rangers again." Enjoy wasn't a word I would have used. Almost getting shot had scared the shit out of me.

Mel Durslag, the sportswriter, came in and joined us. The conversation turned to baseball. He thought the Angels, a Cubs' farm team, were going to have a good year. Lloyd Christopher would hit a lot of home runs with that ballpark's short fences. "That Negro ballplayer from UCLA, Jackie Robinson, had himself a good year for Brooklyn's Montreal farm club. Damn bold move by the Dodgers. He's about to head off to Florida for spring training. Guy's a fine athlete. I hope he makes the big club."

Horse racing had resumed at Santa Anita, which the Army hadn't needed anymore. Mel said he won twelve bucks at the track yesterday.

* * *

Tom Doyle called that afternoon and said he'd been back to the barracks with the FBI and the L.A. police. They'd found no one there. They'd taken pictures, dusted for fingerprints, all those things police investigators do. Two men were left behind on stakeout. When people showed up they'd be hauled in for questioning.

The satchel of surgical tools wasn't there. Otto Woolf, if that really was Otto Woolf, obviously had returned and taken it with him. The man was on the loose somewhere with all those scalpels and things that cut into human flesh. A sick green dread churned in my stomach.

About an hour later, Gretchen called!

"Gretchen what—"

"Jake, listen." Her voice strained, frantic. "Get to your house. Right now!"

I'd never heard such alarm in Gretchen's voice. Or maybe panic was the word. I had no idea what was going on at my house but it couldn't be good. I got to my car as fast as I could. Ran at least three red lights on my mad dash home. If some cop came up behind me with siren whining and lights flashing, he'd just have to follow me there—I wasn't stopping.

THIRTY-ONE

I found out later what happened.

Ilse had been home from school about half an hour. She was in the front room doing some dusting when she heard and saw the front doorknob slowly turning. It was too early to expect one of her parents. Darn, I should have locked it, she thought with a twinge of alarm. *Vati* always tells me to lock up when I'm home alone. I forgot.

The door opened and there stood Coach Schäfer. "Hello, my dear," he said, an ugly leer pasted on his face. Light from a table lamp reflected on his thick glasses. Cold fear ran in Ilse's veins. She saw a long, silvery knife in his right hand, a length of rope in the left.

"Get out of here," she shouted.

"Oh no, my dear." He kicked the door closed with a foot and started toward her. "You will enjoy this . . . and so will I."

Ilse threw the feather duster at him. It bounced harmlessly off his chest. "Temper, temper, my little lovely."

She backed away and grabbed hold of a crystal vase on an end table. Brandished it like a weapon.

"Do not do something foolish, *Liebchen*," the man said. "Put the vase down." He moved toward her, dropping the rope and flicking the knife back and forth like a sword fighter.

When he drew within two feet of her, Ilse swung the vase with all her might. It shattered on his shoulder, close to the neck. Shards of glass went flying. He yelped in pain. "Little bitch," he snarled in German. *Die Miststück.* Spatters of blood appeared on his shirt collar.

He swung the knife forward in a quick jerking movement, slicing into Ilse's left forearm. A hot surge of pain. More blood. Her blood this time.

The man grabbed at her shoulder. A grip of great strength. This big devil had a hundred pound advantage over the girl. He cut her below the neck this time. The gash not deep, luckily blocked by the clavicle from severing the carotid artery. Ilse knew in her gut that she was about to die—without seeing her father again or being able to say goodbye. For an instant, an image of British bombs exploding all around her in a 1942 air raid flashed in her mind. She hadn't died then and didn't want to now.

A primeval fear welled up, an animal impulse for survival. She kicked out with her foot like driving home a soccer goal. She was too close for the blow to hit the man's groin and the kick struck a shin. He staggered back a step.

Momentarily free of his grasp, Ilse spun about and dashed to her parents' bedroom, trailing blood along the way. Inside, she yanked open the dresser drawer where Valerie kept her revolver. She grabbed the weapon and flipped off the safety, as she'd seen her stepmom do at the gun range.

Gun in hand, Ilse saw this monster stalk into the room, face twisted with madness.

No time to think or consider. She had to kill him. No other choice. She took aim and squeezed the trigger. Nothing happened. She pulled again. Still nothing. Her father had told Valerie never to leave the gun loaded at home.

The man smirked. He moved toward her. Slow, deliberate steps. Had his face been contorted like this—in both anger and anticipation—when he was about to cut on a helpless victim at Buchenwald?

Ilse put the gun on the dresser top and grabbed hold of a small jar of something, cold cream maybe. She started to swing it at him but he parried the movement with his dagger, flicking the container right out of her hand. A crimson thread of blood ran across the tops of her fingers. He reached around and grabbed her by the neck. His right hand raised the knife, ready to strike.

Ilse did the only thing she could think of. She spit in his face. He took a step back, freeing her from his grip. He wiped at his nose and eyeglasses with his free hand. Little spider webs of red veined angry eyes behind the thick lenses.

She kicked his leg again and scrabbled toward the closet, hoping to find something, anything, to defend herself with. She thought about shutting the door, but no, he'd just break it down and she'd be trapped. She considered picking up one of her father's shoes, but then her hand felt something thin and round leaning against the door jamb. It was her *Vati's* golf club, the putter with the missing hand grip.

He was in front of her again, a massive bulk of a man filling most of her vision. A black wall of doom. Her heart pounded in her chest as if trying to escape.

Without conscious thought, acting solely on feral instinct and with what strength she had left, Ilse thrust the club's steel shaft at his belly. It broke the skin and penetrated the man's abdomen. An astonished "oof" escaped his mouth. She pushed harder. His eyes rolled back.

And then Gretchen was there! *How in the world?*

Whang! An iron skillet hammered the top of the man's head. He staggered, his eyeglasses fell. Gretchen swung again. The skillet arced high in the air for a second and smashed down on the back of his skull with a sickening thump, a sound like a pumpkin bursting. The man toppled backward and hit the floor with a thud. Two or three feet of silvery spear stood straight up out of his midsection. At the top of the shaft, the putter's clubface looked for all the world like a little gray flag.

Ilse shuddered like a leaf in the wind. Her mind didn't seem to work.

Another man was in the room. It was Nikolaus Eichel, although Ilse didn't know that. "You've killed him," he said, gazing down on the limp form.

Gretchen tossed the frying pan on the bed and took Ilse in her arms and hugged her tightly, never mind the blood soiling her blouse. She began stroking Ilse's hair. "It is okay, Ilse," she said. "You will be all right now—but let us hurry and find some tape and bandages."

Nikolaus Eichel bent over the corpse of Otto Woolf. Eyes as unmoving as stone stared at the ceiling. Two feet away lay a bloody dagger with diamonds sparkling on its hilt.

When I got home, two squad cars and an ambulance were there, lights flashing like neon on the Sunset Strip. I skidded to a screeching stop in the driveway, killed the engine and yanked on the hand brake. A cop confronted me the second I hopped out and wanted to know who the hell I was, buddy. This is my house. I live here. Okay then, go on in.

The front lawns of the nearby houses were filled with gawking neighbors, chattering animatedly. One guy gave me a wave which I didn't return.

Inside, a plainclothes man, notebook in hand, was talking with Gretchen and Eichel. He sat on a chair facing the sofa where the two of them sat.

Gretchen, her face ashen, her blouse spattered with little flowers of blood, said, "She's in there, Jake," and nodded toward Ilse's bedroom.

"Whoa!" the plainclothes said. "Who are you?"

"Her dad," I shouted as I dashed to Ilse's room, almost outrunning his superfluous "Okay then, go and see your daughter."

As I passed the open door to the master bedroom I saw two cops in there, one with a camera. I rushed on into Ilse's room. She lay in bed, bandaged on neck, arm and hand, looking as pale as snow. A nurse and a man I assumed to be a doctor were with her.

Ilse turned her head toward me with wide but lifeless eyes and muttered, "Oh, *Vati*." I knelt and put a hand to her cheek. "Please do not worry," this brave girl of mine said. "It is all right." Her face wore a haunted look and tears dampened her cheek.

I still didn't know what the hell had happened here, but a lump the size of an English muffin had my throat.

The presumed doctor said, "You are the father?" At my nod, he said, "Your girl has a rather serious laceration on one arm and lesser cuts on her neck and hand. She was cut multiple times with a knife." Now I knew Otto Woolf had been here. Ice seemed to form in my veins. "The arm required fifteen stitches," the man went on. "We have cleaned the wounds and I doubt there is danger of infection. With rest and sleep she should be fine. I have sedated her. I would like to hospitalize her overnight as a precaution."

"No," Ilse said drowsily. "I want to be here with you and *Muti*."

I heard movement beyond the door, turned my head and saw two cops carrying a body bag from my bedroom.

"Is that—"

"It is the man who tried to kill your daughter," the doctor said. "He has expired."

"Expired?" Some choice of words. "How?"

"There was quite a struggle. It is a little difficult to piece all this together. The coroner will be able to tell us more."

I touched Ilse's cheek again, bent down and kissed her forehead. "Oh, Ilse," is all I could manage to get out. She clutched my hand—hard, desperately—and murmured, "It is all right, *Vati*. Do not worry about me."

I smiled, turned and said, "No hospital, doc. She needs her

mom and me tonight, and we need her too."

The plainclothes stuck his head in the door and said, "May I see you out here, Mr. Weaver?"

I let go of Ilse's hand and said, "Don't worry, *Liebchen*, I'm not going anywhere. I'll be right back."

In the front room, the plainclothes said, "I'm Detective Wannamaker, sir. The deceased intruder we just took away broke in here and attempted to kill your daughter. She fought him off, as did Miss Siedler here. We've taken the statements of these two. Looks like a clear case of self defense."

Tom Doyle and a man in a gray suit came in the front door just then. I recognized him as FBI Special Agent Warren Grimsby, with whom I'd briefly worked back in '42. This was a break— we'd got along well and he wasn't likely to play tough cop with me. He showed Wannamaker his badge and said, "This case will be ours now, officer. Fill us in."

Wannamaker scowled but complied.

During the next ten minutes I learned that Woolf had attacked Ilse with a long dagger and that she'd speared him with the shaft of my golf club. That may or may not have been fatal but Gretchen had clobbered his skull twice with an iron skillet that scrambled his brains and clinched the deal.

Gretchen gazed at me with a barren look, her face drawn and gray with exhaustion. I gave her a smile and went back to Ilse's room, where I found her asleep. The doctor was closing his satchel. He handed me two jars of pills. "This one contains sleeping tablets and this other is a pain-killer. I will leave her here tonight then. As you suggest, that will be better for her emotionally. One sleeping pill tonight, and the pain pills as needed. The stitches will remain in place for several days. She should be seen again tomorrow. I'm on contract with the police. I can come back or you could have your own physician see her."

"You come back," I said. "You're familiar with her injuries."

"All right, I'll see you tomorrow then." He and the nurse left.

My god, what Ilse had been through. My knees were like Jell-O, barely held me up.

In the front room the L.A. cops were leaving too. "Let me know if you want our pictures or anything else from us," the detective told agent Grimsby.

I caught up with Wannamaker on the porch. I wanted to keep this out of the papers if possible. "Detective, could I ask you not to put this on the blotter?"

"Don't see why not," he said. "It's J. Edgar's case now, not ours." Sounding offended. "No need for me to report it." I was relieved. I could get our police reporter to keep this quiet, but not the *Times* and *Mirror* guys, who checked the cops' blotter every day.

Back inside, Doyle, Grimsby and I sat in chairs around Gretchen and Eichel. They told us their tale.

THIRTY-TWO

Gretchen said she'd teamed up with Eichel because she'd come to trust him, and shared his hope that Germany could recover and grow strong again. She was devoted less to Britain and the MI-6 than to Germany, the Germany that should be, the Germany of music and literature, not the one that existed under Hitler. She had decided that the search for the Buchenwald Butcher would be her last service to MI-6.

"I did not agree with Nikolaus here that obtaining the atomic bomb was important for *Deutschland*, though." The man spread his hands in embarrassment and gave her a wan smile. "Becoming Europe's good neighbor instead of its bully is much more essential. But his fervor was genuine, *is* genuine, and it is people like him who will rebuild our Fatherland."

The look Gretchen and Eichel briefly exchanged made me think there might be more between them than this. She may have found a bedmate after all. If so, good for her. *Anyone but me.*

"What about Woolf?" Doyle asked.

"I was reasonably sure it was him when I spoke with him at that soccer game. You remember, Jake?"

I nodded.

"I had to get closer to him to be certain. When I was convinced he was indeed Woolf—hold on, I must back up. I became convinced, that is, when he began talking about young girls he had seen, especially some of the soccer girls. Strange, almost lascivious talk it was. And then I knew this was the misogynist who killed girls and women. I knew I must stick close to him in order to protect Ilse. Under no circumstances would I allow him to harm our precious Ilse."

Grimsby looked puzzled so I told him Ilse was my daughter and one of the soccer players this guy had coached.

"Why'd you tag along with that monster for several days?" I asked Gretchen. "Why didn't you arrest him as soon as you knew who he was? Or just kill him for that matter?"

"For once in my life, Jake, I lost confidence. I was not sure I could manage to detain him. He was quick, clever and much stronger than I. And wary. He never seemed to sleep."

I wanted to say in that case you should have just shot him, but didn't. I'd probably never figure out women's thought processes.

In defense of his fellow agent, Doyle said, "He was wanted alive or dead, but alive was preferred. For the Nuremberg war crimes trials, if possible. The Pope was clear on that."

"I am sorry," Gretchen said, "that I waited almost too long. Thank goodness Nikolaus and I arrived in time." Said with another kind glance at Eichel.

So Gretchen's motivation for hooking up with these men had been to shield Ilse. I was damned grateful. And impressed. This woman had just killed, or helped to kill, Otto Woolf. I was also impressed that she'd held herself together long enough to tell us all this.

Now she seemed talked out. Tears formed and she slumped against the couch's back rest, looking spent. Who wouldn't?

Nikolaus Eichel took over. He touched Gretchen's hand gently, pulled it away, and said, "I suppose I did go too far in trying to obtain some of *Herr* Oppenheimer's files. I regret that now. I was foolish. I should have listened to Gretchen. There are better ways for *Deutschland* to recover."

He was probably in the clear on his attempted burglary. The Pasadena police wouldn't have his fingerprints on file.

Eichel cleared his throat. "Today now, Woolf was acting more worked up than usual, more—perhaps keen is the word—to get out and do something. There was a queer, frightening light in his eyes. When he left the barracks, he took his kit of surgical tools. Gretchen insisted that we follow him. And so we did, but it was a vain effort. We lost sight of his car in the heavy traffic. At that point, Gretchen said we must go to your home, here we would find him. I do not know how she knew, but her instinct proved to be a correct one. When we reached here and saw Woolf's auto at the curb, she rushed in. I followed, of course. You know what happened next."

Gretchen, her eyes vacant, shook her head, maybe trying not to re-live all that happened next. I knew from experience, though, that she would re-live all that for the rest of her days.

The door opened at that moment and Valerie came in, looking shocked to see Gretchen, and wondering who these strange men were. "What's going on?" she demanded, her eyes wide as silver dollars.

I jumped to my feet, rushed over and hugged her. "We've had some trouble but everything is all right now."

Over the next emotion-charged ten minutes, Valerie learned it all. She was introduced to Tom Doyle, agent Grimsby and Eichel, went in to see her still-sleeping stepdaughter, and looked in dismay at the mess in the master bedroom.

Grimsby told her the cops had completed their crime-scene investigation and she needn't worry about touching things.

When she'd absorbed all that, Valerie said, "Who needs a stiff drink, besides me?" Doyle and Grimsby declined.

I told Valerie to relax, that I'd fetch the drinks. When I came back after pouring four strong Scotches, not much water, I found Valerie sitting beside Gretchen, an arm around her, saying, "How can we ever thank you? You saved our dear, sweet girl."

I handed drinks to Valerie and Gretchen, then one to Eichel. I raised my own glass and said, "Here's to strong, courageous people." I wished I could have come up with something more fitting, more poetic, but it was the best I could do at that moment.

Before he took his leave, agent Grimsby said, "I doubt there will be complications. This was self defense, a justifiable action. We may have more questions for you"—looking at Gretchen—"in a day or two but nothing more at the moment."

Doyle said he would report all this to the Pope.

"The Pope?" Valerie wondered. "Oh yeah, you mean that colonel."

"Tell the colonel he will receive my resignation shortly," Gretchen told Doyle, who was standing by the door, ready to leave. "I will be volunteering with the Social Democrats from now on."

A few minutes later, she and Eichel also left. Going where I didn't know, nor did I ask. The barracks? A hotel? Valerie had hugged the soon-to-be ex-spy and uttered more words of thanks.

I wondered if Woolf had contacted Siegel and tried to make a deal with that valuable stolen dagger. He'd had Bugsy's private phone number.

Understandably, Valerie looked shaken and overwhelmed. "It'll be okay, hon, it's over," I said, taking her hand and leading her to Ilse's room, where we found our girl awake. Valerie drew a chair up to the bed, kissed her and held her hand. As she'd done with me, Ilse said she'd be all right and you mustn't worry, *Muti*. My precious girl was being brave but I knew a lot of tough days and nights lay in wait for her.

We talked for a few minutes, during which I brought Ilse some water. We spoke mostly of how Ilse was feeling, did she have much pain, and so on. Valerie was too wise to ask for details of her terrible struggle with Woolf.

After Ilse fell back to sleep, we began the arduous task of cleaning up. I fetched a dustpan and scooped up the remains of the shattered vase. With tears in her eyes, Valerie took warm water, bleach, and ammonia and began scrubbing at the trails of blood.

"How can we possibly sleep here tonight?" she said.

"If there are bad spirits in this room," I answered, "the way to rid ourselves of them is to *live*, to drive them out by filling this place with normalcy. We could use the guest room, but we'll have to sleep in here sometime, so we'd just as well start tonight."

I took our iron skillet from the bed and returned it to the kitchen, thinking that it was now a murder weapon. No, not murder, I corrected myself. Justifiable homicide. I wondered if we would ever use it again. I told myself that in the days ahead I'd have that psychologist see Ilse for some trauma counseling.

THIRTY-THREE

When I finally got around to checking the mailbox, Woolf's '38 Ford was being hooked up to a tow truck. I didn't know if the cops or the feds had sent it. Their business, not mine.

The day's mail included a letter from Uncle Dieter. He was coming to the States in the spring and would like to see us. That'd be swell. Ilse had known her Great Uncle Dieter quite well in Berlin. He'd become a surrogate father to her after the suspicious death of her mother Winifred at the hands of the Nazis. Visiting with Dieter would be a big help in her emotional recovery.

While Valerie did some more straightening up in the house, I sat in a chair in Ilse's room, gazing at the courageous girl lying there slipping in and out of slumber. One of my big worries had been lifted. The Buchenwald Butcher was no more. But another concern remained: Bugsy Siegel, the bastard who wanted me dead. That realization weighed on me like an anvil.

What could I possibly do?

Around nine o'clock I gave Ilse a pain pill and a sleeping tablet. Though not a complainer, she did admit that the gash on her arm "hurt a little." I knew that meant "a lot." Valerie and I kissed her and assured her we'd be close at hand if she needed us during the night.

I caught myself wondering if Nikolaus Eichel was getting it on with Gretchen somewhere right about then. Why did that thought make me a little resentful? That was ridiculous, but there it was.

* * *

The next day was Saturday so Ilse had no school and Valerie and I were home from work. The doctor came by and took Ilse's temperature and blood pressure, and changed the dressing on her arm.

"Considering everything, you're doing remarkably well," he said. "You can get up and take little walks around the house when you feel up to it, but don't overdo. Spend most of your time in bed. You should miss school for a couple of days but might be able to return by Wednesday."

Detective Wannamaker called that afternoon and said the coroner had found that the crushing blows to the head caused fatal cerebral hemorrhaging. The golf shaft had penetrated Woolf's abdominal aorta but with surgery that would have been survivable.

My voice must have sounded a little off. "Are you okay?" he asked. I was kind of choked up. My girl was not a killer.

I was happy to share that finding with Ilse and Valerie.

In her powder-blue pajamas, Ilse lay reclined on the sofa, her eyes closed, listening to the radio. Her bandaged left arm was splayed across her chest, the right arm dangling to the floor. On the radio Nat King Cole was singing "It's Only a Paper Moon."

Ilse's eyelids rose sluggishly and she muttered, "That is too bad. I wish that I had killed him."

"No you don't," I said. "You mustn't think like that. Just be glad he's gone, out of our lives forever."

"But he violated our home, *Vati*. He stained it with his evil presence."

"Stains can be washed away, Ilse. There are vicious, abnormal people in the world, people who somehow are just wired to be bad. You've seen some of that. But there are many, many more good people. We'll put all this behind us."

"You and *Muti* are two of the good ones. Two of the very best, and so is *Grossonkel* Dieter. I am glad that he is coming . . . Say, is Nat King Cole a Negro?"

"Yes, but what's it matter?"

"It does not matter at all. I just wondered. He has a nice voice."

"One of the best," I said as I went to the door.

"Where are you going, *Vati*?" Concern in her voice.

"Out to mow the lawn and trim the oleanders, *Liebchen*. I'll be right outside. I could put it off, though."

"No, no, you go ahead." Her eyes closed again. Jo Stafford's voice had replaced Nat Cole's.

When I'd taken the hand mower from the garage and wheeled it onto the lawn, the sun hung low in the sky, throwing long shadows across the street. I reflected again on how fortunate I was to have a daughter with such a special combination of openness and strength.

A Buick Super drove by. My mind's eye saw a scoped rifle poking out from the lowered rear window. I dived and flattened out on the grass. *Not again.*

The car, it was black—not maroon—passed on by. The back window was closed.

Christ, my mind was playing tricks on me. Dirty tricks.

THIRTY-FOUR

I called Ilse's home-room teacher to tell her my daughter would be absent a few days on doctor's orders. She arranged to have some assignments sent over so Ilse wouldn't fall behind.

My girl grew better each day, at least physically. She returned to school on Thursday, six days after the attack. "Everyone kept asking about the dressing on my arm," she said that evening. "I told them I fell off my bicycle. I could not think of a better story."

The gash actually was healing nicely, and our doctor removed the wrapping that weekend.

During that month, I took her to the psychologist for two trauma-counseling sessions. His astuteness and gentle manner seemed to help her a great deal. During one of the visits he asked how I was doing, did I have any more bouts of short-term amnesia?

"I might have had one after a bad moment down at El Segundo recently," I said. "I'm not really sure."

This came as a surprise to Ilse, so on the way home I told her about the odd blackouts I'd had a time or two after some bad experiences, not mentioning that the bad experiences involved my shooting some Germans during the war.

At work I was busy carrying out my military writer duties. President Truman had issued an executive order racially integrating the services. He was sore as hell at the Russians, who'd set up puppet communist governments in East Germany, Poland and other eastern European countries they'd occupied. Truman told them in no uncertain terms to keep hands off Greece and Italy. A relief program for war-torn nations was being drawn up by Secretary of State George Marshall.

Although the Unholy Trinity was out of business, crime and corruption continued on its merry way in Los Angeles, and there was plenty of non-military stuff to write about.

Mickey Cohen survived an assassination attempt, a vicious car bombing, simply because the wind blew his hat off and he'd gone back to get it. Our police reporter wrote the story. Mickey and I got together two days later at Musso & Frank to talk about it.

"I think it was a cop who's been tryin' to shake me down," The Mick told me after drinking off some of his martini. "Hell, I can't pay off the *whole* force. That fucking bomb blew my Caddy to pieces. Tony Flores, poor bastard, was my best driver. Lucky my hat come off. I tell you, Scribbler, I been shot at, knifed, and now bombed. Wonder if I got any of my nine lives left."

"Maybe you're in the wrong line of work, Mickey."

"Hell, I'm too old to change my line of work now. Maybe just a little change, though. Gonna open a haberdashery on Sunset. Next few months. Strictly legit." He finished his martini and signaled for another. "Damn sorry to lose Tony. He was a good man. I sent a bunch of dough over to his wife. Gonna give him a nice service at Forest Lawn."

I didn't tell Mickey, but I was going to write a follow-up about this senseless event.

He asked if I'd like to go to an upcoming exhibition game between the Coast League Angels and the Chicago Cubs at Wrigley Field. I said sure. Phillip Wrigley, the chewing-gum millionaire who owned both teams, had named the Angels' ballpark for himself, same as he'd done in Chicago.

* * *

Valerie'd had some bad moments over all that had happened, but was mostly cheerful, even though Tool Design had been whittled down to just six people. Fortunately she was one of the six.

Ilse was feeling more like herself every day and was doing well in school. Tom Doyle called and asked how she was, darn nice of him. His stay in Los Angeles had been extended. "The Pope wants me to look into one or two more things before I'm recalled," he said. "Some procedural things were involved but we now have a property receipt from the FBI on that dagger, and we'll see that it goes back to its rightful place in Paris."

One day when Valerie got home before me, she greeted me with, "Look here, Jake, we got a postcard from Gretchen in Berlin. She's back in her old townhouse in Schöneberg, in the American Zone. She says there's a lot of damage nearby, but her place is okay." I had vivid memories of that townhouse – maybe *too* vivid.

"Does she mention Nikolaus Eichel?" I asked. "I wonder if they're together."

"No, not a word about Eichel. I was wondering that, too."

I still wanted to know if Otto Woolf had tried to make a deal with Siegel over that bejeweled dagger. I had Bugsy's unlisted number, and had promised my source at Ma Bell I wouldn't call it. But promises are meant to be broken, the old saying goes.

At the office in the morning, I called that Crestwood number. Damn, Bugsy himself answered. I quietly put a finger on disconnect. I waited an hour and a half before trying again.

"Siegel residence," said a voice I thought I recognized, a voice belonging to a pretty young woman who'd brought me coffee back in December.

"Is this Hilda?" I asked.

"Yes, who's calling?"

"Dominic Amato, from Mr. Lanksy's office. I'm in town for a few days. I got a question for you—in strict confidence."

The line went silent for at least ten seconds. "In confidence, Mr. Amato?" she said at last.

"Right kiddo, Lansky wants it that way."

"Well, uh . . . okay, sure then."

"What we wanta know is if a German guy, Otto Woolf, husky, thick glasses, has had any contact with Ben?"

"Awhile back I think that maybe a man like that was here for about half an hour. I served them drinks. They had a normal conversation at first, but then it got kinda heated. Ben said something like no deal, he was asking way too much."

"Too much for *what*, Hilda? What was Woolf trying to peddle?"

"I don't know. I didn't hear the whole conversation. I'm not an eavesdropper." I rather doubted that. "Ben asked if he had it with him, whatever it was. The man said no, he wasn't a fool, just look at this picture. Does that help you, sir?"

"It sure does, Hilda. You're a doll. I'll tell Lansky you were real helpful." Putting a touch of menace on it, I added, "Remember, not a word to Ben about this."

"Of course not, Mr. Amato." Sounding nervous.

Well, Sherlock, I told myself after hanging up, now I know Woolf tried to sell Bugsy that dagger but couldn't make a deal. That's why he still had it when he attacked Ilse. I stashed that away in the old memory bank.

It was a beautiful spring, so that weekend we took a day trip to San Diego to visit the zoo. The three of us trudged all over that sprawling place, seeing lions, polar bears, snakes, exotic birds—you name it—and a trained-seal show.

"This is wonderful, *Vati*," Ilse said when we stopped at the elephant enclosure. "This reminds me of the Berlin Zoo. Do you remember the day we spent there?"

"I sure do, *Liebchen*. We really got to know each other that day." That was shortly after I'd learned she was my daughter. Valerie smiled at us as we reminisced.

Afterward, we strolled through the main part of Balboa Park, admiring the many Spanish Revival buildings. The gals had packed a picnic lunch, so we spread a blanket on the lawn outside the House of Germany. That place reminded me of Sachsen Haus in L.A., and it rekindled memories of all that had happened in the recent months.

Picking up her tuna sandwich, Ilse said, "Guess what? Dave Honeycutt came up to me yesterday. He said he'd been doing a lot of thinking and that he was wrong to say what he did about Aaron Epstein. He said he'd decided that his father's opinion of Jews is all wrong. He asked if I could forgive him. I said yes I could. Then he asked if he could date me again."

"And?" Valerie prompted, her face alight with curiosity.

"I said not right now, that I would have to give that some thought."

I took a bite of apple and said, "Good for you."

"I hope that he was sincere, *Vati*, but he may have said that just so I would date him again. I cannot tell. So I think we should wait awhile. I am also thinking of asking Aaron Epstein and his aunt over for dinner with us. Would that be all right?"

"It certainly would," Valerie said. "That's a very nice idea."

"Thank you, *Muti*. Say, Uncle Dieter is coming soon, isn't he? I cannot wait to see him."

Just south of us a United Airlines DC-4 droned in toward Lindbergh Field, passing by the El Cortez Hotel.

On our drive back on Highway 101 that afternoon, Ilse amused herself reading the Burma-Shave signs. One of the couplets that had us laughing went: *Big mistake . . . many make . . . rely on horn*

. . . instead of brake . . . Burma-Shave.

As we passed through Laguna Beach, I thought about the poker game Marko Janicek had arranged for next week. My first reaction was that I shouldn't go, not at this time, although it had been several weeks since Otto Woolf's invasion of our home. A night out with the boys might do me some good at that.

My sanguine mood was shattered two days later when Cohen and I went to the Cubs-Angels game. While the managers exchanged lineup cards at the plate before the top of the first, Mickey said, "Scribbler, you gotta start bein' real careful again. I had a drink yesterday with Bugsy at the Brown Derby. Never saw the guy so upset. Talked a mile a minute. Lansky called him to New York again and came down on him real hard. Demanded to know where the hell the money was, all that dough he owes 'em. Bugs said he was mad as hell at you for puttin' that in the paper the way you did, and for writin' that he bankrolled Ginny Hill."

That hit me like a brick in the face. I'd hoped that after all this time Siegel might have cooled off some. I thought about Howard Jones's admonition that the best defense is a good offense. Maybe I should act first, do something to Bugsy before he could do something to me. Last thing I wanted was to leave Valerie and Ilse alone in the world.

I had trouble following the ball game.

THIRTY-FIVE

Bugsy beat me to the punch. Literally. I walked to my car after work the next day, a block away on Georgia Street near the trolley-car barns. I'd found a space there with no parking meters.

As I approached, two punks were standing by my car, beefy guys, Mob guys if I'd ever seen any. One of them had scar tissue in his right eyebrow, a sure sign of an ex-boxer. The other wore a watch cap and had gold chains around his neck. Both had blacksmith arms. My gut quivered at the sight of them. No one else was around.

"Hi fellas," I said. "Can I help you?"

The ex-boxer type launched a bolo punch at my midsection. I dodged it and drove a left to his chin, my own boxing days coming back to me. Followed with a right cross to his gut. I'd drawn first blood, but I knew I was overmatched.

From the side the other guy slammed me with a kidney punch that sent an electric shock spinning up my spine. Still, I twisted and hammered a couple of body blows at the first guy. But the kidney puncher grabbed me from behind and locked up my arms. I squirmed and kicked but took punch after punch to chest and stomach. Then a stinging blow to my cheek. A galaxy of stars exploded in my eyes.

"Not the face, not the face," Watch Cap shouted. "Don't mark him up." Now came a rain of blows to my midsection. I was queasy, dizzy.

Finally, they stopped. I bent over and wretched up my lunch

right there on the sidewalk. "The message is stop writin' stuff!" the ex-boxer snarled. I sank to my knees, inches from the puddle of vomit.

They straightened up, the guy I'd hit rubbing at his stomach. At least I'd hurt him some. "Remember the message," Watch Cap said. They stalked off.

I dry-heaved a couple of times, then managed to get to my feet and lean against the car. The trolley barns across the street were spinning around in slow motion. When those buildings finally dropped anchor, I realized these guys had made one mistake. I'd seen one of them before. He was the guy on Siegel's porch when I'd left his house that day. The one who'd given me his version of the evil eye. I now knew for certain this dirty work had been Siegel's.

Their warning had the opposite effect of what was intended. Yeah, I'll write something, something that'll burn Siegel's ass.

I ached all over as I drove home. Slowly, carefully. Each breath caused a hurt inside my chest. My ribs ached. I hoped none of them were broken, but they sure were sore. One knee on my slacks was torn. I checked my face in the rear-view mirror and saw a purple and black bruise blossoming on my right cheek. Little rivers of blood seemed to fill that eye.

When I dragged in, Valerie and Ilse were shocked at my appearance. "Oh, my Lord, what on earth happened?" Valerie asked, rushing toward me.

"A couple of Siegel's punks worked me over. Told me to stop writing."

"But you *have* stopped," Valerie said. "Those bastards!"

"These guys don't know the Unholy Trinity's out of business, Val. We didn't publicize that, just let it go away quietly. Hell, the only story I've written about mobsters lately was the follow-up I did on Cohen's car bombing."

Ilse got a cold, wet cloth and held it to my cheek and Valerie brought me a strong drink. "How do you know these were Siegel's men?" she asked.

"Because I'd seen one of them at Bugsy's house when I was there. Guess he thought I wouldn't remember that." I took a gulp of Scotch. Then another.

"*Vater*, I want to take a baseball bat," Ilse said, "and pay a visit to Mr. Siegel."

"Thanks, *Liebchen*, I appreciate the thought, but you'd best leave Mr. Siegel to me."

"Let's call the doctor," Valerie said.

"Nah, another one of these"—raising my glass—"and a hot bath will do the trick."

But of course they didn't. I had trouble sleeping that night, just couldn't find a comfortable way to lie. I hurt in places I hadn't known I had.

It was during that tossing and turning that I reached my decision. The story I'd write would say Bugsy was connected to a vicious Nazi criminal who'd been on the lam in the U.S., a sadistic murderer known as the Buchenwald Butcher. This Nazi had Siegel's unlisted number in his possession, and they had met. The article would speculate that Siegel was sheltering this murderer. I didn't like writing such flimsy stories, but this was a special case. This piece would finish the bastard. Hearst would love it. And I would have a soaring sense of satisfaction.

Two days later I was almost back to normal. The bruise on my face had lightened from reddish black to a pallid yellow, and I felt only the occasional stab of pain in my ribcage. I'd written most of my story but we hadn't printed it yet.

Before breakfast I went out and picked up the morning *Examiner* from the front steps. A black headline shouted **GANGLAND SLAYING.** The subhead read **Racketeer Bugsy Siegel Gunned Down**. I was stunned, had to read it twice. Bugsy dead?

I took the paper in to the kitchen table. A gruesome photo filled three columns, Bugsy sprawled on a sofa—the very sofa I'd sat on a few months before—his face and torso splattered with blood. One shot had punched a hole next to his left eye. He wore a tie and a beige or tan suit, now stained by ribbons of his lifeblood.

The story included such words as "unknown assailant" and "police manhunt."

Where had I been last night? Suddenly all that was a litte foggy. I recalled the brief blackout I'd had after shooting that Nazi infiltrator during the Battle of the Bulge, and how the psychologist later told me that kind of reaction was not uncommon. I put a hand to my face and kneaded my forehead. Was my mind playing tricks again? Could I possibly have . . . No, now I remembered where I'd been.

The phone on the wall rang. I grabbed the handset fast because Valerie and Ilse were still sleeping. It was Mickey Cohen. The Mick was sure up early today.

"Did you punch Bugsy's ticket last night?" he said.

THIRTY-SIX

Valerie came in moments later, sleepy-eyed, and said, "Who was that?"

"Nobody," I said.

"Nobody? Is nobody named Mickey? I heard you say Mickey."

"Okay Val, it was Mickey Cohen. He'd just seen this too," I said, gesturing at the front page of the paper.

She looked and gasped, "Oh, my Lord." She put a hand to her throat. Slipped unsteadily into a chair beside me and began to read, making little clucking noises with her tongue.

"Where were you last night?" she asked after a long silence. I'd been playing poker with Marko Janicek, Shaker the bartender, and two other guys. "At that card game like I told you. You surprise me, Val."

"Are you positive?"

"Oh, come on, babe, surely you don't think . . . look, you can ask Marko if you want."

"No, of course not, I believe you. I'm ashamed I ever said that. I know this anti-crime thing's been tough on you, so many brushes with bad people. You held a grudge against this hoodlum, a very justified grudge. I just thought—"

"That's okay," I said, though I was disappointed. I leaned close and kissed her cheek. "I've never killed anyone," I lied, "and I'm sure not going to start now."

"Forgive me, Jake, please. Would it make you feel better if I told you I wanted to kill Siegel myself? I'll never get that near collision on La Cienega out of my mind. Sometimes in my sleep I see that big car slamming into me . . . Well then, Mister I'm Not a Murderer, who do you suppose did this?"

"The New York Mob, most likely. He'd become a real loose cannon, and Lansky and Genovese were mad at him, his Las Vegas fiasco, big debts, all that. Other possibilities come to mind, though. It might've been Jack Dragna. Those guys hated each other, had a real turf war going on. Who knows? It might even have been Bugsy's wife. She had to know about him screwing the shorts off Virginia Hill."

I even wondered if that Hilda babe who'd poured coffee for me had done it. Maybe she'd been a plant put there by Lansky.

Speaking of coffee, I got up to make some. While I scooped some Maxwell House out of the can, I relived Cohen's call. I'd told him, "Hell no, I didn't kill him, but I bet you have a pretty good idea who did."

"Don't even ask," he'd said, then changed the subject. "When you told me Siegel's boys took a shot at you at El Segundo awhile back I already knew it."

No wonder he hadn't sounded surprised when I'd told him about that. "How?" I asked. "You have that car followed?"

"Yup. Lansky told me to keep a close eye on him."

"You have his place staked out last night then?"

"We called it off at ten. You or somebody came by later. Bugs got plugged around midnight, the cops say."

"Damn it, Mick, it wasn't me!"

Ilse came in at that moment, ending my little flashback. "Shall I make the eggs?" she said.

"No dear," Valerie replied, "you just sit here and relax. It's my turn to do breakfast."

"Dieter comes tomorrow, doesn't he?" Ilse asked. "May I come to the station with you to meet him?"

"I don't see why not," I said. "His train's due to arrive at three-thirty. We can go right after school."

As Valerie cracked eggs and dropped them into a hot skillet—no, not *that* skillet, a brand new one—Ilse said, "Why are you both so quiet? Usually you are chatty in the morning. Well, I will read the funnies in peace then." I didn't stop her as she turned over the paper. She'd find out soon enough.

Ilse visibly shook on seeing the big headline and the bloody picture. "*Mein Gott,*" she uttered, then said nothing more for almost a full minute. "He was a bad man," she said at last. "His criminal enemies did this, didn't they? I am glad it was not you, *Vati.*"

I wanted to say at least someone around here believes in me, but didn't. Valerie shot me a sheepish, apologetic look.

"I'm glad it wasn't me too," I said, "though I can't say I'm sorry. Bugsy Siegel was evil through and through."

Ilse gave me a smile that spoke volumes, and turned pages till she found the comics. "Let us see what Li'l Abner and Pappy Yokum are doing today in Dogpatch."

"Who's ready for some scrambled eggs?" Valerie asked.

I remembered that the card game had broken up at 10:30. I'd come straight home after the game, hadn't I? My alibi for midnight was Valerie. I was in bed with her then. Wasn't I?

I told myself to tear up that story about Woolf being connected to Bugsy when I got to the office. The man was dead.

After breakfast I went to the crawl space above the closet and took down my Luger. Checked it closely. No smell or residue of gunpowder, not that I could tell. It hadn't been fired recently, not since that day at the gun range. So I hoped.

THIRTY-SEVEN

This sudden murder of Bugsy Siegel had me off my feed. I thought about calling in sick, but that wasn't my style, so I forced myself to go to the office, where I found the newsroom crackling with activity. Aggie was busy giving out assignments, and a couple of extra men were put on rewrite. We'd have lots of follow-up stories that afternoon.

Our police reporter was the lead guy and would write the main story. Marko Janicek, Dick Lafferty and Richie Millsap would produce sidebars covering various angles and theories.

"How about you, Jake?" Aggie asked. "What would you like to take on?"

"Nothing," I said. "It's in good hands with Richie and these guys. I've got some military calls to make," I dissembled. Normally I'd be like a racehorse jittering eagerly for the starting bell. The truth was, though, I was a little shook up. I'd been too close to these mobsters—to all of this—for too long.

She shrugged, gave me a hard look, said, "Well, this is a first," and turned back to Lafferty.

I went through the motions, trying to shut out the big-story hubbub buzzing all around me. Made a few phone calls, jotted down some notes.

Shortly before lunch, Detective Wannamaker, the cop who'd been at our place after Otto Woolf was killed, showed up. I wasn't surprised. The police would be out in force today, looking into everything they could think of.

He said, "Hello, Weaver, where can we talk?" I led him upstairs to a vacant office in the circulation department, where we each took seats.

"I imagine the feds will take over and yank us off of this," he said. "Probably today, but for the time being it's ours, so I've got to ask you some questions. We're talking to everybody we know who's had contact with Siegel. That includes you, so . . ."

Letting that sentence hang, Wannamaker took out a pen and a small notebook. He leaned forward and proceeded to ask most of the questions I'd expected, and I answered meeting his eyes and trying not to look nervous.

Had I been to Siegel's home? When was the last time I'd seen him, and why? Was it last night? What did we talk about? Did I own a firearm? Did I know of anyone who'd want him killed? (Oh, come on, Detective, only about half the Cosa Nostra.)

Where was I last night? (Playing poker till 10:30, which a guy downstairs can confirm, and in bed with my wife at 11:30.) He jotted that down, then asked his last question: "Did you have any quarrel with Siegel, any reason to be unhappy with him?"

"Yeah, I lost a little too much at blackjack last winter when he opened that Vegas hotel of his." Putting a grin on it.

Wannamaker gave a world-weary, half amused smile and got to his feet. "Okay, Weaver, that's all I got. We're asking the same questions of lots of people today, least till the FBI kicks us offa this, which they will, sure as death and taxes."

I'd answered him with honesty and just enough levity to look relaxed and, I hoped, innocent.

On his way out, he gave a little wave and said, "I hope your daughter's doing okay. Terrible thing she went through." I thanked him and said Ilse was getting along real well.

Back in the city room, John Campbell asked why I didn't want to work on any of the Siegel stories.

"Sorry, Johnny, I'm just burned out on writing crime stuff, but if any of the fellas want to ask me some questions, fine."

* * *

When Uncle Dieter arrived the next day, Ilse and I collected him at Union Depot.

After dinner, he and I were sitting on the sofa in our front room, glasses of beer in front of us on the coffee table. "Dieter, it was great to see you getting off that train today," I said. "We're so glad you could come and visit."

"*Ja*, and so am I. The ice cream cones we had on the drive here were delicious. It was grand to see Ilse again after all these years. She looks good in spite of all that she has gone through. She's become quite a splendid young woman."

"She sure has. I couldn't agree more."

I'd told Dieter everything. The Unholy Trinity. The attempt on Valerie's life. My getting abducted in Detroit. Klaus Schäfer, who was really Otto Woolf. Ilse's immense courage in the face of that monster. Why my face wore the remnants of a bruise. I didn't have to bring up Bugsy's slaying—he'd seen the newspapers.

"Now, about this Siegel business," Dieter said. He glanced down at the paper opened on the coffee table. "You surely had cause. Are you certain—"

"*Jesus*. You and Valerie, what trusting souls you are. Although I might have wanted to, I did not do this!"

"No, of course you didn't. Then who did, would you say?"

"The Mob. Meyer Lansky and Vito Genovese were fed up with this guy's shenanigans. These people are beyond vicious. I think Lucky Luciano ordered them to have this punk taken out."

"No doubt you are right, my boy. Say, this Hamm's beer is not bad. Not as good as German beer, mind you, but not bad."

"I guess so," I said. "Now, Uncle, tell me how you managed to keep safe all that time and finally surrender to the British at the end."

"Oh, why go into all that? Let us just say that I was lucky—and also at times clever," he added with a sly wink.

"You're a crafty old devil, you. So you're completely retired now?"

"*Ja*, as you know, I was a police detective in Berlin this past year, but I've resigned."

"Good. You deserve to relax."

"Relax, Jacob? *Nein*, there is work to do. When I return I will help in the clearing of rubble and the rebuilding."

"We're sure glad you're here now," I said. "You're up to date on all that's happened to us."

The phone rang. "Excuse me, Dieter." I answered and found Colonel Freeborn on the line from London. The Pope of MI-6 himself. The transatlantic connection was surprisingly clear.

"Scoutmaster informed me of your recent difficulties," he said. The Pope still loved using those code names. "His majesty's government owe your daughter and Tapestry—and we are sorry to lose the woman—a great debt of gratitude, as do all the wartime Allies. Eliminating that beast Woolf was a service to mankind."

"Thank you, sir. I'll tell Ilse what you've said."

"Yes, do. And I'm delighted that your problem with that Siegel fellow has been sorted out. Tom Doyle is a capable chap."

Doyle? What was Freeborn telling me?

■